The Ivy House

The Queensbay Series - Book 3 - Phoebe & Chase

Drea Stein

GirlMogul Media

Contents

Title Page	
Chapter 1	1
Chapter 2	6
Chapter 3	10
Chapter 4	19
Chapter 5	23
Chapter 6	29
Chapter 7	41
Chapter 8	47
Chapter 9	56
Chapter 10	66
Chapter 11	72
Chapter 12	82
Chapter 13	98
Chapter 14	101
Chapter 15	122

Chapter 16	124
Chapter 17	134
Chapter 18	144
Chapter 19	148
Chapter 20	158
Chapter 21	167
Chapter 22	173
Chapter 23	180
Chapter 24	191
Chapter 25	194
Chapter 26	201
Chapter 27	220
Chapter 28	223
Chapter 29	226
Chapter 30	232
Chapter 31	235
Chapter 32	242
Chapter 33	250
Chapter 34	254
Chapter 35	263
Chapter 36	267
Chapter 37	270
Chapter 38	273
Chapter 39	276

Chapter 40	284
Chapter 41	287
Chapter 42	292
Chapter 43	297
Chapter 44	303
Chapter 45	305
Chapter 46	309
Chasing a Chance – Book 4 of The Queensbay Series – Lynn & Jackson's Story	313
Books In This Series	321
About The Author	323
Copyright	325

Chapter 1

Phoebe Ryan could feel the real estate agent eyeing her as she surveyed the house. "It has charm," Sandy Miller said. "Perhaps if you added a fresh coat of paint, cleaned out the backyard..."

"Hmm." Phoebe just made a noise, wishing the woman would be quiet and let her think. She was still bleary-eyed from the time difference. She had left Los Angeles yesterday morning, landed in New York, hit the lawyer's office, rented a car, and finally found her way just after dark to the Connecticut shore. She had checked in at the Osprey Arms, the only hotel in town, and after a surprisingly delicious salad and a glass of wine, had curled up on the big four-poster bed and cried herself to sleep.

Now, less than twenty-four hours after she'd left California, she was getting her first view of it. Ivy House was a short walk up from town, at the end of a little lane that jutted off from the main road, commanding a prime piece of property on a bluff overlooking Queensbay Harbor.

Phoebe breathed in deeply. She could smell the fresh tang of salt, see the white caps that flecked the blue-green surface of the water, hear the gulls cawing as they wheeled around the clear sky. It was beautiful, and she could already see herself here, watching the boats come and go, enjoying the sunset while sipping a glass of wine. At least that's how she had imagined it back in Los Angeles.

But if Queensbay Harbor and town were New England charm personified, Ivy House was not. It was the eyesore, the black sheep in the town's collective spic-and-span family. It was Victorian in style, seeming taller than it was wide, with a steep slate-covered roof, pointed gables on either side, and a tall, thin square tower topped with the classic widow's walk. A deep porch wrapped around the front, and a black iron picket fence separated the house from the street.

Paint peeled, the porch sagged, shingles were missing. Weeds choked the front yard, and the iron fence was rusted through. The flagstone path was uneven and while there had once been an extensive garden, now everything was wildly overgrown. The plant that had given the house its name covered one side almost completely, even the windows. Everything about it screamed genteel decay and Phoebe took a moment to ruminate about the prospect of fully renovating the place. It wasn't as she had imagined it. But then, things seldom were.

Phoebe had only glanced toward the side yard, but she could see stuff. Some old wicker furniture, perhaps a refrigerator, plastic jugs, maybe even a beer keg. It was hard to imagine the late, great Savannah Ryan having anything to do with this place.

The thought of her grandmother threatened a fresh onslaught of tears, but Phoebe forced them away.

"The major appliances are all there," Sandy said and then corrected herself, "I think."

"Electricity? Water, heat?" Phoebe asked. If she focused on the details, the little things, she could avoid thinking about the big things. She closed her eyes briefly, ready to sense the possibilities. That was her gift, a vivid imagination, a mind that saw things in pictures, one that could turn those pictures into reality. She envisioned the house as Savannah had described it to her, as it had been, when the sun set across the expanse of the harbor and the backyard, with the sloping lawn leading to the sandy bluff.

"You'll have to have all the utilities switched to your name, but I have the numbers for you to call. Shouldn't take more than twenty-four hours for it all to come on once you do," the agent assured her.

Phoebe nodded, ready to walk up and into the house. She put a foot on the first step to the porch, tested it with her weight, and was pleased to find that it was solid. Good bones, she thought. All the house needed was some TLC.

"Here are the keys," Sandy said, dropping them in Phoebe's outstretched hand. Phoebe closed her hands over them tightly, afraid perhaps that it wasn't true, that the house wasn't hers.

"I did a walk-through after the tenants left and there are some scrapes and scuffs and a hole in the wall. They left it broom clean, though, if you want, I can give you the name of a local cleaning service I use. In my opinion, you'd be better off gutting the place first."

"Gutting it?" Phoebe tried to keep the horror out of her voice. How could you consider destroying a masterpiece like this? The house was living history and she could already feel herself falling in love. Visions of fairy lights in the trees, the setting sun, a table set up outside, and some friends to share it with. Still, she shouldn't get too attached yet. Her home, her life was three-thousand miles away. Imagination couldn't always overcome reality.

"Oh, well," Sandy blinked, then resettled her oversized sunglasses more firmly on top of her head. "I mean, you'll see. As I said, everything's perfectly sound, but things haven't been updated in a while."

Phoebe smiled. All the better, she thought. So many people ruined old houses by trying to update them too much, trying to drag them kicking and screaming into the modern world, while not respecting their expert craftsmanship and clean, simple lines.

"I like old houses," Phoebe said. "They have character." In California, old was a relative term, but here she was dealing with a jewel built in the nineteenth century, before planes, cars—electricity, even. It would need to be respected, cherished. And more so because it had belonged to Savannah.

Sandy was about to say something when her phone rang. Holding up a finger, she checked the screen and then excused herself to take the call.

Relieved to be alone, Phoebe moved up the porch, imagining how it would look with some fine old wicker rockers, instead of those hideous, rusty folding chairs. She stood in front of the door. It was the original: a fine wood-paneled door, painted a bright blue. Cheerful, but to her trained eye, a little too bold. Something softer, duskier would suit. She tried to peer through the sidelights on either side, but they too were original and the glass, wavy from age, made it difficult to see inside.

She put the key in the lock and turned. The lock was stiff from disuse, but she wiggled until finally it opened. Perhaps there wasn't much cause to lock your door here and that thought pleased Phoebe immensely, who lived in the city and always made sure to triple-lock the door.

Swinging slowly back, the door opened with a scream on its hinges, a slow, protracted squeal. It was a sunny day, but as Sandy had mentioned, there was no electricity and the sun only just touched the interior.

Phoebe took a step in, smelling mustiness and dampness, the scent of a closed-up house. Her eyes poked through the gloom and she was finally able to see.

"Oh, my..." she said out loud.

"I told you." Sandy had come up behind her, her phone call done. "In my business, it's what we call a tear down."

Chapter 2

The agent left and Phoebe let herself have a full-blown moment of panic. She managed to breathe despite the filthy atmosphere and explored the rest of the house. She took the sight of the inside in stride, telling herself it was what she should have expected. After all, considering the way Savannah had handled her affairs, it was a miracle there was anything left for Phoebe at all. And this was more than she could have hope for, she decided, as she reminded herself of the house's basic sturdiness.

Unfortunately, despite what Sandy had said, the house had been subjected to a number of redos throughout the decade, the latest of which had left lots of linoleum, probably covering the original, wide plank-wood floors; peeling wallpaper; and mirrors, lots of mirrors.

The paint colors throughout were faded or jarring or both, as though the rooms had been painted by someone color-blind or using the clearance colors from the local home improvement store. Definitely both, Phoebe thought as she opened the door to a smallish room, the dining room perhaps, and took another look.

The rest of the house wasn't much better—it

was dusty and dirty, and the tenants had left piles of things, from old bedding to stacks of newspapers, in various places. A few of the windowpanes were broken and had been covered up with pieces of cardboard.

Finally, she found herself outside in the backyard, taking in the view. There was a flagstone terrace out here, with a fire pit, ringed by a low rock wall, perfect for enjoying cool spring nights and watching the water. A strong breeze blew through the trees and she wandered down to the edge of the bluff. A picket fence ran along it, and there was a set of stairs going down to the beach. She looked over it. Apparently, this was the only thing the tenants had decided to keep in good repair, the beach access, because here and there were pieces of new wood on the stairwell. This was what Sandy had meant when she said it was a million-dollar view.

Carefully, she made her way down to the beach, stopping when she got to the bottom. The shore was a mix of sand and rock, and there was a large driftwood log pulled up around what looked like the remains of a fire. She sat on the log and breathed in, the smell of the charred wood assailing her senses.

The sun was getting warm and she needed to think, figure out what to do next. The water, the sand, and the sun were working their magic. Already, less than a day out of the city and she felt calm, rested. The sadness of Savannah's death, the stress of dealing with her estate, and that big looming question—*What do I do now?*—seemed to fade away. Phoebe took a deep breath, her grandmother's words coming back to her: *Enjoy the moment.* All that mattered was that it was sunny and she was enjoying the view.

She tried not to think about the wreck that was looming, both figuratively and literally, above her head. Ivy House was a disaster. It would take a small fortune to fix it up, that much was clear, and Phoebe didn't know if she had it in her. Either physically or financially.

The agent had already dropped hints. Despite its decrepit condition, it would attract some serious buyer interest. Just because of its "historical significance." Phoebe had almost burst out laughing at that one. A torrid love affair wasn't exactly world peace. Savannah and Leland had been more infamous than famous, but that still didn't stop legions of people from obsessing over them. All the more now since they were both dead.

But Phoebe was a Hollywood girl. She knew that the public's obsession with the life of movie stars was never quite rational. Any little thing, be it a prop or a costume piece, could be fought over by a serious collector. And now, if now, the chance to own the actual house that had been the love nest for the "Romance of the Century" became available, Phoebe knew she'd have more offers on her hands than she could handle.

Phoebe was still taking it in. She had thought that Savannah had sold the house years ago after Leland's death. Instead, she had kept it, renting it out year after year. Despite the fact that Savannah could have used the money, she had not sold the house. She had left it, mostly intact, for Phoebe. What had Savannah been thinking, leaving Phoebe with a wreck of a house three-thousand miles away from her home?

I'll just have to figure it out as I go, Phoebe thought to herself, her natural optimism returning as she trekked back up the steps. There was always a way to salvage a disaster.

Chapter 3

That was strange. Phoebe was sure she had closed the back door to the house behind her, but here it was, open again. Tamping down a wave of panic, since this was charming Queensbay and not the big city after all, Phoebe pushed open the door a little wider. It was probably one of the former tenants, maybe with an extra key, coming back for something they left behind. Hadn't she seen an old stuffed animal—a teddy bear or maybe a bunny rabbit—in one of the rooms upstairs? Couldn't leave Floppy behind now, could you?

"Hello," she called. Her first attempt was weak, so she cleared her throat and called out again, "Hello, is someone there?"

She heard the floorboard creaking and looking up at the ceiling, she could see the floor sag as feet made their way across.

"You don't look like you're from the electric company," she said, keeping close to the door just in case.

Feet, shod in Converse sneakers, and legs, in jeans, emerged down the steps, followed by a large brass belt buckle, a blue windbreaker, and finally, a head.

Phoebe watched as the man crystallized into view. A pair of sunglasses, aviator-style, hung in the v of the t-shirt that poked up through the collar of his jacket. The man loomed, Phoebe thought, as he reached the bottom step and casually supported himself by putting one hand on the wall, the other crooked at his side.

"Lovely place you've got here," he said in a smooth voice that sent shivers shooting through her, despite the sarcasm.

He was taller than Phoebe by several inches, even in her high-heeled boots, which put him at well over six feet, and she could see that his arms were muscular underneath his jacket. He wore a smile though and Phoebe didn't feel threatened so much as aware, hyperaware of his presence.

He was every inch a male and was assessing her, conducting a slow survey, starting with her face, running down the length of her body, and back up to her face. He stopped there, his gaze lingered, narrowing, and then a slow grin spread over his face.

Phoebe could only guess that he liked what he saw because he rocked forward a bit on his feet and leaned in.

She found herself pinned to the wall by a set of the darkest blue eyes she had ever seen. They were set in a tan face, a face that obviously spent a good deal of time outside. His hair was black, an inky, undiluted black. Dark brows slashed across a wide forehead, which ran down to a straight nose and then tapered to full lips and a charming cleft chin.

"It needs some work," Phoebe admitted, because it was true and the only thing she could think of saying. Witty responses had never been her thing, especially when faced with a grin like that—cocksure and confident—which had a strange, tingling warmth spreading over her. She'd never had such a physical reaction to the very presence of a man before.

He touched the wall with the palm of his fist, and she could hear the plaster gently falling down behind it.

"Please stop wrecking my house," she said, feeling her heart pump a little faster.

"That was just a light touch." He took a step closer and she almost wanted to rear back.

"You need to leave right now," she said, trying to hold firm. She had felt an instantaneous shock of attraction and knew that she needed to get rid of him.

"Sorry, the door was open. I thought I heard someone crying for help, so I just let myself in. Wanted to make sure you hadn't fallen through the floor or something like that." His tone was light, joking.

He laughed then, and the grin came quickly and he looked almost mischievous. "It was probably just the cry of a seagull. Were you down by the beach?" He took a step forward and Phoebe felt the need to step back, but she stopped herself, holding her ground.

She shifted the leather bag she was holding from one hand to the other and almost back again before she stopped herself. What had Savannah said? It is the small gestures that give you away. It was her way of saying *never let them see you sweat.*

Because this guy was making Phoebe sweat. Not nervously, as in he wasn't a creep or causing her to wonder why she was alone in an empty house with him, but more along the lines of how she couldn't stop herself from looking at his beautiful face, or the way, even in the jacket, she could see how his waist tapered in and then how his long, powerful legs were encased in his jeans. She hadn't been this aware of a guy in a long time and the feeling was totally disconcerting.

He moved closer and she caught the scent of him. Something woodsy and spicy, just a hint of soap, nothing too overpowering. God, she was a twenty-eight-year-old woman, not some teenager, and already she could feel her heart start to flutter.

His eyes glinted down at her and Phoebe wished that she had closed the top button of her blouse, but to do anything now except meet him head on would betray the way he was making her feel.

"Can I help you with something?" She lifted her chin and met his eyes boldly, the way Savannah had told her to. Phoebe had never been much for channeling her inner femme fatale; still, the man had the grace to look a little ashamed that he had been caught staring.

"You just remind me of someone. Not sure who. Do you get that a lot?"

Phoebe smiled, but her back stiffened. It was a question she got so often that it annoyed her. Too bad, because before he had gone for the obvious line, she had felt that spark of interest on her part, her vivid imagination working overtime, wondering just how his wide, sensual lips might feel brushing against hers.

"Not really," she demurred, while cursing the Ryan genes that showed so plainly in her face.

"Are you sure?" he said, snapping his fingers. "Because I swear, you remind me of someone. Let me see, someone famous. A model?"

Phoebe managed to arch an eyebrow. She had a swimmer's body, moderately tall, wide shoulders and slim all over, but she'd never been mistaken for a model before.

"Nah, not quite tall enough, though those shoes make your legs go on forever," the guy said, his eyes twinkling. He was smiling so outrageously that Phoebe almost didn't mind that she was being blatantly hit upon. Perhaps his recognition of her had been fake, a cheesy come-on. Maybe he had no idea. "A singer?"

"Tone-deaf," Phoebe countered.

"Too bad—you'd look pretty bad-ass up on stage." Somehow, the guy had moved closer to her, invading her space and yet, Phoebe didn't mind at all. He had lines around his eyes, as if he squinted too much in the sun, and his hands, one of which was splayed on the wall, like his clothes, were not those of a man who spent all of his time inside.

He snapped his fingers. "The stage. That's it. You're an actress. Theater? TV. A cop show. I can see you arresting the bad guys."

Phoebe shook her head, feeling the smile that was lighting up her face and the buzz in her body as she decided to play along.

"Medical drama?" He tried again.

"Hate the sight of blood."

"You're sure I don't know you from somewhere?" The guy leaned over her, his eyes looking into hers. Thoughts, none of them coherent, raced around Phoebe's head and she was aware that it was warm, very warm in the house, where before it had been cool, almost too cool.

"No, I'm nobody," Phoebe said and managed to take a deep breath, almost willing that to be true.

"I don't believe that for a second, miss." He leaned in close to her and his voice dropped to a dangerous whisper. "With a face like that, you're surely someone."

Phoebe didn't know what to say to that and she didn't have to. Her phone beeped and, eager to break the intense connection between herself and this man, she pulled it out of her bag and saw that there was a text from Sandy, the real estate agent.

Have interest from buyer, heavy hitter, wants to see house ASAP

Phoebe cleared the text in frustration. She thought she had been very clear. She wasn't ready to entertain any offers for Ivy House yet. But some people were rude and didn't take no for an answer. Phoebe looked up. The guy, this "heavy hitter," apparently hadn't gotten the message because he was already looking around the place as if he were measuring how well his flat-screen TV would look above the fireplace in the living room.

Phoebe texted back, *"Not interested...send away..."*

Fast and furious came the text message back: *"Too late, he's already on his way..."*

Phoebe gritted her teeth in frustration. *"Fine, I will take care of him."*

She put the phone away just as it started ringing. It was Sandy, but Phoebe decided to ignore her. She wasn't interested in hearing the woman try to save her own commission.

"Excuse me, sir." Phoebe found him in the back room, the one she had already imagined would be perfect as the studio study, looking out the full wall of windows.

"Quite a view," he said with an easy gesture, seemingly unembarrassed at having been caught roaming around the house.

"I'm sorry, I think there's been a misunderstanding. The house is not for sale," Phoebe said, drawing herself up to her full height.

The man looked over at her, a lazy smile on his face. "Is that so? It's a prime piece of property. I've had my eye on it for a while. The old owner never would give me the time of day, though, no matter what I offered."

"Well, guess this isn't your lucky day either because I have no intention of selling," Phoebe said. It wasn't exactly true. Last night, she'd had every intention of glancing the place over, getting a price from the real estate agent, and heading back to the city. But now...she'd already imagined sipping wine on the terrace.

She heard the ping, but before she could reach for her own phone, she saw the man take his out of a pocket. The conversation was brief, but Phoebe was almost certain Sandy, the real estate agent, was on the other end of it.

He hung up, looked at Phoebe, a sharp, appraising look.

"Well, I guess I was mistaken. But you know what they say: the harder you work, the luckier you get."

Phoebe stiffened. The real estate agent's meaning had been clear. Waterfront property in Queensbay was a highly sought-after commodity. There would be plenty of people who would be willing to take it off her hands, even in this economy, so there was no reason she needed to be grateful to the guy for being the first.

She drew herself up. "Ivy House is not for sale. I have no intention of being taken advantage of just because I'm not from around here."

He only smiled again at her huffy tone, unperturbed by it.

"Trust me, I would never try to take advantage of a lady. I will be happy to offer a fair price for a fair bit of property."

Phoebe looked into his eyes. So he was only interested in the property, not the house. She guessed he couldn't see the house for what it was—a diamond in the rough. Did he not know? Or was he playing it cool?

He pulled something from his pocket, a white envelope, and held it out to her.

She looked at it, puzzled.

"I know I'm supposed to go through the real estate agent, but sometimes I find it easier to just deal with the other party directly."

"What is that?" Phoebe said, trying to keep her voice level.

"A very generous and more than fair offer for the property." He said, still holding it out towards her. She crossed her arms, feeling childish, but refusing to give in even an inch.

"I told you that Ivy House isn't for sale."

He cocked his head to one side and put the envelope back in his pocket, a wise move Phoebe thought.

"You keep calling this place Ivy House. I haven't heard it being called that in years."

"It's what my grandmother called it," Phoebe said. Savannah could only be persuaded to talk about Ivy House and Leland after a glass or two of wine and even then, it was a tricky subject.

His mouth dropped open and a look that Phoebe didn't understand crossed his face.

Chapter 4

"You're Savannah's granddaughter," he said, as if everything came together.

"Who did you think I was?" Phoebe asked with real curiosity. In Los Angeles, the recognition was almost immediate mostly because people there knew their celebrities, even the older ones.

"Well, I told you, you looked like someone. I didn't realize Savannah still owned the property, that's all. I've been sending offer letters to a lawyer in New York the past couple of years and getting pretty strong nos."

"So you thought you'd take your chance with the new girl in town," Phoebe said, wondering just how outraged she should feel.

"I always like to make newcomers feel welcome." He had inched closer and the cocky grin was back.

Warning signals chimed in Phoebe's head. She was in no condition to have anything to do with a man like this. He was all male and obviously a huge flirt. Definitely not what she needed right now.

"Well, very thoughtful of you, but like I said, the house is not for sale and I have some work to do."

He looked around again at the dusty floor and

the empty room.

"I'm sure you do. Still, I think you should consider my offer. I'd be happy to take the house off your hands, as is. You wouldn't have to do a thing to it. You could be back on a plane and back to your life by tomorrow."

"Listen, Mr...." Phoebe realized that she had never gotten his name.

"Please call me Chase. All my friends do," he said with another one of his grins. Phoebe had the feeling that Chase was the kind of guy with plenty of friends. And she had no intention of becoming one of them.

"Why are you so interested in the place?" she asked.

For the first time, she saw that he hesitated, his feet doing a little dance. "Let's just say the property has always spoken to me."

Phoebe looked at him. With the broad shoulders and the constant grin, Phoebe didn't think Chase looked like the kind of guy that let anything but tall blondes speak to him, but she supposed you never could tell. But that wasn't her problem. Ivy House had also spoken to her, and she wasn't about to let the legacy Savannah had left her go so easily.

"Well," he said after a moment, when he realized that Phoebe wasn't going to say anything else, "it was nice to meet you, miss..."

It was her turn to hesitate, though she supposed it didn't matter. All he needed was the internet. He could find out anything else he wanted to on the internet.

"Phoebe Ryan." She couldn't be invisible, not if she expected to spend any amount of time in Queensbay. Word was bound to get out.

"Well, it's nice to meet you. And I'm sorry for your loss." She gave a quick nod. It had been almost six weeks since Savannah had died, but it was the sympathy from strangers that still got her. She managed to blink away the tears that were forming.

"Here, please take the envelope. Like I said, it's a good offer. More than fair and, well, you'll be getting more of them, so I just want to make sure that you have mine."

"Listen, I told you," Phoebe started, her anger quickly replacing her tears.

"I know, Ivy House isn't for sale," Chase said, his face serious now. "But just in case."

He practically shoved it into her hand and she had no choice but to accept it. She gritted her teeth as she took it, their hands brushing, and she felt an unfamiliar thrill of electricity run through her at his touch. Chase must have felt it too because he looked at her and time seemed to halt for a moment, and then Phoebe became hyperaware of everything around her. The small settling sounds of the house, the chirps of the birds outside, the gentle sway of the branches.

Then the moment broke because he picked up her hand, brought it gently to his lips, and said, "Perhaps you'll come around. Until we meet again."

He dropped her hand finally and brushed past

her on his way out the door. She heard the fluttering sound of more plaster falling as he walked down the hallway. Reluctantly, she trailed after him and watched him as he strolled with his hands stuck in his pockets, whistling as he made his way out the front door, down the steps, out onto the path, and through the rickety gate. He turned once, gave a wave, and then kept walking. Phoebe watched him go and then found herself leaning against the wall, hearing the whisper of dust as it fell down behind her.

She had no intention of selling Ivy House, at least not anytime soon, but she couldn't get the wild thoughts out of her head, thoughts of how it would have felt if she had stretched upwards a little farther and let her lips brush against Chase's face and feel his perfectly-formed lips upon hers.

Chapter 5

"Hi there." Phoebe turned to see a woman standing on her porch.

"Sorry, I didn't want to intrude. I'm Lynn Masters. I live next door." Lynn was shorter than Phoebe by a couple of inches, with long, wavy brown hair and dark chocolate-colored eyes. She was wearing blue hospital scrubs and had a welcoming smile on her face.

"Hi. Phoebe Ryan," Phoebe said, stuffing Chase's envelope into her pocket. How long she had been standing there, in the hallway, dazed, with the front door wide open, she didn't know.

"Are you related?"

"Excuse me?" Phoebe braced herself. Her brush with anonymity was truly over, she supposed.

"Your last name. Were you really related to Savannah Ryan?" Lynn asked, excitement sparking in her eyes.

"Yes. I'm her granddaughter." Phoebe said, stepping onto the porch. The sun was out in full force and the porch was warmer—much warmer—than the inside of the house, and Phoebe realized it felt nice.

"Wow, that is so cool. My parents moved here about two years ago. My mom was so excited when the real estate agent told her that Savannah Ryan lived here, she nearly had a cow, but of course once we moved in, she realized that it didn't mean Savannah still lived here."

Phoebe gave a small smile. Lynn was chatty and, apparently, a fan, or at least her mom was. Once people found out the relationship, they usually pumped Phoebe for information. Over the years, Phoebe had learned to keep quiet about the family connection with Savannah if she didn't want total strangers asking her bizarrely private questions, like if Savannah really spent all day in pink silk pajamas.

"Looks like you have your work cut out for you," Lynn said and Phoebe forced her attention back to her.

"What?"

"This house. It's such a great-looking place, but the last couple of tenants were a little crazy. College kids. Threw some great parties though."

"Oh." Phoebe looked around, remembering the condition of the property. "Yeah, it will probably take a while to clean it up."

"Did you know Savannah well? Oh gosh, where are my manners. I am so sorry for your loss. I just couldn't believe it when I read about her death."

"Thank you." Phoebe had to smile at Lynn's openness and lack of pretense. Lynn's face radiated sincerity, and instead of feeling the onslaught of tears, Phoebe was able to summon up a bit of lightness.

"Well, she was well over eighty." All the years of cigarettes and champagne had finally caught up with Savannah. And in the end, it had been time for Savannah to let go.

"Well, it's nice to know that the house will still be in the family. Are you going to be moving here alone?" Lynn shook her head, her brown hair moving with her.

Phoebe gave a noncommittal shrug. She didn't know what she was going to be doing. The next couple of months stretched wide open in front of her, but the truth was that except for this wreck of a house and her room at the Osprey Arms, she had nowhere else to be. But she didn't need to explain that to anyone, did she?

"Oh. Well, like I said, it would be cool if someone young moved in. Queensbay's pretty and all that, but it's not exactly a big city."

"So you live next door?" Phoebe asked, glad the subject had veered away from her family.

"Yes, I'm finishing my last year of residency. Pediatrics," Lynn said, waving a hand to explain the scrubs, "So I'm living with my parents to save money. Plus, I'm rarely home, so it doesn't make much sense to have my own place. And," Lynn dropped her voice, "my mom is a great cook."

Phoebe smiled at the conspiratorial tone.

"Which is one of the reasons why I'm here. When my mom heard that there was someone closer to my age moving in, well, she wanted to make sure I invited you over for dinner."

As an afterthought, Lynn added, "...if you don't mind, that is. Like I said, she's a really good cook. And she's not as meddling as I might have suggested."

Phoebe was disarmed by Lynn's friendliness. Phoebe was happy being on her own and she had envisioned a quiet few days in a new place to get her head on straight. It was on the tip of her tongue to say no, but Lynn's open smile and friendly manner had her changing her mind.

"That would be nice," Phoebe agreed. The thought of a home-cooked meal suddenly sounded very enticing.

"Great," Lynn said. "I have to run out to work now, but how about six tomorrow night? My mom's making something Italian, is that OK?

"Sounds great," Phoebe nodded. She would bring a bottle of red, she decided, as a thank you.

Lynn stole a glance around Phoebe and into the house. "Good luck with the place. Everyone's excited that someone's taking an interest in it, after all these years. Not that all renters are bad, but I think it's time this place had someone who really cared about it." Lynn put her hand on one of the columns of the porch and, as if on cue, a part of it fell off and bounced on the porch.

"Oh, dear," Lynn started to reach down to pick up the piece of rotted wood.

Phoebe laughed. "Don't bother. I am sure it

won't be the last thing that falls down around here."

"Well, I guess it's good you have a sense of humor about the whole thing."

They shared a laugh and Phoebe said goodbye to her new neighbor. Lynn squeezed through an opening in the bushes and a moment or two later, Phoebe saw a car drive past, with a hand waving out the window.

Not trusting the rusty chairs and wanting to enjoy the sunshine, Phoebe plopped herself down on the porch step, drawing her knees up so her chin rested on them, thinking. The house was both more and less than she had bargained for.

She remembered it from when she had been young and visited. Everything about the place and the town had seemed magical from a little kid's perspective. But now the house seemed smaller and dingier and it needed a lot of work. Savannah, though, had loved it so—must have—to keep it all these years, without letting on that she still owned it.

Phoebe sighed. She knew why Savannah had left it to her. Phoebe's parents had been Hollywood types too—her father an up-and-coming director, her mother a soon-to-not-be struggling actress—when they died in a car crash. Savannah had taken her in, her only living relative, but Savannah had never been the maternal type. Ivy House had been a part of Savannah's history, her happiest times. A place where Savannah had believed that anything was possible, until it wasn't.

The reasonable, solid, practical thing to do would be to sell Ivy House. Phoebe had built her own life a whole country away, in Los Angeles, and if her prospects there were somewhat in flux, it made more sense to stay there than to think about moving her whole life here. Her practical, reasonable half pulled the envelope Chase had given her from her pocket, because selling Ivy House, even to someone who only wanted it for the view, was the smart thing to do. She didn't belong here. This was Savannah's history, not hers.

A picture of Savannah from long ago flashed into her mind, when Phoebe had been little, her red-gold hair in pigtails. She had been whispering to Savannah about how the house was magical. And Savannah had been in full, solemn agreement and had made her promise not to tell anyone else. Their secret.

Phoebe sighed again. Just what had Savannah gotten her into?

Chapter 6

Chase Sanders spun around aimlessly in his office chair. He was supposed to be looking over quarterly reports and making some decisions on what to include in the new product line, which, at this point, was looking pretty dismal. But he couldn't concentrate. Not even the sight of the stiff breeze kicking up whitecaps on the harbor could distract him from thinking about her. The blond at Ivy House. Phoebe Ryan. He should have known the minute he'd seen her, but he had acted like a fool, making all sorts of inane remarks that had probably sounded like cheesy come-ons, which, in a way, had been just that.

The sight of her, it was a bit like staring at a ghost. Except he'd had an entirely different reaction between his legs than fear. Nope, no doubt about it. Phoebe Ryan was almost as much of a looker as her grandmother had been in her day.

Still, that was all it was—a fully physical reaction to her. Her red-blond hair, the splay of freckles over her nose, the light blue eyes, the long, strong body. The way she had glanced at him coolly, obviously put out by his presence, but keeping her cool. She'd been wary, wondering what his game was. But he hadn't told her anything beyond the fact that he was interested in the house.

He had at least remembered to offer his condolences, which were sincere. He didn't hold anything against Savannah. In fact, his entire family just ignored the whole thing. Sort of pretended that Leland had never existed. His grandmother had even remarried, so Chase hadn't realized that Grandpa Sal was really just a stepgrandpa. And with a different last name than Leland, Chase had gone through most of his life without giving his connection, however tenuous, with Leland another thought.

Well, she'd probably figure it out soon enough, and then the game would be up. Well, the game would be up as soon as she would look at his card. If she ever did. She seemed adamant about not wanting to sell the house, which meant that the Historical Commission would be up in arms. They were naturally distrustful of outsiders, and a blond Californian had them all in a dither. They were afraid the new owner was going for a tear down. So, Chase had valiantly decided to play the white knight and rescue Ivy House from the West Coaster who didn't know a gable from a cupola.

It hadn't worked quite as smoothly as he hoped. Phoebe had seemed a bit stuck-up, not melting into his charm. Chase, with some satisfaction, had yet to find a red-blooded female who didn't give in to it. But Phoebe had just kept looking at him like he had two heads. He was trying to concentrate on paperwork, but all he could do was shuffle around the documents so incoherently and roughly that he knocked over his paperweight, which hit the floor like his jaw had when he first glimpsed Phoebe Ryan.

"That's a way to make a mess," Noah Randall said as he walked into Chase's office, "and not much else. What's eating you?"

Chase felt sheepish as he looked at his oldest friend. "It's nothing."

Noah, tall, slim, with light brown hair, laughed. "Sounds like girl trouble to me. What's her name? Beth, Bethany?"

"Ha." Chase gave a halfhearted laugh as Noah threw himself into one of the chairs on the other side of his desk. "It was Bethany and we broke up six months ago." Chase got up and picked up the paperweight, a solid glass orb with a replica of the schooner *America*, the winner of the first America's Cup.

Noah shook his head. "That long? Wasn't she some sort of model?"

"Wasn't my type," Chase answered curtly.

Noah shot his friend a look. Bethany had been a swimwear model and Chase had met her at a photo shoot for the spring catalog. "I didn't know there was a girl who wasn't your type."

"Well, let's just say she seemed to be more interested in what I could do for her than in my sparkling personality."

"Wow, sounds like you're maturing. Good thing since you're turning thirty in another couple of months and all that," Noah said with a laugh.

"Very funny," Chase said, managing to keep

the sarcasm to a low boil.

"Are we going to spend all of lunch talking about your love life?" Noah asked, one foot swinging casually off the side of his chair.

Chase gave a half smile. Noah was his oldest friend, and they'd been through a lot of things together, including girls.

Chase shook his head. "There's nothing to tell." Once he had grown tired of Bethany, who, like most of the other women he'd dated, seemed more interested in his wallet than him, he'd decided to take a break. It had been refreshing—six months of not worrying about what someone else thought—but a man had needs. And right now, there was a certain blond up on the hill who was occupying more than her fair share of his brain space.

No wonder she had looked at him down her nose. He was dressed like a dockhand. He should have put on a suit and tie, the kind that he kept for meetings, but he'd been so excited when the agent had told him that Ivy House might be available that he rushed up there, sure that fate was handing him his chance.

"I keep telling you: dating models and actresses isn't the key to lasting happiness," Noah said, shaking his head, bringing Chase back to his present predicament.

"Just because you're married now doesn't mean you're the expert," Chase shot back.

Noah gave a small laugh. "Isn't that the truth? I've known Caitlyn just about all my life and been married to her for over a year, and she still surprises me."

Chase took a long appraising look at his old friend. The surprises must have been good ones because Noah looked happy, at ease. Of course, it was easy to be that way when you were a successful tech entrepreneur, had reconnected with the love of your life, and were expecting a baby.

"Congrats, by the way, for real. I haven't seen you since you guys announced the news," Chase said.

He meant it too. He and Noah had grown up in Queensbay together, thick as thieves as kids. Noah had lived in the big house on the bluffs high above the harbor, while Chase, his brother, and parents lived down in town, near the marina.

Noah and Chase had learned to sail on the harbor at the Yacht Club and had hated each other at first sight. That had led to a game of chicken, in boats, which resulted in one boat sunk and the other one in dry dock for weeks. To help pay for the damages and learn a better way of handling their feelings towards each other, their dads made them work at the marina, scrubbing down boats and pumping gas. Since that hadn't helped their relationship, they decided to settle things the old-fashioned way—with a race. Chase had beaten the pants off Noah, and Noah, always one to use brains over brawn, shook his hand and offered to be his crew for the Club's Junior Cup. They'd won that year and every year thereafter.

Since then, they'd been inseparable on the water and off, he and Noah making a powerful team. After high school, Noah had headed to college for a couple of years and then dropped out to go to Silicon Valley, California. Chase, too, had gone to college, but spent most of his time with the sailing team, and finally, after a few semesters, the lure of sailing in the big leagues caught up with him.

Chase had focused on racing, on winning, driven by the money it made him. He'd been doing just fine and hadn't thought much about it when Noah, turned down by his own father, had asked for a loan. Chase and his brother Jackson had scraped together everything they had, and Noah had given them a bunch of papers in return.

And then his dad had gotten sick, and with his brother still in college, Chase had to come home. The family business had needed help and Chase assumed the helm. He'd discovered that the papers that Noah had given him meant he was a part owner of Noah's company and that had been all he needed, besides his own winnings, to take the family's boating supply store, North Coast Outfitters, and grow it into an upscale catalog, a chain of stores, and a website catering to the yachting crowd. The success and the hard work it had taken left him with no regrets about giving up his racing career. Sure, a chance at the America's Cup was probably out of the question now, but he had a good life, and his father, while not in perfect health, was doing OK.

Chase had his own membership at the

Queensbay Yacht Club, a forty-foot sloop in a slip at the marina, which he now owned to boot, and he was the hometown boy made good. There was just one thing missing to make his dream complete.

"Thank you. Caitlyn's been down with morning sickness for the past three months, but she says it's easing up. Either that or she can't stand being cooped up anymore. Watch out, I'm sure she's planning some sort of party soon." Noah ran a hand through his hair.

Chase had nothing to say for a moment, lost again in thoughts of Phoebe and her downright refusal to sell the house to him. Well, she hadn't been subjected to a full-on campaign of his persuasive powers yet, had she?

"Hey there, Earth to Chase." Noah was looking at him curiously. "OK, from what I can see, your business is doing great, so that means that something else must be bothering you. If it's not a lady, what is it?"

Chase grimaced and ran a hand through his hair. "It's the house. Ivy House. Would you believe it that Savannah Ryan owned it all these years and left it to her granddaughter?"

Noah shook his head. "I don't get why you're so fascinated with that house. You would think the fact that your grandfather once shacked up there with a movie star would make it off-limits for you."

"Very funny. That's history. And who cares about that?" Chase pointed out. It had been a scandal over fifty years ago, and because of its tragic end-ing, it still got dragged up now and then on some entertainment shows. "That house, with the tower, the gables, and the view...Do you know how often these waterfront properties come up for sale? And with that size lot? I've wanted it ever since I could remember."

"OK," Noah said, nodding, playing along, "So you said the owner is Savannah Ryan? I thought she sold the place years ago."

Chase shook his head. "Guess not. That's why all of my offers must have gotten rejected. I guess she didn't have any kind feelings towards the family. But she's dead, and now someone new owns it."

"You know if you want to tear down the house, the Historical Commission is going to have a fit," Noah told him.

"Well, that won't be a problem since the new owner swears she isn't selling." Chase didn't defend the house. He had no intention of tearing it down, but he didn't want to seem too sentimental. Truth was, after poking around there a bit today, he realized that Ivy House wasn't so bad. Of course, it wasn't as big as some of the newer bluff homes, but it was big enough, with its distinctive tower and widow's walk. And it was perched high above the harbor, a guardian overlooking the town and the marina. And he had always loved it, imagined himself owning it from the days when he'd been looking up at it from the water below. Ivy House had been a commanding presence in his life even before he realized the family connection.

"Weren't the last tenants pretty rough on it?" Noah said.

Chase nodded. "Yup, and the new owner, Savannah's granddaughter, is from California. No way she's going to commit to fixing this place up, not if she wants to get back home anytime soon. Or, worse yet, I bet she wants to build some modern box-type thing with a thousand windows."

Chase focused on one of the photos he'd hung in his office. North Coast Outfitters had grown so fast because of who he was, or at least the image he'd played up. It was a picture they'd used in last year's catalog: Chase at the helm of a sleek racing yacht, the seas foaming and looking rough around him. He could remember the feel of power, the sheer strength of the boat beneath him, the sense of rightness. He'd always felt the same way about Ivy House, the way it watched over the village with a quiet dignity, even as its condition took a turn for the worse.

"Savannah Ryan has a granddaughter?" Noah said with a low whistle. "Now *that* I find hard to believe."

"Well, believe it because here she is."

He turned his laptop around to show Noah. He'd been doing a little internet research on Phoebe.

Noah's eyebrows shot up in appreciation. "Wow, so that's Savannah Ryan's granddaughter. Nice to know sometimes the apple doesn't fall far from the tree."

Noah pursed his lips as he thought through things. "Wait a second. Isn't there a problem? Since her grandmother and your grandfather were married, does that mean you two are related? That could be a little weird."

Chase shot his friend a withering look. "We're not related. Leland left my mom behind when he ran off with Savannah Ryan, and she already had a kid. So, there's no weirdness there and no blood relations. I guess we're like stepcousins or something."

Noah laughed. "Weird, no, but trust me, the media would eat it up. If they got wind that the two of you were even talking. And that Phoebe was living in *that* house. I can see the headlines now." Noah held up his hands as he intoned, "The Romance of the Century, Part Two."

"I'm not interested in her. Just the house." Chase groped for words. There had been an unmistakable spark between them, but she had stayed curiously immune to his teasing, to his flirting. Phoebe Ryan was a cool customer, and well, dammit, if he didn't like a challenge, which had to be the reason why the thought of her kept distracting him.

"Well, that should be fine then. She probably has to head back to Los Angeles soon though. That is sort of your type, isn't it? Someone who isn't looking for any sort of long-term commitment?" Noah said.

"We will see," Chase paused. "She flat out told me she wasn't interested in selling the house. Her house, she called it." Maybe that was what was bothering him, the fact that Phoebe had never even seen the house Chase had loved since he was a kid and was now getting all possessive about it.

Noah smiled. "Well, hearing 'no' never seemed to stop you before. Let me know what I can do to help."

Chase shook his head. "Well, I'm not sure she's put it together, who I am, you know, since Leland had a different last name and all that.

"That's a good thing, isn't it? Kind of awkward, right? Savannah and Leland came to a bad end. Not something I would want to bring up in casual conversation."

Chase pulled the computer back to him, looking at the picture of Phoebe Ryan. He had done a basic internet search on her and was surprised by the amount of information that came back. First off was the website for her company, Ivy Lane Designs. Apparently, she was some sort of designer.

And then there were a bunch of image results and press releases.

"Isn't that guy on some TV show?" Noah said, pointing to one of the pictures. Chase looked at the headline.

"Yeah, some cop show. Looks like he and Phoebe are an item."

Noah pulled the computer back to him. "Hmm, Caitlyn likes that show. She says it's because of the acting, but I swear, that guy always seems to be taking his shirt off."

"Lucky for Phoebe," Chase muttered. The guy's name was Garrett McGraw and he looked like the standard actor type: tall, dirty blond hair, artful stubble. He and Phoebe looked good together, Chase thought.

"Well, if she has that to go home to, maybe she won't be so eager to stick around. Come on, it could be a good thing."

Chase shot his friend a look, but Noah was busy scrolling through something on the computer screen.

"You know, once word gets out that Ivy House belonged to Savannah Ryan, the price will go up." Noah looked up.

Chase smiled, thinking about the envelope he had given her. "That's why I've made her an offer she can't refuse."

Chapter 7

Phoebe stared at the envelope. It had been delivered by a courier service from the lawyer's office in New York. She had opened the package and first read the typed note from Savannah's lawyer, the one who had informed her about Ivy House.

Dear Ms. Ryan, your grandmother asked that you get this letter after you had a chance to visit Ivy House. As I understand you have done this, I am now releasing the letter to you.

The letter wasn't dated, but it couldn't have been too recent because Savannah's script was firm and legible, before her body had been ravaged by the cancer.

My Dear Phoebe,

If you're getting this, it means I'm gone. I don't know how much will be left, but I have ensured that I have one thing to leave you. Ivy House. I found it hard to live there after Leland's death, and after your parents died, it seemed cruel to move you away from the only home you had ever known. But Ivy House was always special to me. It always seemed to have a touch of magic about it. I am told it needs some repairs. And probably some love and care after all these years. Leland Harper was very special to me, and the time we spent at Ivy

House was some of the best, though all too brief, years of my life. How it ended with Leland was a tragedy, a twist of fate.

Ours was a passionate affair and our love burned brightly. I do not know if it would have lasted, but he was the love of my life, even though the press had the world believe otherwise.

I know that I have not always been the best mother or grandmother. To be an artist requires a bit of selfishness, I always felt, especially an actress. You belong to your fans and it's hard to be everything to someone else, especially a child. I didn't always do right by your father, but he turned out fine—better than fine. My only regret is that he too was taken from this world too soon.

And he and your mother did just fine by you, giving me the most precious gift. I know you haven't always enjoyed the life you had to lead with me, and, to be frank, I am not sure it suited you. But you did the best you could with it and that is all anyone asks.

So now, when I can bear to part with it, I give you Ivy House. It was a safe port for me and Leland when times were rough. I hope you may find it to be your own safe haven and a place of happiness and magic. While I was there, I found out who I was…I hope it holds the same promise for you.

Phoebe dropped the letter onto the desk. She was in her room in the Osprey Arms. It was a decent size, with a nice view, and the feeling it was supposed to encourage was one of colonial charm, but the mix of toile and floral fabric was a bit overdone and dated.

She flopped down in the wingback armchair and looked out the window. It was a sunny day. Gulls wheeled in the sky and there were boats leaving the marina heading out for a day on the water.

I give you Ivy House... How very Savannah, Phoebe thought. *I hear it needs a little work...* Also very Savannah-like, Phoebe thought, to give something that wasn't quite fit for gifting. Savannah had left her with many obligations.

Phoebe looked at her phone. The story had hit the papers just as she was getting ready to leave Los Angeles. She didn't want to endure the pity of all her friends. But there it was, in black and white: "*Savannah Ryan Dies Broke...*" was the most succinct. After Savannah died, Phoebe had faced a mountain of paperwork and bills, which the Los Angeles lawyers had summed up for her nicely: sell everything or come up with a mountain of cash to keep it.

While Phoebe wasn't broke herself, Savannah, what with her illness and the nursing home costs, had depleted all her savings quickly. She had already moved out of the house in Malibu and had been living in an apartment. It was on a lease, but the landlord had been happy to let Phoebe out of the contract. That had left furniture and clothes, most of which Phoebe had put into storage, and the rest she had arranged with a dealer friend to sell.

At the end of the day, there had been just enough to cover Savannah's final expenses with a bit left over. So much for the remains of a long career spent entertaining the masses. Savannah had never been interested in anything other than making movies. She had never attached her name to any product or cause. And for the last decade or so, she hadn't been working.

Phoebe glanced over the story. It had the basic details down right, and it included a notice about the sale of some of Savannah's furniture at the gallery. But that was just a sentence or two. The author of the piece had decided to fill the story with some salacious details, rehashing all the details of Savannah Ryan's life: her scandalous child out of wedlock and then her determined wooing of Leland Harper, a married man quite a bit older than her, and their stormy and passionate marriage, which had resulted in his messy divorce and a relationship that kept the media hopping.

She sighed and kept reading. Savannah and Leland's relationship, always heated, turned almost violent, with Leland drinking and accusing Savannah of hooking up with her costars. Before things could get really ugly, Leland had died in a plane crash. Sympathy swung in Savannah's favor, as she became a tragic figure, the lover left bereft, and her career had slowly revived.

Savannah had had a fortune, both from Leland's money and her own work, but she had let it all slip away. Worse, though, was that she had spent Phoebe's inheritance too. Her parents had died in a car crash on the way home from an awards ceremony. Phoebe had been only eight when it happened and Savannah had been awarded custody, moving from Queensbay back to Hollywood, trying to be a mother, while also trying to revive her career.

Phoebe hated the papers. She'd managed to stay out of them and, after a while, so had Savannah. But she'd known enough people, friends and acquaintances, who were hounded by them; the merest indiscretion fodder for endless days of stories, the loss of privacy unbearable.

Phoebe looked at the other envelope on the small side table. Chase had given it to her the day before. He had said it was an offer for the property. As if that was all Ivy House could be.

Her practical side warred with her outrage. And then she thought about what Savannah had done. She had left her a dilapidated house requiring immeasurable investments of time, money, and energy.

She reached for the envelope. It was a simple white one and she slid open the flap, giving herself a nasty paper cut in the process. Strike two against him, Phoebe thought, as she stuck her finger in her mouth, trying to soothe the pain away.

A single sheet of paper fell out. It was a heavy bond and there was a simple, solid dark blue type on the letterhead. But her eyes glossed over that as they fixed on the number. Sure, there were a bunch of words surrounding it, outlining terms and details, but it was the number that got her attention.

"Holy shit," she mouthed and looked again to

make sure she wasn't mistaken. Sandy, the real estate agent, had been right. It really was a million-dollar view. More than a million dollars.

She read over the terms and saw they were simple. The offer was for the house and lot, as-is conditions, no questions asked. All cash, possession to be taken as soon as possible. Phoebe knew that if she accepted this offer, she could be on her way back to Los Angeles and her life within a day or two.

Tempting. Yes, very tempting. She had left Los Angeles at loose ends, and while it didn't mean she needed to get back there right away, she didn't think her absence would make getting her life back together any easier. With that kind of money, she wouldn't have to go back to Los Angeles with her hat in hand, wouldn't have to rely on Dean to sort things out for her. She could be independent, really independent for once, be able to work for herself and not rely on the whims of clients.

She took another look at the letterhead. *Chase Sanders*. The name niggled at her, like the face of someone you saw in a crowd, but couldn't place. Perhaps she needed to do a little more research on this guy.

Chapter 8

Phoebe made her way through the lobby of the Osprey Arms. Like her room, it was elegant in a bland sort of way, with reproduction antiques and a rug that that did nothing for the place except hide the dirt. The effect was a sort of cheap imitation of what elegance should be. It could be so much more.

She was more intent on checking her bag, making sure she had remembered her pencils, her sketchbook, and her laptop, than in noticing her surroundings, which is why she was so startled when she connected with a wall.

"Ouch," she said and then looked up. It wasn't a wall at all, which made sense, since she had been quite sure she'd been walking in the middle of the lobby. Now the contents of her bag, including her sketchbook, were scattered across the floor.

"You," she said. It was Chase. "Chase Sanders," she corrected herself. He was standing there, looming above her.

"You weren't looking where you were going," he said, but she could see that he was more amused than angry. No, she decided quickly. He wasn't just amused. He was openly laughing at her. Not surprising, since she was so startled that she had popped back about three feet upon coming in contact with him. He was a lot more solid than he looked and a definite lurker.

"Do you always stand in the middle of hotel lobbies?" Phoebe snapped back, knowing that it wasn't much of a comeback. She had to look up at him and wished she were wearing higher heels. The Chase of jeans and a windbreaker were gone. This Chase had on tailored slacks, a white button-down, and a dark blue sweater. The expensive sunglasses hung in the v of his sweater and she wondered if he ever went anywhere without them.

He shrugged, the laughter gone, but the amusement still in his eyes. The preppy outfit couldn't hide the broad shoulders and well-developed biceps, even more apparent because he was standing with his arms crossed.

"Here, let me help you with that." And before she could tell him to leave her alone, he was on the floor, casually gathering her things up.

It was too much. She had told herself that she would be calm about the whole thing, but, really, this was too much.

"I don't know who you think you are," she said, finally, as he stood with her sketchpad and some pencils in his hand.

"And what sort of scheme you're trying to run." She felt emboldened and crossed the distance between them. Her finger found his chest and she jabbed it into him, hoping to make her point perfectly clear. "You must be up to something. And just to make it clear, Ivy House is not for sale."

A puzzled look crossed his face. "Is that what you think the offer was? Some sort of scheme?" He stepped back a little from her poking finger. Phoebe noticed that the guy behind the desk—blond, with a stubby little ponytail and one small gold earring—was paying close attention to them, while pretending to do anything but.

"Yes, that's what I think it is exactly." Phoebe felt herself beginning to get worked up. Why else would he have offered so much money for a decrepit house? He was trying to bribe her. That had to be it. Get her to sell and move out and leave Ivy House to the fate of the wrecking ball.

"I don't think when one is set out to scheme against someone, they make such a generous offer," Chase said, his voice mild even as he stopped her pointing finger from stabbing him in the chest again. He held her hand for what seemed like a minute too long, and Phoebe was distracted by the thought of how nice and big it felt wrapped around her own. And then she realized she was close enough to smell him and that he smelled good. Fresh soap and some sort of spicy aftershave.

She swallowed. There had been a point somewhere in there. Ah, yes, Chase Sanders was a conniving bastard with a too-sexy-for-words smile. Phoebe drew herself up to her full height. She had fallen for the sexy smile once too often, but this time she was forewarned. If he thought he could try and sneak Ivy House away from her, then he was surely mistaken.

"I don't know if you think you can steal Ivy House away from me, or what you're planning on doing with it, but I'm no fool. I've done my research. I know what it's worth and trying to sneak in and steal it from under me is a dirty, underhanded trick."

"I take it then that you didn't look at the offer. Because if you had, you would be aware that I offered more than what it was worth."

Chase released her hand and gave her back her pencils. She took them and shoved them in her bag. He still had her sketchpad, and it was with alarm that she watched him start to flip through the pages.

"What are you doing?" Phoebe knew her voice had risen and also knew that the guy at the reception desk was no longer pretending not to notice what was going on in the middle of his lobby. No, he was avidly staring at the both of them.

Chase looked up at her face and then back down at the pad. He had stopped at one of her latest designs, something she had come up with on the plane. Phoebe held out her hand, feeling her face start to grow red. Finally, after what seemed like forever, he handed the sketchbook back to her. She dropped it into her shoulder bag, relief flooding through her now that it was safely back in her possession.

"I assure you, Ms. Ryan, I wasn't trying to steal or sneak anything from you." Chase was smiling again, easy and confident as his blue eyes roamed over her face. Phoebe was aware that her foot was starting to tap impatiently. This encounter wasn't going quite as she had imagined it.

"I'm sorry. I didn't mean to deceive you. I was simply making a fair offer for the house," he said smoothly, and Phoebe took a deep breath.

"I meant what I said; I am interested. It's a great piece of property and ones like those don't come on the market very often."

"Well, I think you might be surprised to find out that you can't just charm your way into everything." Phoebe had done a little more research. Chase's offer had been good, but there was always room to negotiate. That wasn't what Phoebe intended, but she needed to know where she stood.

Chase smiled a slow, lazy smile, and Phoebe felt her stomach do a little flip-flop. Chase was not handsome, at least not in the pretty-boy Hollywood way she was used to. But he had as much presence as any movie star, and it was hard to keep her mind focused when he turned his dark blue eyes on her.

"Oh, you're right. I don't expect charm to work in this case. I figured it was going to take some cold, hard cash to get what I wanted. What do you say? I know I'm breaking one of the first rules of deal making, but that was just my first offer. Care to hear my second?"

There was something almost casually obscene about the way he made the remark, and Phoebe felt herself taking a step away.

"Really, I..." She spun on her heel and walked over to where the guy with the blond ponytail was sitting behind the reception counter. Jim, his nametag read, all of a sudden seemed to be very busy with his computer.

"Excuse me." Phoebe thumped her hand on the scratched wooden surface of the desk. Jim looked up, an embarrassed smile on his face.

"Can I help you miss?" He asked, sounding like he was anything but eager to do so.

"This man," Phoebe did a half-turn and pointed to where Chase was standing, arms folded, rocking slightly on his heels, a very amused expression on his face, "is bothering me. I am a guest at this hotel and I demand..."

Before she could continue, Chase spoke up. "It's quite alright. Sorry to bother you, Ms. Ryan. I'll be going now. But please, think about what I said."

The smirk was back on his face and so were his sunglasses, and if Phoebe wasn't mistaken, she was almost certain his shoulders were shaking ever so slightly as he walked out the swinging double doors and onto the wide porch.

Phoebe turned back to look at Jim, who seemed to be having some sort of choking fit. His face was bright red and when she asked if he was OK, he waved his hand and managed to cough out, "Fine, just fine."

She left after that, satisfied that she had made her point to the lurking and looming Chase Sanders. Ivy House would not be for sale to him. Savannah did not want her to sell it, at least not to someone who probably only wanted it for the view.

Phoebe started out across the village, taking Hill Road, aptly named because it snaked up the high bluffs that circled the harbor. A mix of colonial and late Victorian houses lined the road, and as she got to the top, it flattened out and little lanes jutted off, leading to the water's edge. Ivy Lane was just a half mile up from Queensbay, but it was a steep hike, and she was just a little bit winded when she made it to the front gate.

Ivy House stood there, starkly white against a bluer-than-blue spring sky. It had beckoned to her since yesterday. All of last night she had dreamt of it, strange dreams that had played out like one of Savannah's black-and-white movies. Looking at the house now, the images came back to her. Savannah had appeared, dressed in a simple flowing dress, an elegant blonde. Stepping into the frame had been an older, distinguished man, Leland Harper, dark haired, white suited.

Savannah and Leland's affair and marriage had been so passionate that books had been written and even a miniseries had been based on it. Phoebe's grandmother hardly ever talked about Leland, so Phoebe had done what any kid would do. She'd gone to the internet, watched the miniseries—filled with B-list actors—read the books, and tried to imagine what it had been like.

Savannah and Leland had decided that the best way to quell the uproar was to appear normal.

So, they had stayed in Queensbay, Leland's hometown, and had tried to live like normal people for a while, as normal as a movie star and millionaire could be. The happily-ever-after hadn't lasted, of course. They were too close to Leland's ex-wife, who wouldn't leave them alone, and Savannah couldn't be kept from acting.

No one knew if it would have lasted since Leland had died in an airplane crash, making the story tragic and epic. Still, from the dreamy look Savannah got on her face whenever she talked about Leland and Queensbay, Phoebe knew that Ivy House had been a special place.

Now looking at the house, Phoebe tried to sense the magic Savannah had written about in her letter. The house was beautiful, at least if you looked past the cosmetic blemishes. The white tower that shot up lent the house a quirky sense of possibility. Magic, though? Phoebe looked around at the overgrown garden, the rusted fence, and the broken flagstones. She closed her eyes, breathed in the scent of the water, and let the movie play again in her mind.

Ivy House was gleaming white, the sky blue, the water bluer. Seagulls wheeled in the sky and a light wind rustled the oaks. Foxgloves and lupine bloomed, and the fence was a gleaming black. There was the sound of laughter and the porch invited you to sit. The door was painted Phoebe's favorite color, a slate blue, and the brass knocker shone.

Smiling, Phoebe opened her eyes. Perhaps

this was it, what she needed. Maybe Savannah had truly meant to give her something that needed to be put back together again. She could restore Ivy House, whether for herself or to sell it; maybe that didn't matter. But it would be a project, real, honest work while she sorted out her life. It was the perfect reason to disappear from her old life for a while. And if she decided to sell it, she could be choosy, sell it to someone who didn't want to tear it down, someone who would respect it.

Chapter 9

She tried to push away the thought of Chase Sanders laughing at her as she spent the day at Ivy House, starting to make a plan of what needed to be done. She looked down at one point at her to-do lists and saw that she had drawn his face. And not just once, but several times. She had drawn him once with his eyebrow quirked up, another one with the beginnings of a smirk, and finally one that focused on his shoulders. She sighed and drew bad-guy, villain-type mustaches on all of them, hoping it would get the thought of him out of her mind.

Halfway through the day, her creative energy had taken a turn, and Phoebe abandoned the plans and the numbered lists, grabbing her sketchpad and drawing, designs coming easily to her. She felt that her creative energy was sapped while she was trying to care for Savannah, and she had given up designing everything after the incident with CallieSue Owens. But now, on Ivy House's stone terrace, with the light breeze ruffling her hair and the gentle lap of the waves in the background, she felt absorbed, and a plan, one that included the house and her dream, began to take shape.

Phoebe had been so caught up, she'd looked

up in surprise when Lynn found her, sitting on the low stone wall, sketching the way the setting sun purpled the sky. It was just a way to capture the colors around her, the way everything seemed so bright and vibrant.

"Ready for dinner?" Lynn had asked cheerfully, and Phoebe realized she was. She hadn't eaten since breakfast and the idea of a home-cooked meal was definitely appealing. Gathering all her stuff, she shoved it into her bag, jumped up and stretched.

"Do you ever get tired of it?" she asked Lynn as they both looked over the bluff and toward the water.

Lynn sighed. "No, not really. I know that I'll have to move out soon and I'll miss it, but maybe someday I'll find my way back here."

Phoebe had lived close to an ocean all her life, but there was something soothing and calm about this harbor, the way the bluffs were like arms encircling you in a hug, the simple beauty of lights twinkling in the windows of the houses that ringed the shore. It was comforting, she decided, as she and Lynn walked through a break in the privet hedge that separated the houses.

Phoebe was welcomed into the Masters' home as if she'd grown up there. As promised, Mrs. Masters, who was a doctor as well, was an excellent cook. She was also a huge Savannah fan. Mrs. Masters was just as open and friendly as Lynn and the pasta fra diavolo was so good that Phoebe decided she didn't mind supplying all the information

Mrs. Masters was after.

Lynn's father, also a doctor and chief of the local hospital, drifted off to watch a baseball game right around the time Phoebe started to give details about Savannah's eating habits. It was after the mixed-berry pie à la mode that Lynn had to put a stop to all of her mom's questioning and declared that she and Phoebe were going out on their own.

"These margaritas are delicious," Phoebe said, taking a sip. She and Lynn were down in the village at a place called Augie's. It was different from the Osprey Arms, with a younger, more fun crowd. There were a few families finishing up their dinner, but mostly it was couples and singles, groups of people at tables, some people milling about by a pool table. There was even a jukebox; someone popped in a new song, and people were starting to dance.

"It feels so good to get out," Lynn said, her dark hair curling around her delicate face. They were leaned up against the bar, so she was swaying to the music and sipping her drink.

"It must be tough, all the hours you put in," Phoebe said, also feeling herself starting to sway to the music. It was a nice atmosphere, totally low-key, but fun, and even though she was stuffed from Mrs. Masters' meal, she was eyeing the potato skins someone had ordered a few chairs down.

"Well, at least there's a light at the end of the tunnel. One more year and I'll be a real doctor. I am so excited. It's been a long slog. College, medical school, then residency. But it will all be worth it," Lynn said. Phoebe thought she detected a note of wistfulness in Lynn's voice.

"What do you think you want to do?" Phoebe asked. She had known a few doctors in Los Angeles, mostly plastic surgeons or dermatologists. Not bad people, but they were always working an angle once they found out who she was, trying to see if Savannah would be interested in endorsing them. One guy had even gone so far as to promise Phoebe some "free work" if she could get Savannah to recommend him.

"Well, my dad knows a few people who would be happy to bring me into their practice. Or I could get a job at the hospital. Since he's the chief of staff there, it might be a little weird though, you know, like everyone would think I only got the job because of him."

Phoebe shook her head. "In Los Angeles, it's all about who you know. No one would think twice of using any connection they could to get ahead. My last boyfriend was an actor." She thought briefly of Garrett and the way photographers had always seemed to be around when they went on dates. "And it turned out he was all about my connection to Savannah."

"Sounds like you were burned by someone." Lynn looked at her. "Come on, spill. If you tell me about yours, I will tell you about mine. Can't be worse than someone who got turned on by 'playing doctor.'"

"Dumped me about a week after Savannah's funeral."

"What?" Lynn said, her voice disbelieving. "That creep. What reason did he give you?"

"It was him, not me, you know. The same old stuff. I realized I had just about outlived my usefulness, especially since he had just gotten cast on a new show. And I had this rule: no dating actors. I thought I had learned my lesson, but Garrett was so charming, I just couldn't resist."

Lynn's nose crinkled. "Do you mean Garrett McGraw, the one who's going to be on the new medical show?"

Phoebe looked at her glass. It was almost empty. There was a group of guys, late twenties, early thirties, casually dressed. One of them tried to catch their eye. Phoebe sent a quick smile and then turned to Lynn. Somehow, a blond cutie in a fleece wasn't doing it for her tonight, not when she had spent the afternoon drawing pictures of a dark haired, blue-eyed lurker.

Phoebe shook her head. "He's the one. I thought he was different. We actually went to high school together and, believe you me, he was not that cute back then. So when he showed up looking all yummy and delicious, fresh off that other show, I thought I was being the shallow one, you know, giving him a second chance."

"But let me guess, he was just using you?" Lynn said, her eyes wide and knowing.

"He wanted to impress Savannah. Turns out,

he wanted her to make a few phone calls to some producers, which I guess she did. She never could resist a cute face. Or tight abs. And before I know it, he goes from having a few bit parts in a TV show to being cast as the charming yet deep doctor on the most anticipated show of the season, 'Mercy.'" Phoebe shook her head and looked into her drink. She had managed to finish her entire margarita.

"Well, if it makes you feel better, real doctors hate those shows. Everything's always so dramatic and over-the-top. And trust me, none of us look that good in scrubs," Lynn said.

"Thanks, but I don't think that makes me feel better."

"So did you ever act?" Lynn asked.

"No way. Not for me. Let's just say I am definitely a behind-the-scenes girl. I worked as a set designer for a while and then as a graphic designer and then a designer. Pillows, fabrics, and things. I have my own company, but I mainly do consulting work."

"Would I have bought any of your stuff?" Lynn asked, and Phoebe could tell she was curious.

"Sort of," Phoebe answered.

"Sounds like another story."

Phoebe sighed. Not even tequila could make this story better. "I told a client that she had the taste of a hillbilly."

"A client?" Lynn was puzzled.

"I was hired by a certain celebrity, one with her own cooking show, to help her develop a line of dinnerware. She and I had different ideas on what things should look like," Phoebe said simply. The taste of that defeat was still far more bitter than what had happened with Garrett. She had gotten what she asked for when she dated an actor. But the breakup of her professional relationship had come out of left field.

It had hurt when CallieSue Owens hadn't bowed to Phoebe's far superior design sensibilities. And that manufacturing company, the one paying Phoebe's fee, had chosen CallieSue's white-trash design sensibilities over her own.

"You don't mean CallieSue..." Lynn started to guess.

"Shh. No one is supposed to know she's not designing it herself. But yeah, I mixed it up with a gal from Texas and guess what?"

"What?" Lynn asked.

"You really don't want to mess with Texas," Phoebe said.

Lynn hooted with laughter. The blond guy in the fleece was starting to make his way over to them, and Phoebe decided she didn't care if he came over or not. Perhaps a preppy guy in fleece was just what she needed to block the thoughts of Chase out of her mind.

"Did you get another job?" Lynn asked.

"No, not at the moment. I am clientless." Phoebe only hesitated for a moment. CallieSue Owens had made sure of that. Phoebe had underestimated the amount of pull the woman had and, now, no other celebrity would touch her. Dean, CallieSue's agent and a friend of Phoebe's, was trying to smooth things over, but she was pretty sure that it was a long shot.

"Then what were those sketches I saw you working on?" Lynn asked.

Phoebe hesitated. She had, in between consulting gigs, been working on her own designs, her own lines. It had been sort of a sideline, the pillows, but the designs had started to take off around Los Angeles. Someone she knew, an interior designer, had used a few in a client's home, and that home had made it into a style magazine and Phoebe had gotten credit. She had a website, of course, and before she knew it, people were trying to order pillows from it.

So far, Phoebe had done everything through phone and email, but now that she had no other commitments, she was thinking that perhaps it was time to get serious about it, about her own line of home goods. Still, the decision was so new that it felt weird talking about it aloud. But if there was one person who would certainly not judge her, it was Lynn.

"No, I've been working on a business idea. I think I was getting tired of coming up with all these great ideas and having other people take the credit for it. Quitting my job, taking care of Savannah, coming here—it all feels like maybe it's a part of a journey, some journey to find what I really want to do with my life." Phoebe stopped.

"Well, Queensbay is about as small and real as it gets. Not that we don't have our little society here. There's the Garden Club and the Yacht Club—Friday night barbeques, not to be missed…" Lynn gave a laugh. The guy in the fleece, joined by a friend in a ball cap, was edging closer.

"I guess it wouldn't be such a bad place to try and blend in," Phoebe said, twirling the stem of her oversized margarita glass. She realized that she was really considering the thought. Sure, Ivy House needed work to make it fit for habitation, but not that much. After the renovation, she could keep working on it while living there and running her business.

"You totally could. It would be great. And in the summer, the place really picks up. Plenty of guys with absolutely no ambition of becoming actors. You could go incognito."

Augie's was filling up, the energy rising. Phoebe could feel the tequila in the margarita starting to loosen her up. It would be nice to be somewhere. Put down roots, start over, far away from the too-bright sun of Los Angeles. Savannah had always said Ivy House was magical. Maybe it just needed a little love to bring the magic back.

"I could do it," Phoebe said, emboldened by the liquor. "I can fix up Ivy House and live there. Why not? I'm twenty-eight years old, I have some money in the bank. I don't have to be anywhere I don't want to be."

Lynn threw her head back and laughed. "You

go girl."

They clinked their glasses. "And here's to dating people who have no idea who we are," Lynn said.

"Here, here. No real names and no real professions tonight!" Phoebe agreed, already feeling the smile starting to curve up her lips.

Chapter 10

Phoebe woke up with a throbbing headache, cursing the curtains that had been left open. Sunlight, bright and harsh, streamed into her room. The margaritas. She and Lynn had had more than a few, and then they had walked back to the Osprey Arms, after collecting more than a few phone numbers, all of which they had dumped in the trash can. Lynn had crashed on the couch in Phoebe's room, and sometime in the morning, while Phoebe was still sleeping, had left to get ready for work.

She'd left a note, scrawled on the pad from the desk: *"Take two and call me later. Lynn."* A packet of headache medicine was on top of the note, and Phoebe decided that she must have just been subjected to some sort of doctor humor.

She had dreamed of Ivy House last night. It had been a full, richly layered dream, startlingly vivid to her, fueled no doubt by the alcohol. But it had seemed so real, and in it, Ivy House had been perfect. Gleaming wood floors, comfortable couches, color, and light. And there had been laughter drifting through the house. This time, there had been no Savannah. In fact, everything about the dream had been modern, very present day. It had felt right.

Phoebe looked at herself in the mirror. She felt much better now and she sent a silent shout of thanks to Lynn and her medicine. Time to decide what to wear. She tried to open the windows to see what the temperature was, but the paint was so thick that they were effectively sealed shut. She tried applying some force, but that only made her head hurt, so she flopped down in the little wing chair that looked out over the docks and picked up her phone.

She checked the weather first. Another perfect spring day here on the East Coast. Jean capris, she decided, and her pink-and-white-striped Oxford shirt. A pair of canvas sneakers. She still had some cleaning to do at the house, so she'd pull her hair back in a ponytail. And she had a nice lightweight fleece in case it was cooler up there.

That decided, she glanced through her emails. She'd set an alert to go off whenever her name or Savannah's came up on the Internet. The phone had been buzzing all morning, as more papers picked up on the sad state of Savannah's financial affairs. Her phone buzzed with texts and calls, none of which she answered. They were from friends and colleagues asking if she was OK. It would have been nice, except she could sense the avid curiosity. They were all wondering what it felt like to be poor.

Her phone rang at that moment. She almost didn't answer it, but the temptation was too much, and she glanced down to see who it was.

"Dean," she said, feeling a smile form on her face. Dean was one of her closest friends, the kind of guy who was always there for her. They had met in college when Phoebe had signed on to design the sets for the theater department's production of "Anything Goes." Dean had been in the chorus and they'd formed an instant bond, poking fun at the self-important lead, sharing the same taste for bad action movies, and a love of ice-cream shakes.

After college, Dean had realized he couldn't handle the amount of rejection and poverty it took to be an actor, so he had started working at a talent agency. His good looks coupled with a killer business sense had him quickly rising up the ranks. He'd been responsible for a lot of Phoebe's more interesting and lucrative gigs, whether they were set designs or movie posters, and since he was CallieSue's agent, it was he who had suggested they work together on CallieSue's own line of country chic placemats, tablecloths, and other things.

Too bad CallieSue couldn't see the chic through the forest of tackiness she lived in. But even though CallieSue was Dean's biggest client, he had fought hard for Phoebe, so hard that Phoebe had to quit before Dean could ruin his own career trying to help hers.

"Phoebs, I saw the article, are you OK?" His voice radiated concern even over the phone. It was early on the West Coast, but she knew Dean rarely slept more than a few hours a night. He was seemingly married to his job, always dealing with clients, crises, and other issues. Phoebe knew he was angling for a big promotion.

"I'm fine. It's nothing." Phoebe tried to brush his concern off. He'd been a great friend for her the past few months as Savannah's decline became apparent, checking in on her, sending over takeout, sending flowers, and even his own housekeeper when Phoebe needed help sorting through Savannah's stuff. Still, she had come all this way so that the news from Los Angeles wouldn't bother her, so that she could have time to think, to be herself.

"So are you really out there, in the middle of nowhere? Sure I can't convince you to come back to the Los Angeles? Tinseltown misses you."

Phoebe tensed. After Savannah's death, Dean had told her that he would find a way for her to get her job back, that he could smooth things over with CallieSue, but she had resisted, asking for more time to sort things out. He hadn't thrown a fit, but it seemed like they had come dangerously close to having a moment, to him telling her how he "really felt" that she had panicked and started talking about her need for a strawberry shake. Emotional honesty averted, they had been able to part as friends.

"Dean," she said carefully since she didn't want anything to change between them. She looked out at the water because she found the view, the sky blue with only a few wisps of milky white clouds, and the surface of the harbor cobalt, flecked by the tiniest of white caps, calming.

"I know, I know. You're on a leave of absence from your life. I get it, but let me know if you get bored and want to come back. CallieSue is busy terrorizing someone else and I'm pretty sure she has forgotten about you. I wouldn't be lying if I told you I already have some other opportunities brewing for you. Maybe another movie set, a big-name director. It can be just like old times."

Phoebe smiled wanly into the phone. That was the problem. She hadn't been happy with old times and always working on someone else's vision, and Savannah's death had only brought that into focus.

Sensing her hesitation, he hurried on. "Well, whatever it is, I'm here for you, Phoebs. You know that, right?"

Phoebe took a moment to picture Dean's face. He was fair, blond, with green eyes and high, sculpted cheekbones. He was a good-looking man, gym-fit, with a nervous energy and driven ambition. She had seen him be both charming, with clients, and ruthless, when it came to winning a deal.

"I know that." Phoebe closed her eyes.

All the time they had known each other, they had never managed to both be single at the same time, so the question of getting together had never come up. But now it was out there. Dean was a great guy and, unlike Garrett and a string of others she had dated, didn't need anything from her. But she wasn't sure that was enough.

After a few more words of support from Dean, she clicked off and leaned back again, closing her eyes, trying to soothe her troubles away. Could three-thousand miles really change her life? There was little for her in California. To focus on taking care of Savannah, she had even given up her apartment, putting most of her things in storage, and ever since she'd sold Savannah's house, she'd been couch surfing. She had no house, no job, and perhaps no future.

Savannah's words came unbidden to her: *We make our own destinies.* If anyone could truly believe a saying like that, it would have been Savannah, who'd been sublime at reinventing herself. From the girl next door to an ingénue to a stately matron, Savannah had played every role and then some.

Phoebe took a deep breath. Perhaps she was where she was supposed to be. She was free. For once in her life, she had no ties. She had money in the bank and a roof over her head. *Count your blessings,* Savannah's voice whispered to Phoebe and she laughed.

Phoebe checked the email on her phone. There was only one email from a reporter asking for a comment on the state of Savannah's affairs. She ignored it. It would be better if that story died out.

Right now, she needed to focus on her legacy and her future.

Chapter 11

The fall line was bothering him. Or it wasn't, which was part of the problem. It was boring. North Coast Outfitters was growing fast and that was good, but perhaps there were only so many ways to make a raincoat look sexy.

Chase slowed his steps as he headed up Main Street towards The Golden Pear. They had the best chocolate-chip cookies in town, and he had promised his staff that he would spring for a box of them at the next meeting. It was too nice a day to be cooped up inside, and he had welcomed the chance to walk up towards the restaurant. But it wasn't the smell of cookies that had him slowing down.

It was the sight of her. He hadn't seen Phoebe in a few days, ever since she had literally run into him in the lobby of the hotel, though he'd done his best to keep an eye out for her. Short of walking up to Ivy House, where she had made it clear he wasn't welcome, he hadn't quite figured out a way to run into her again.

But his luck, as it usually did, was holding. He could see her, but only from behind, through the large plate glass window of The Garden Cottage, Queensbay's furniture and knickknack shop. Joan

Altieri, who owned the place, was a friend of his mother's, so it only took Chase a second to come up with a plausible reason for wandering in there. The chocolate-chip cookies would have to wait.

A bell tinkled overhead as he pushed his way into the store. The Garden Cottage had a nice collection of stuff. Lots of things for the garden, of course, and then the usual doodads—candles, candlestick holders, dishes, glasses, plaques, centerpieces, and the like. It was the kind of place women loved and men only stepped in under duress or if they were shopping for a present. His mother's birthday wasn't too far away, and this time, instead of remembering at the last minute, he could kill two birds with one stone: find something for his mother and bump into the perfectly delectable Phoebe Ryan again.

He gave a little wave and a nod to Joan, letting her know that she shouldn't interrupt what she was doing to bother with him. Chase scanned the shelves, desperately trying to think of how his mother had decorated her new place in Florida, seeing if there was anything that she would like, all the while trying to inch closer to Phoebe.

Phoebe hadn't noticed his arrival yet, since she was so intent on what she was showing to Joan.

"Barrel stitched. All hand done. I have some great seamstresses working for me. And this size is available in five different fabric options."

Chase moved through the wine lovers section and angled himself so he had a good view of what

Phoebe was holding up. Rectangular, plump. A pillow he surmised. He watched as she dropped the pillow down on the counter and held up her phone to Joan to show her something.

"And you said these have appeared in *Pacific Living*?" Joan asked, but even Chase could hear the doubt in her voice. Joan was not really a risk taker when it came to stocking her inventory. He'd often thought the store would play better with a slightly fresher sensibility. It was definitely the place to buy your mother or grandmother a gift. No man would ever think of buying his wife or girlfriend something from here.

He came up close enough so he could peer over Phoebe's shoulder. There were five or so pillows laid out on the glass counter and they were fun and bright. A nice pop of color against the muted palette of The Garden Cottage.

"Well, they're certainly bright," Joan said. She was chewing on the end of the earpiece of her glasses and Chase knew that was never a good sign.

"You know, I was thinking that's exactly what my mom needs for her new place." Chase emerged out of the shadows and was rewarded with a huge smile from Joan and a frown from Phoebe.

"Well, they're certainly beachy." Joan agreed, perching her glasses on her nose and running her fingers along the fabric of an azure blue-and-white-striped pillow.

"They're inspired by coastal living," Phoebe said. "West or East Coast." She offered Joan a smile after deliberately turning her back on Chase.

"Well, the summer season is coming up," Joan mused.

"And I'll take two for my mom," Chase said, already reaching into his pocket for his credit card.

Joan looked flustered at that response, and Chase knew that she and Phoebe hadn't quite talked terms.

"Well, I'd be happy to give you the standard wholesale price," Phoebe jumped in quickly and pushed a piece of paper towards Joan, who glanced down and smiled.

"And perhaps," Phoebe finished up smoothly, "you can take a few more on consignment. Showcase them for a few weeks, and when they sell, you can pay me then. You seem quite trustworthy."

"Oh, she is," Chase said, putting his credit card down on the counter. "Why don't you ring me up and I'll pick them up on my way back from the bakery."

Joan flashed him a brilliant smile, and he realized he'd probably been a bit foolish not to ask the price, but hey, he was trying to impress the girl. He hazarded a glance at Phoebe, who was looking at him coolly, arms crossed, chin up slightly. Apparently becoming a customer hadn't changed her mind about him.

Phoebe was pleased with what she had managed to accomplish. It was a small accomplishment, of course, just a few pillows, but Joan had certainly seemed a lot friendlier towards her once Chase had appeared on the scene.

A shadow fell across her path and she looked up. He was standing there or, rather, leaning against the front of one of the shops, waiting as if he had nothing to do but to worry about the large white box he held.

Phoebe swallowed, not sure whether she should follow her nose, which was currently fixated on the smell emanating from the box, or focus on the smug look on Chase's face as he looked down at her from behind his sunglasses.

"You're welcome," he said, his grin turning positively cocky.

"What for?" she said, tucking her sample book back into her bag, trying to feign indifference, though she knew exactly what she should say thank you for.

"Are you always this unfriendly towards your customers?" he asked.

Phoebe pursed her lips. No she wasn't. When someone bought one of her designs, she prided herself on saying thank you. But somehow, the words were having a hard time coming where Chase was concerned.

"Thank you," she managed to say, turning and starting to walk. With catlike grace, Chase was up from the wall and following her. Her nose twitched and she couldn't help but glance at the box he held.

"The Golden Pear's chocolate-chip cookies. Best on the planet," he said, his tone sober.

She stopped. "You're serious?"

"I never joke about these chocolate-chip cookies. The recipe is some old family secret and is guarded better than the gold in Fort Knox here," he said and easily peeled open the box. The aroma of baked goods was overpowering and Phoebe swallowed her desire.

"Try this." Chase held out a cookie.

"No way. That thing is huge. It's practically the size of my head."

He looked down and shrugged. "Half the time they're the size of my head. But that never stops anyone. Trust me."

Chase had pushed his sunglasses back up on his head and she could see the teasing look in his eyes. Good sense and fear of death by chocolate warred against the goddess of hedonism as she took the cookie.

She took a bite, aware that Chase was watching her intently. She chewed, swallowed, and took another bite.

"Oh, wow," she said, around a mouthful of sinfully velvet chocolate and smooth dough. "That really is good."

She took another couple of bites, letting the chocolate chunks sit on her tongue and melt. Phoebe was aware of something. She opened her eyes and saw Chase staring at her with a heated look. She was aware that she had let every nuance of how the cookie was affecting her show on her face. Hurriedly, she swallowed, took a deep breath, and tried to compose herself.

"I told you so," he said, smiling. Phoebe barely listened to him. Here she was in the middle of the street eating an entire chocolate-chip cookie. There was pretty much no way Chase was going to get this back from her.

"Sinfully good," she muttered, letting her tongue find another bit of chocolate to melt away in her mouth. A couple, strolling hand in hand, walked past them, the woman giving Phoebe a strange look.

Phoebe glanced up at Chase. He was leaning in again, watching her, and there was the unmistakable air of amusement about him.

Self-conscious, she looked down. She'd eaten more than half the cookie, which wasn't a surprise since she'd skipped breakfast this morning. Too keyed up about the sales call, she'd only had coffee.

"What?" she asked, feeling shy all of a sudden. It was not like her to take cookies from someone she barely knew. Especially someone she'd recently been yelling at.

"You have a little bit of chocolate there," he said. She licked her lips, trying to find it, and Chase straightened up, his eyes on her.

"Not quite there," he said. "A little farther up, towards the corner." She found it and it was gone, but she saw that Chase's eyes had lost their amused spark and that he was now looking at her entirely differently.

"What?" Phoebe took another bite.

"Just a bit there," he said and reached in, his finger hovering near her cheek before it gently made contact. It was a feather-light touch, but it made her insides sit up and take notice. Her stomach clenched and rolled, and the two of them were frozen for a moment, looking at each other.

"Excuse me," a voice broke in and Chase's hand was gone from her cheek. Phoebe's stomach seemed to right itself, but not without leaving her feeling a bit dizzy. Too much coffee, she thought, even as the voice kept talking.

"I was wondering from where you got that cookie." It was the woman who had just walked past with a look of disdain on her face, and now she and her husband were standing there, looking at them, the woman's mouth slightly open, the man sending Chase a knowing look.

"It looks amazing," the woman added.

Chase recovered first. "From The Golden Pear, one block up. Make a left onto High Street."

"Best I've ever had," Phoebe said and then wished she had kept her mouth shut.

The couple left, and she and Chase were alone again. He had taken a step back and was no longer leaning, and his sunglasses had slipped down from his head and she could no longer see his eyes. It was hard to read him, and then his mouth quirked up in its typical smile.

"I guess I'll be seeing you," he said.

"I guess so," Phoebe agreed, though she didn't know why. Unless he needed more pillows. Still, she wasn't in the right frame of mind to disagree with him.

He backed away a few paces before he turned and walked in the direction of the harbor. Phoebe stood there, the remains of the cookie still in her hand, unabashedly enjoying Chase's rear view.

Head turning, he caught her looking at him and flashed her a grin. She was almost certain that he threw her a wink behind his sunglasses. And then he turned and was on his way.

Phoebe leaned against the cool brick of the building. It was a shady and ideal place for her to just stand still. Her brain was a puddle of mud. And her stomach was flip-flopping again, probably from the giant cookie she had eaten. Right, that was it. It had nothing to do with the way Chase Sanders kept showing up when she least expected it. And doing her favors. Phoebe shook her head, trying not to get too worked up. In Los Angeles, nobody did favors for nothing. Chase's help had to come with a price.

Chase did his best to keep his cool as he made his way back down towards the marina and his office. He'd only meant to give Phoebe a helping hand with the pillows. He stopped, almost started back, and then thought better of it. Joan still had his credit card and his pillows, but he knew they'd be safe. He'd go by later and pick them up when he was sure that Phoebe would no longer be anywhere in the vicinity.

One glance of her eating that cookie had been enough. The cookies were famous enough around Queensbay. Heck, even Noah swore by them when he needed to get out of the doghouse, but Chase wasn't sure he'd ever seen someone, well, a woman, get so much pleasure out of a cookie. It was like… no, he wouldn't—couldn't—go there. Already he was having too much trouble concentrating without any more thoughts of Phoebe Ryan breaking into his head.

Chapter 12

Phoebe retreated to Ivy House. She had discarded the rest of the cookie and was now eating an apple while she doodled. The internet had been set up in the house, and Lynn had let her borrow a couple of sawhorses and a large piece of plywood from her father's garage. It was serving as a temporary desk and that was just what Phoebe needed.

Joan Altieri had called just after lunch, while Phoebe was busy scrubbing kitchen cabinets. A customer had seen the pillows Chase had bought and wanted some just like it. Did she have more?

Phoebe took a deep breath, lied, and said yes. There was no way she was going to say no to another sale. As soon as she got off the phone with Joan, she called up her workshop in California.

Angela, the manager there, was nice, but always fretting, and Phoebe had to stop herself from screaming with frustration. That would only make Angela fret more and delay the process of her getting any more pillows. Finally, Angela admitted that they did have some stock in the warehouse space that Phoebe rented from them, and that she could send out some pillows by tomorrow morning.

Triumphant, Phoebe fist-pumped and got off the phone before Angela could change her mind. Walking over to her computer, she tapped on the keyboard until her website came up. She sighed. It was a piece of crap. Well, not exactly. It looked good, with beautiful pictures of her designs and even a pretty good headshot of her on it, one that she had bartered for. A duvet cover captured her in a slightly sexy, somewhat just-woke-up kind of look. Phoebe's only quibble was that her resemblance to Savannah was too evident. Dean had suggested that she mention her relationship to Savannah in her bio, but Phoebe had balked. She wanted people to buy her products because they liked the design, not because she was related to someone famous. Dean had smiled at her and shook his head at her naiveté.

But Phoebe wasn't being naive. She knew that putting the Savannah relationship out there could only help her, but it still didn't sit well with her. Savannah too had thought her silly not to make use of her fame, but Phoebe knew that she had also admired her determination to make it based on talent.

Nope, the problem with the site, Phoebe thought, was that it was hard for people to order something from it. Sure, they could email her with inquiries, but there was no way for people to add things to a shopping cart, pay with a credit card, all of that stuff everyone else seemed to have. Something would have to be done about it.

"You look like you're on cloud nine," Lynn

said, appearing in her doorway. "I did knock, but you didn't hear me."

"Sorry." Phoebe stood up and stretched. Work and pillows had been a nice distraction from Chase Sanders and his chocolate-chip cookie. "I was on the phone."

"No problem. So you got the internet up?" Lynn asked, nodding at her computer, and before Phoebe could say anything else, she continued. "By the way, my futon from college is just sitting in the basement. It's not much, but my mom wants to lend it to you if you'd like, until you get a real bed. That's if you're serious about not wanting to stay at the Osprey Arms. She also told me to tell you that you're more than welcome to the guest bedroom."

Phoebe looked up. "That would be great. The futon, I mean. I don't suppose we could move it ourselves."

Lynn smiled and her dark ponytail bounced as she held up her arms, muscle-man style. "With these guns, we can move anything we want."

Phoebe laughed, but she knew Lynn was serious. She'd already received a lecture from Lynn on the importance of weight training and been subjected to a rundown of just how much Lynn could bench press.

"Well, sounds good." Phoebe would be happy to move out of the Osprey Arms. The view at Ivy House was better and it was, for the moment, free.

"Whatcha looking at?" Lynn said, coming around to the computer.

"Oh," Phoebe said, her mind going back to the morning with Chase. "I sold some of my pillows to The Garden Cottage. You know, that shop in town."

Lynn nodded. "Sure do, my mom loves that place. My brother calls the owner around Mother's Day, gives her a spending limit, and tells her to pick something out and wrap it up. Looks like a champ every year."

Phoebe laughed. She'd only seen pictures of Kyle, but knew he had a job that kept him traveling a lot.

"Well, tell him this year, he wants to order a Phoebe Ryan original."

"Will do. Is that your website?"

Phoebe nodded. Lynn was looking at the picture of her.

"The resemblance is really uncanny when you look like that." Lynn was looking at the picture of her. The dress was a lot sexier than she would normally wear, and Dean had made her get her hair and makeup done before the shoot. Normally, Phoebe was a lip-gloss-only type of girl.

"I know. But luckily, I don't wear stilettos and plunging necklines. Hard to be creative when you're uncomfortable. At least it is for me. But," Phoebe said, thinking maybe Lynn could help her, "I do need some help with the website. I need to put a shopping cart in and be able to accept credit cards and the like. Do you know anyone around here who could help me with that?"

Lynn looked up, lips pursed, and then she

snapped her fingers. "Yeah I do. Tory. She's some sort of computer whiz. She helped out with the website for the clinic, and she works for Chase Sanders."

"Chase?" Phoebe said, trying to keep her voice neutral, but Lynn picked up on it immediately.

"You know him? Well, I mean, of course you know him, you must."

"What do you mean?" Phoebe asked, a moment of panic coming to her as she thought about the cookie on the street. It had been good and she had been into it, but really, people couldn't be drawing conclusions, could they?

"Well, you're kind of almost related." Lynn saw the look on Phoebe's face and backpedaled. "Well, not really."

"What are you talking about?"

Lynn looked at her, confused. "You mean you really don't know who Chase Sanders is?"

"He's some guy who wants to buy this house. And he bought pillows from me. And gave me a chocolate-chip cookie." Which was so good, Phoebe thought, that she had to lean against a wall to catch her breath.

"And that's all you know about him?"

"Well, he's cocky and arrogant..." Phoebe added, remembering how Chase's finger had brushed against her cheek in search of an errant piece of chocolate.

"And a total player." Lynn nodded. "Pretty much everyone agrees on that score. But that's not all."

Phoebe shook her head in ignorance.

"Here, let me." Lynn pulled the computer to her, typed in something, and stood back. Phoebe stared down at the image on the screen.

"Why am I looking at a picture of Savannah Ryan and Leland..." Phoebe trailed off, not believing what her eyes were telling her.

"Can you see the resemblance now?" Lynn asked.

"What...How..." Phoebe sat down on the rusted folding chair.

"Chase Sanders is Leland Harper's grandson. You know, from his daughter from his first marriage. She married a Sanders."

"And he lives here in Queensbay?"

"Yes...has lived here his whole life, I heard. I guess his grandmother remarried and stayed here. You mean you never saw how much he looked like Leland?"

Phoebe shook her head. "Savannah didn't keep many pictures. At least not the ones that were out. She didn't like to be reminded of him. Too painful."

It took a moment for it to all sink in. Chase Sanders, he of the ridiculously high offer for Ivy House, he of the pillow buying, chocolate-chip-dispensing charm was Leland Harper's grandson. And he had known all along.

It took about a moment for the shock of it all to wear off and be replaced by searing hot anger.

<<>>

Outrage propelled Phoebe out of the house, down the hill, and towards the marina. She brought herself up short at the top of the marina's docks, her eyes scanning for dark hair and sunglasses.

"Can I help you, miss?" She looked up. A boy, blondish hair, an earring in one ear, and a polo shirt embroidered with the words "Queensbay Marina" was looking at her.

"Chase Sanders," she barked.

He glanced her over, then decided that she was harmless, and pointed down to one of the long narrow docks.

"The *Windsway*, berth eighty-nine."

"Thank you," Phoebe managed to say.

A hand touched her arm, and Lynn pulled her around.

"Phoebe, are you sure you should be doing this?" Lynn's brown eyes were round with concern.

"Oh, I am sure," Phoebe said, starting down the ramp. The dock bobbed as she stepped on it, and it took a moment for her to catch her footing.

The slips were all numbered, and she walked carefully along. Lynn followed her, calling out suggestions. "You know, maybe you should phone him first."

"What, and give him a chance to come up with some story?" Phoebe said. They were at slip eighty, and she practically jogged the rest of the way to his boat, drawing up short when she came to it. Now that she was here, she wasn't quite sure what to do next. She could hear voices coming from inside the boat. It was a sailboat—long, sleek, with a white hull and a blue sunshade over half of the cockpit. The chrome gleamed and the wood shone. Lines were neatly coiled around cleats and winches.

There was the sound of laughter, high, girlish, and then a lower, deeper, answering chuckle.

She hadn't expected him to have company.

Lynn came up beside Phoebe and looked at her. Phoebe knew there was no turning back.

"Chase Sanders."

"Try again," Lynn suggested. "Louder. Let him know how riled up you are."

Lynn seemed to be enjoying this way too much.

"Chase Sanders, I need to talk to you." Phoebe called and this time her voice was loud and true.

There were sounds of rustling and then a head popped up, one with long, light brown hair, the color of caramel, followed by eyes of the same color, and then came the rest of the body, goldenly tanned, dressed in a pink polo shirt and straight-leg khakis.

The girl, who looked like she could have been a college student, swung her eyes between Lynn and Phoebe, gave a nod to Lynn, and then stuck her head down from where she had come.

"Chase, there's someone here to see you."

Another bit of rustling and Chase appeared.

"What?" His hair was mussed, and he had a finger in his mouth, as if he'd hurt it.

"Oh, thank God, a doctor," he said when he saw Lynn. He pulled his hand up and they saw blood flowing freely.

Lynn went into doctor mode, and Phoebe was left on the sidelines.

After a brief examination, during which Lynn told the other girl to get the first aid kit, Lynn pronounced Chase fine.

"Just keep it clean and a bandage on it for a day."

"I don't need a tetanus shot?" Chase asked. He was sitting in the cockpit, looking like he was used to women hovering about him. Phoebe had stayed on the dock, arms crossed, kicking at it harmlessly with her toe.

"I don't know," Lynn said, cleaning up the supplies from the medical kit and handing it back to the girl. "When was the last time you had one?"

"Not a clue."

Lynn snorted. "How rusty a nail?"

The other girl rolled her head. "It was a paper cut. Chase was pushing papers and I was trying to calibrate his radar system."

"I think it was a splinter." Chase said, his eyes turning puppy-dog round, but Lynn was unmoved.

"A paper cut is more likely."

Phoebe looked up and caught Chase gazing at her, his blue eyes filled with interest. She turned and paced another length of the boat.

"Look, I gotta get back to the office, Chase. I have a call with the West Coast over online promotions."

"Great, Tory, thanks for trying to fix the radar

system."

"Trying?" the girl, Tory, Phoebe supposed it was, tossed her caramel-color hair as she easily landed on the dock. "It's fixed. You can bring me a mocchachino later. See you, Lynn."

The girl shot a smile at Chase and Lynn, gave a nod and a wave to Phoebe, and walked back towards land without another look.

Lynn glanced uneasily between Chase and Phoebe. "I think the clinic just buzzed me. I'll catch you later."

She too jumped lightly on the dock and made a discreet "call me" gesture before leaving.

Phoebe drew up near the little step stool that Chase had set up to make it easier to get on board the boat.

"Glad you came by. Tory's a genius with computers, but I think the sight of blood makes her faint." Chase smiled at her, as if nothing out of the ordinary was happening.

Phoebe said nothing, trying to fight the trembling that had come over her.

"You know you're supposed to ask permission to come aboard?" Chase said, the know-it-all grin back.

"I don't think I need to ask anything of you," Phoebe said. Her tone almost wiped the smirk off Chase's face.

"How dare you?" she began and found that she was trembling.

"Whoa, what did I do?" He stood up and the

boat moved with him. Phoebe thought better about climbing aboard as he crossed the space of the cockpit and was now standing at the railing looking over her. She didn't need to be in a confined space with him.

"It's more like what you didn't do."

"What are you talking about?" He sounded genuinely surprised.

"How could you have not told me?" Phoebe found that she had gone from angry to upset and her voice showed it. If Savannah had been here, she would have known how to play to the scene. But she wasn't. Instead, Phoebe was facing Chase Sanders, Leland Harper's grandson.

"Told you...You mean you didn't know?"

"Of course I didn't know. You're Leland Harper's grandson."

"So?" Chase said, and he jumped lightly onto the dock. It moved gently underneath them, and a seagull that had been posed on a piling took flight into the warm blue sky.

He was there, right in front of her, standing too close to her. She took a step back and found that her way was blocked, that there was something, a large pole, behind her. To step around would make it obvious that she was trying to get away from him, and she wasn't going to give him the satisfaction of knowing that.

"Don't you think you might have mentioned it?"

Chase shrugged. He didn't have his sunglasses

on, and she could see just how blue his eyes were, the sapphire of them surrounded by little lines that fanned out from the corners.

"I guess I was waiting for the right time. Besides, it's a bit of an awkward way to open a conversation, don't you think?"

Phoebe didn't say anything, so he continued. "Anyway, what does it matter?"

"Matter?" Phoebe knew her voice sounded shrill even to her own ears. "Matter. Why do you want the house? Some sort of evil vendetta?"

"Vendetta?" Chase looked puzzled. "What are you talking about? It's a house..."

He didn't get any further than that.

"I know what you Harpers are capable of. And if you think you can drive me out of town, make me miserable, just like you did to Savannah, you have another thing coming."

"What...Make you miserable...Your grandmother was the home wrecker."

"Home wrecker?" Phoebe fought for control. "She was an amazing actress, an American legend."

"God," Chase rolled his eyes. His nonchalant grin had been replaced by something more like annoyance. "You're starting to sound like those crappy Hollywood tribute programs, 'Savannah Ryan, the golden child, blah, blah...'"

"Well, at least she wasn't some dried-up prune of a woman who hounded her ex-husband when he wouldn't take her back."

"Oh, please, like you would know. What is

that, the Savannah Ryan Hollywood version of the story?"

They were yelling at each other full on. Phoebe realized that more than a few people had popped their heads out of boats and were looking at them with open interest.

Chase was also very close to her, so close that she could see the way the blue of his eyes was pierced by lighter flecks. They were like pools of water, great, deep, inviting pools of water, and she felt hot all of a sudden, even though the day wasn't that warm, and she was in the shade of the boat.

Now it was Chase's turn to point his finger and, though he kept it from touching her, it wagged annoyingly in her face.

"You might think you can come here, all high and mighty, Ms. Hollywood, but not everyone in this town wants to see that house torn down."

"Torn down?" she said, puzzled, not quite sure where this conversation was going.

"It's practically a piece of history, and maybe all you people from California want new and shiny and modern, but here in Queensbay, in my town..."

"Your town?"

"My town, that's right, we believe in preserving history, not destroying it."

"I don't want to destroy it..." Before Phoebe was able to go any further, there was the sound of pounding feet and an anxious voice.

"Chase." Phoebe looked over Chase's shoulder. It was that girl again, Tory, with the caramel-colored hair.

"Not now, Tory," Chase said without turning.

"Ahh, I think you're going to want to come. There's an issue down in Florida."

"Take care of it," Chase said, but he turned to look.

Phoebe saw that Tory was wringing her hands and looked genuinely distressed.

He turned back to Phoebe. "This," he said, "isn't over." He spun around and walked up the dock, Tory talking to him urgently. The surface under Phoebe swayed a little and she leaned back into the piling. What had just happened?

<<>>

"Do people think I want to tear down Ivy House?" Phoebe asked Lynn. They were sharing a bottle of wine Lynn had brought over, along with cheese and crackers, sitting on the low stone wall that marked the border of the terrace.

"Well," Lynn said.

"Come on, tell me."

"I guess the thought was that you were some big Hollywood hotshot. What would you want with some big old pile like this?" Lynn trailed off.

"You look guilty," Phoebe said. Lynn had brought along some chair cushions, but still the ledge was not the most comfortable thing in the world. There was an old garden bench tucked under a tree. It was rickety, but with a little work, it would be serviceable. Maybe that should be one of her first projects.

"Who me?" Lynn popped a cracker with a wedge of cheese on it into her mouth.

"Is that why you were so friendly to me? What, did the Historical Commission send you up to make sure I wasn't going to tear the place down and put up some ultra-modern white box?"

Lynn shook her head. "No, of course not. Well, not exactly. But they did ask me what I thought. And I told them you didn't plan on it. Sorry, I didn't mean to be a gossip, but seriously, you do not want these old biddies on your case. Look, it's your house and if that's what you want to do…"

Phoebe shifted as a pointy bit of stone was jabbed her thigh. "So why does Chase Sanders think that's what I'm going to do?"

Lynn considered for a moment and then a smile spread across her face.

"What is it?" Phoebe knew Lynn was onto something.

"Didn't you say that Chase offered an obscene amount of money for the house?"

"Yeah, I thought he wanted the view," Phoebe said.

"No way. He loves the house. Totally thinks the family connection is cool. I mean, at least that's how I heard him talk about it at one of the Yacht Club things."

"So he's serious about wanting the house. He doesn't want to tear it down as part of some sort of revenge fantasy against Savannah?"

Lynn shook her head. "No, but there is someone who benefits if you sell this place. More so if she has an eager buyer who thinks you might need a ridiculous offer to be persuaded to part with it?"

Phoebe almost smiled too. "Ahh, a little negotiating ploy by the real estate agent." The sun was setting, sending soft rays of light out along the water. The harbor was calm, almost glasslike, which seemed to happen often at dusk. It was quiet and peaceful, and soon the lights in the houses sitting on the bluffs would start to wink on. Most of the boats were safely back in port for the night, and the only real sound was the gentle bell tolling on one of the channel markers.

"Well, both of them will be very sorry. I'm certainly not going to be tearing this place down." Phoebe turned to look at the house behind her. She had taken Lynn up on her offer of the futon. By tomorrow night, she would have moved in enough at Ivy House to give up her room at the Osprey Arms.

"And what about Chase Sanders?" Lynn asked, taking a sip of her wine, her brown eyes twinkling above the rim.

"What about him?" Phoebe tried to forget the way his blue eyes had flashed at her, raising her body heat through the roof. "I think Queensbay is big enough for the two of us. And if I don't intend to tear the house down, I don't suppose the natives, including those old biddies, will have anything to complain about, will they?"

"Not likely," Lynn said, and Phoebe decided to ignore the doubt she heard in her voice.

Chapter 13

Chase sat in the meeting, listening to the bickering going on between the creative director, his PR director, Tory, and assorted staff. It was one of the few things he hated about running a company. Decision by committee. As North Coast Outfitters had grown, he hadn't been able to keep a finger in every pie. Too many locations, too many moving parts. He'd had to do what he did best—be a captain and manage his crew. But right now, his crew was getting on his nerves, and he wished he could make them walk the plank, metaphorically speaking, that is.

The windows of the conference room had a good view of town. He'd been able to watch Phoebe make her way off the docks and head up the road back, he presumed, to Ivy House. She had been angry and had been yelling at him, her eyes bright, the color high in her cheeks. Phoebe had looked lovely and he had wanted to kiss her. There, he had admitted it.

But his meetings with her never quite played out the way he thought. He'd offended her at the first, had her angry at the second, almost won her back at the third, and now she was all riled up again.

So what if he was Leland Harper's grandson. The man, except for passing on some DNA, had been a blip on the screen as far as his family was concerned. At least the ones now. He knew Grandmother had never quite forgiven Savannah for stealing her husband. But that was history.

Now they tossed the story around like it was a joke, a legend, history, but of the more colorful sort. Every family had some of that, right?

Chase shook his head. He'd made the offer on Ivy House because his mother had called, saying what a shame it would be if the new owner, an out-of-towner, came and tore down a local landmark. And then Joan Altieri had clucked over the same thing, and before he knew it, Mrs. Sampson, the head of the Queensbay Historical Commission, had ambushed him on his way to get coffee and said the same thing. And then Sandy Miller, real estate agent extraordinaire, had swooped in and told him, for a price, he could have the best view in town.

So much for a done deal. Phoebe Ryan was having none of him.

He sighed and turned his attention to the pictures in front of him.

"The preview emails received a dismal click-through rate," Tory was saying. "I just don't think anyone was very excited about the new designs."

"I know, I know." His creative director looked annoyed. "Look, this is the first time we've ever attempted to branch out beyond our core of sailing and sporting goods. Maybe we need to start over?

These designers are great with raincoats, but," she gestured at the portfolio in front of them, "I don't think they're getting it."

Even Sam Waterstone, the PR director, the one who always had an idea on how to make something look fun or sexy or useful or all three, was shaking his head.

"Not getting it?" Chase repeated, looking at the images. Nope, they were certainly not getting it. Everything was blah, boring, and definitely not hip. They needed something fresher, lighter, younger.

Suddenly, Chase felt instinct take over. "I have an idea." He leaned back in his chair, feeling victory within grasp. He knew just the person who could help them.

Chapter 14

The note came the next morning with a large bunch of flowers, creamy white lilies. Looked like Chase had written the note himself, she thought. Thick black marker, simple printed letters.

I think we got off on the wrong foot. Do over? The Osprey Arms, seven o'clock, tonight.

Phoebe held the note, remembering the last time she had seen Chase, his blue eyes flashing, his legs spread apart, hands on his hip, looking for all the world like he was the captain of a ship about to face the maelstrom. Did she want to see him again? Phoebe placed the flowers on the edge of her desk, looking at them.

Of course, she wanted to see him. Her whole body was practically itching with desire at the thought of seeing him, the thought of looking into his eyes, watching his lopsided grin staring down at her, the thought of running her hands through his too-long black hair. She could pretty well imagine the silky feel of it.

Phoebe sighed deeply, inhaling the light, fresh smell of the lilies. Yes, she was going to go. There was no way she could stay away; both her interest and her curiosity were aroused. Chase Sanders, Leland Harper's grandson. A link, however tenuous, to Savannah.

<<>>

Phoebe awoke with a start. She checked her watch. She had worked all day at the house, both on her website and on cleaning the kitchen. It was dirty, hot, and exhausting work. Another day or so and she would be ready to move in, but for now she was happy with the clean bathroom and soft bed at the Osprey Arms. It had been so inviting that when she had come back, she had intended only to close her eyes for a moment, but she'd fallen fast asleep, and now she realized with a rush of panic that she had only a half hour to get ready.

A quick shower and only a few minutes to figure out what to wear. It certainly wasn't a date, so anything with too suggestive a neckline or too low a back was out. But would looking too casual send the wrong message?

Finally, she had decided to keep it simple, a pair of dark wash blue jeans that stretched nicely over all the right places and a purple v-neck sweater. No heels, since she was tall enough already, but a pair of ballet flats and scarf tied at her neck pulled it all together. It was her go-to outfit, she supposed, simple, with the sweater highlighting her eyes.

She felt flushed and slightly embarrassed when she entered the darkened room. It was closer to seven thirty than seven, and as a rule, she didn't like to keep people waiting. The bar at the Osprey

Arms was mildly crowded for a Thursday night. There was a couple leaning in towards one another, heads close, hands intertwined. There was also a group of older men, in khakis and sweaters, white-haired with red cheeks, so Phoebe figured they had probably come in from a round of golf.

And there he was, in the far corner, with an empty stool next to him. He saw her and one hand went up. She swallowed. She worked her way down the bar, nodding at the bartender.

Chase stood up when she turned the corner, his hand held out.

She stopped and looked at it.

"What are you doing?"

He smiled, but this time it was genuine, an almost friendly grin. "Like I said, starting over. See, I'm Chase Sanders. Nice to meet you."

Her eyebrows arched up, but she decided to play along, "How nice to meet you, Mr. Sanders. I'm Phoebe Ryan."

"Please call me Chase."

"Thank you." Phoebe let herself be guided into the high chair at the bar, the wide palm of his hand splayed across her back, creating an instant contact burn with her skin, right through the thin cashmere wool of her sweater. No flushing, she ordered herself, glad the dim lighting in the bar would offer her some camouflage for the way her body was reacting to him.

"What will you have?" Chase asked, catching the bartender's attention.

"A white wine, please."

Chase ordered a wine for her and a pint for himself. She was surprised at that, but decided to say nothing. At least he wasn't pretentious in his choice of beverage.

"So..." Phoebe said during the uncomfortable silence that had settled between them after their drinks were delivered.

"To new beginnings," he said, raising his glass in a toast. She smiled. She could agree to that.

Phoebe took a sip of her wine. It was cool and crisp and was probably from a better bottle than whatever the house wine was. She glanced at Chase again. His hand was wrapped around his pint glass and she could see the fine light-colored hair on his tan knuckles. It was not a hand that looked like it stayed inside all day pushing papers around. For a brief instant, she remembered how it had felt on her back, large, warm, almost possessive, as he had guided her onto the bar chair, and she let herself imagine just what else it might be capable of.

"First off, I was sincere when I offered my condolences about your grandmother. Whatever else she was, she was certainly a talented actress," he said.

Phoebe scanned his face, trying to see if there was a hint of sarcasm. She saw none, so she smiled. "Thank you. But did you know, from the first meeting, who I was?" Phoebe asked, curious.

He shook his head. "No, not until you said something. I mean, I was sincere too. You did look familiar. Of course, I realize that it was the family resemblance that had me thinking you were someone."

"Thank you, I guess."

Chase smiled, showing a set of nice, straight white teeth. She felt her skin warm under his gaze. "You're welcome. It was a compliment, however backward it might have seemed."

"It's just I was hoping to be somewhat anonymous, you know, here. Thought it might be possible. To just be myself."

"Yes, of course," he raised his glass again. "Though I think your cover might be blown. The real estate agent is pretty much buzzing with excitement. Apparently she was a big fan."

Phoebe smiled. "There aren't many who weren't. I'm told it makes the house more valuable."

Chase gave her that cocky grin, and she felt her heart bump against her ribcage. "So I would have gathered. Though some may say that it didn't play host to the happiest of couples."

Phoebe smiled. "Happy is probably too mild a word. They were wild for each other, a burning passion. And then it all went downhill. Is that why you're interested in the house, because your grandfather lived there?"

"Leland Harper wasn't my grandfather," Chase said. Phoebe was about to disagree when he continued. "At least not in any way that mattered. When he left, my grandmother apparently never spoke his name again. She remarried Sal, who ran the marina here, and she was very happy. Happier than she was with Leland. So happy she waited her ex and Savannah out, and Queensbay was her town until she died about ten years ago."

Phoebe did the math. Savannah had been much younger than Leland, so the timing made sense. "So, no hard feelings?" Phoebe asked, curiously.

"Do you want me to blame you for something your grandmother did? I assume you didn't have anything to do with it."

Phoebe shook her head. "No. Savannah did what Savannah wanted."

Chase laughed. "I gathered that. Supposedly, Leland was a bit like that too. Perhaps the two of them were perfect for each other."

She liked the way he laughed and had to look down into her wine to fight the warm clench in her stomach.

"And the house?"

"Always loved it. There always seemed to be some sort of mystery about it, but of course, no one in my family would ever talk about it. It took me a while to figure out the history behind it and then I just kept my interest in it to myself."

"It is a great house," Phoebe agreed, thinking of the vision she'd had earlier, it perfectly restored, filled with light and laughter. The feeling of happiness had been so real.

"So you don't want to tear it down?"

"No." Chase looked truly shocked by the idea.

There was a pause and then he asked, "You?"

"No. Savannah said it was a magical place. I just didn't know it was such a dump. Or how much work it would take to restore it. I'm not about to tear it down."

"Does that mean you're going to fix it up, live in it?" Chase asked.

Phoebe smiled, hoping she wasn't giving too much away. "I'm definitely going to fix it up. As you mentioned, I'm not from around here, and I'm not quite sure I'm up for the East Coast winters."

He shrugged, grinned. "They can have their charm, when the harbor's rimmed with ice and the trees sparkle against the winter sky."

"You sound like a poet."

"I'm a sailor. I notice the weather." There was a pause while they studied each other, and then Chase said, "If fixing it up becomes too much or you get too cold, you know the house would be safe with me."

Phoebe shuddered. "You'll probably want to put in a black leather couch and a giant TV."

Chase laughed. "And what's so wrong with a TV?"

"Fine if it's for screening black-and-white classics. But if it's for watching every game being played, then you might as well be in some place where you're not paying for the view."

"Noted. I'll make sure the couch isn't black."

Then, because her senses were raised and she was aware that she had been feeling too much at ease, too much under the spell of his charm, she asked, "It's awfully presumptuous of you to think you might get a crack at decorating it. Do you always get what you want?"

He looked at her, his eyes dark, smoky in the dim light. There wasn't a hint of a smile as he answered. "Always."

Phoebe swallowed, wondering how one simple word could have her hot, her body tingling with excitement down to her core.

She didn't know what to say next, the art of small talk escaping her as she tried to get her emotions under control, since his closeness was making her feel too hot, too aware of everything going on around her.

"So what brings you to Queensbay? Besides a free house?" Chase asked. He said it casually, his eyes actually on the flat screen showing a baseball game, but she sensed he was deeply curious about the answer.

"You said it yourself," Phoebe replied.

"I did?" He looked at her now, and she felt the force of his presence wash over her. He had, she decided, a very commanding one.

"New beginnings. It seems like it's the perfect time in my life to start over to make a change. I don't have any family, anyone waiting for me in Los Angeles, so I thought it might be time for a change. Savannah claimed the house was magical."

"Magical?" Chase asked, and she looked closely to see if she was making fun of her.

"Well, perhaps not magical, as in witchy magic. But I think for the first time in her life, Sarah Jane Ryan felt like she belonged."

"Sarah Jane?"

"Her given birth name. Legally changed it to Savannah when she was of age. I never did find out why. But Savannah grew up in a small town, in the middle of nowhere, where no one believed in dreams. And to her, Ivy House was the embodiment of every dream she'd ever had, even if it only lasted for a while. Ivy House meant that your dreams could come true."

Chase nodded, but he didn't say anything and was watching her intently. She felt a surge of heat wash over her under his scrutiny.

"It's just a house," he said, a faint trace of amusement evident in the way his lip curled up.

"It wasn't for Savannah and Leland."

At that, Chase tossed his head back and laughed; then he lowered it and looked down at her. "I don't think there was anything magical about them."

Phoebe let the hint of a smile ghost across her face. "Well maybe you only heard one side of the story. Savannah always said Leland was the love of her life and they were happiest here. They were out of the limelight; they could be themselves."

"Savannah was an actress. Was she never not acting?"

Phoebe could feel herself smiling at the memories. Chase had a point. Savannah never did anything by halves. Even sitting by the pool was a production. She would be in a sexy two-piece, with some gauzy swim dress thrown on, with a huge hat and big glasses to hide her face and keep it sun-free. Still, there were times, like when she made a big bowl of popcorn and they sat down to watch a movie, that Savannah had been herself. Just a woman, almost a grandmother. There was something sublime in it, to be in the presence of a legend, yet have her be relatively down-to-earth.

"Savannah knew that most of the time, there was someone watching her. And she was right. Makes it hard to be yourself. But she could sometimes be just herself with me. And that's when you could get the real story."

"Didn't stop her from hooking up with just about everyone under the sun," Chase pointed out.

"Well, she always said you couldn't kiss a ghost."

Chase smiled at that, a genuine smile, and Phoebe felt her stomach do a quick flip-flop. She was finding it very easy to forget that this was a guy who admitted he wanted something from her.

"Guess there's something to that," he said, taking another long sip of his beer.

Two menus had appeared in front of them, but Phoebe didn't touch hers. She wasn't sure it was a good idea to stick around with him. She was pretty certain that Chase Sanders didn't do things just to be a nice guy. He wanted something from her.

"So when are you most like yourself?" he

asked.

"What do you mean?"

"When you're not being the ice queen?"

"Ice queen?" Phoebe realized her mouth was set in a firm line.

Relax, she told herself, *don't let him get to you.*

"Yeah, when you're not all pissed about someone trying to buy your house. Or being possibly, sort of related to you. What do you like to do for fun?" Chase stood there, a big grin on his face as he watched her try to make sense of that.

"I thought you said we were trying to start over?" Phoebe stammered.

"We are. I want to get to know you. I want to get to know what makes Phoebe Ryan tick." He leaned in as he said it and casually brushed her cheek with his hand as he tucked a strand of hair that had fallen out of place back behind her ear. His touch was electric and Phoebe felt her skin burning. She looked up at Chase, who was no longer smiling at her, but looking at her speculatively.

She leaned back in her chair, aware that all of a sudden the taproom of the Osprey Arms was feeling crowded and warm. Chase gave her another smile, this one wolfish, as he looked at her with interest.

The heat, the intensity she had felt before, she hadn't just been imagining it.

"Me, I like to sail," Chase said slowly.

"Sail?" Phoebe managed to croak out. That would explain the expensive sunglasses and the way he was tan, even in the early spring in the Northeast.

"You know, a boat, with sails." Chase had moved in closer so that he was almost whispering in her ear. The side of his face touched hers, his skin rough and charged against hers.

"Do you like the water?" he asked.

"I was a swimmer in high school," Phoebe managed to stammer out.

"I kind of prefer to be on top of the water." He had taken a step back, and she felt the pressure of the air around her lessen, felt able to breathe again.

"Is that what you do all day, sail?" Phoebe managed to ask.

He smiled. "Not exactly. Of course, I still have the boat. She's a fine little sloop, pretty fast."

"So you're sleeping down at the marina?" Phoebe tried to imagine Chase crammed into the small cabin of his boat. Perhaps he swung a hammock up on deck and the thought almost made her giggle.

Chase nodded, a smile playing on his lips. "Sometimes. It's refreshing to be out on the water, even when you're docked."

There was an angry shout and a cheer from along the bar. It was mostly men, a cluster of young and old, mostly professionals, in button-downs and work slacks. Just about everyone's attention was focused on the baseball game, and Phoebe figured that they were a group of mixed fans.

Phoebe realized that she and Chase had slid

closer to each other, to hear better in the bar that was growing more crowded and becoming louder by the minute. She was sure she felt his knee pressing into the side of her thigh. When she looked up at him, she saw he had a lazy smile on his face.

She pushed herself away. Chase was an attractive guy, maybe a little too brawny for her. Unfairly, she compared him to Dean, who was lean, ripped, but could carry off skinny jeans if he had to. One of Chase's thighs would barely fit into Dean's jacket.

"Want another?" Chase nodded towards Phoebe's glass. She looked down, realizing it was more than half empty. She'd been drinking fast, probably because she was nervous. Chase's pint was almost gone.

"I really shouldn't..."

"But you will," Chase said, waving his hand, and the bartender appeared almost instantly.

"Hey Paulie, we'll have another round."

"Sure thing, boss." Paulie flashed a quick smile and was gone.

"Boss?"

Chase shrugged. "I'm sort of a regular."

"Will you and the lady want something to eat?" Paulie had returned with their drinks.

Phoebe was about to protest that it wasn't a date, when Chase spoke up. "We'll have a plate of the calamari and salad to start."

"I thought this was just drinks," Phoebe pointed out, annoyed that he had ordered for her.

Chase shrugged. "Shouldn't drink on an empty stomach. Besides, their calamari is amazing. There's a pretty amazing chef here. Unless, you don't like squid?"

"Is it fried?" Phoebe asked.

"Of course."

"Fine, I'm in. But this isn't a date."

"Who said it was? Maybe you have a boyfriend. Maybe I have a girlfriend." He said it casually enough, but she could see that he was waiting for the answer.

"I'm not involved with anyone at the moment." Phoebe thought of Garrett and wished she hadn't. And then she thought of Dean. Good old reliable Dean, who was always trying to help her and her career. He had told her he would always be there, but she needed to ignore that if she was going to figure out what she wanted to do with her life.

"Even better," Chase said and she felt the pressure of his hand along the back of her chair, as he smiled roguishly down at her. Roguishly...where had that even come from? Who did that? It was almost predatory, as if he were sizing her up, seeing how she would taste. Phoebe felt her body tingle with attraction, a rush of heat between her legs, while her brain screamed *no, no, no.* So, she followed her brain and moved her shoulders around to give him the hands-off message, while her hands tightened around the stem of the wine glass.

"Besides swimming and making pillows, what else do you do?" Chase asked, his arm steadily in place. Phoebe stopped trying to shrug it off, realizing that he was too solidly built for her to get him to move it.

"I'm a designer. For a while, I worked with at Shelby Hill, the furniture catalog, and then I went freelance. I've designed movie sets, posters, then I did a lot of work for Doran Industries."

Chase nodded. "You mean the people who take a celebrity's name and slap it on a bunch of stuff and sell it in the big-box stores."

Phoebe smiled thinly. She didn't think that's how CallieSue Owens would like to describe her newest business venture, but that was pretty much what it was.

"Pretty much."

"But not anymore?" he asked.

"No, I stopped when Savannah got really sick, to help look after her. And now, there seems to be a lot of loose ends to wrap up, so I am not sure what I am going to do." Phoebe had her plan, but she wasn't quite ready to share it with Chase at the moment.

"That was nice of you. Hard for someone your age to give up her social life and career for a dying relative."

Phoebe gave a thin smile. "Savannah raised me. We were all each other had. It wasn't hard at all to take care of her."

"I'm sensing a 'but' there," Chase said, his dark eyes holding a connection to hers. Something warned her not to give too much away, but the way he was looking at her, his attention fully on her, compelled her to be honest.

"There's no 'but.'" Phoebe thought about all she had found when sorting through Savannah's affairs. And then she shrugged. It didn't really matter, so she told him.

"Well, after I was around, I started to take a closer look at things. Her papers, bills. I wasn't snooping, at least not at first. She needed someone to handle all of that stuff."

"Of course," Chase nodded in encouragement.

"I should have stepped in a lot sooner."

"Really?"

"Savannah was pretty good at making money, but sucked at holding onto it. She managed to spend just about all of hers."

"What did you do?"

Phoebe laughed at the memory. Savannah had been in bed then, in and out of it, the cancer moving quickly through her body. Phoebe had been so angry with her, she had wanted an explanation, but in the end, she had chickened out. Or didn't want to hear the truth.

"I realized that there wasn't much to be done about it. But at least she left me one thing."

"I'm sorry," Chase said. "I know it's probably not what you expected, the house I mean."

Phoebe almost felt the sting of tears against her eyes. How had he known what to say?

"Sorry." Phoebe dashed a quick hand against her eyes and then took a deep breath. "I'm not usually like this. I can't talk about them, my parents and Savannah, without breaking down in tears."

"My parents died in a car crash," she said to his unspoken question, "a long time ago."

"Were they actors too?"

"Yes. Well, my dad was a director and my mom, an actress. Their careers were just starting to take off when they died. My mom didn't really have any family, so that left Savannah."

"It sounds tough, being alone like that," he said, his dark blue eyes holding hers. Once again, she was hyperaware of everything around them.

Phoebe took a deep breath, determined to move away from her own story. "OK, so that's me. What about you?"

"Me? Well, let's see. I grew up in Queensbay, close to the water, with my parents and my brother. They're retired now and live in Florida. My brother's still around the area, but travels a lot, so we don't get to hang out much."

"Sounds nice, normal."

"Pretty normal," he said with an easy smile, and Phoebe knew he was waiting for her to ask him what he did.

"I learned to sail right here. Spent some time as a sail bum and then came home to take over the family business. We sell boat stuff to boat people."

"Perfect job for a guy like you."

Chase smiled. "What can I say, I'm a simple guy."

"I don't buy that for a second," Phoebe said.

Chase gave a shrug as if to say "no biggie," but

Phoebe thought there was a lot more behind those last words than he was letting on. Maybe she had misjudged him earlier. And it made him undeniably sexier.

"So you said you were working. Are you or aren't you?"

"What do you mean?" Phoebe said.

"You said you were, then weren't...which is it, working or not?"

Phoebe stared down into her drink. Exactly the territory she didn't want to veer into right now.

"I'm taking a break. To think things over."

"What sort of things?" he pressed.

"You know, what to do with my life now that I am well and truly on my own."

Phoebe didn't know why she told him. Perhaps it was the two glasses of wine, or the calamari, which she hadn't touched, so intent had she been on their conversation.

"Well, as you saw, when I was in The Garden Cottage, I've been designing my own things, housewares."

"What are housewares, exactly? Plates?" Phoebe felt her eyes narrow as she looked him over carefully. A trace of a smile ghosted across his lips.

"Plates, pillows, curtains, sheets..."

"Sheets?" The full lips definitely curved up. "I like sheets. Better than plates," Chase said, his voice dipping low, along with his head as he almost breathed the suggestion into her ear.

Phoebe forced herself to take a sip of the cool

wine. Never had talking about sheets affected her in quite this way, she thought. Somehow, just that one word carried a whole lot of weight to it.

She squared her shoulders one more time, this time quickly and with enough force that Chase's arm fell off the back of her chair. Feeling the weight lifted freed her, and she let a small smile of triumph grace her features.

"So you design things and, what, sell them?" He had taken her flinging his arm off the chair as a challenge because he had moved in even closer so that all she could smell was him. Nothing else but his clean scent, a combination of something spicy and fresh, almost windblown.

Phoebe smiled. "That would be the point."

"You know my boat has beds, except we call them bunks..." he trailed off as he looked at her face.

Phoebe flushed. Chase was so close to her, almost as if they were the only two people in the whole bar. Everything about him oozed sex and suggestion, and she knew that if she let herself, she would be swept up into him, let his big, strong hands pull her towards him, let them roam over her. Thoughts of just where that might lead had her coming to her senses. He was someone who wanted something from her, no matter how rakish his grin or how much she wanted to kiss him.

With every ounce of self-control she could muster, she pushed her wine glass away from her. "This, whatever this is, is over." She was off the bar chair in a flash, only stopping to say something to

Paulie, the bartender.

"We're finished here. You can just add it to my room tab."

With that gesture, and hoping Chase didn't take it upon himself to order a steak dinner, Phoebe stalked up to her room, fumbled with her key, and got herself in. She half-expected Chase to follow her, but when he didn't, she was torn between being relieved and disappointed. Still, she made sure the door was double-locked as she threw herself down on the bed, eyes open, staring at the ceiling, willing her body to calm down.

Why was her heart racing? When she closed her eyes, why could she only see his face, close up, dark, intense eyes, searching into her? God, she had pretty much bared her soul to him after one glass of wine. She could talk about her family, but she almost never did, and certainly not with some guy she had just met.

She rolled over and pulled out the card Chase had given her from his purse. She almost snorted.

Slowly, as the wine settled in her stomach and her heart slowed, she thought that perhaps Chase Sanders, as the president of a major sporting goods company, really had been talking about the bunks in his boat and actual sheets for them. Perhaps she had just blown a chance for a design deal with a major catalog.

Sighing, Phoebe rolled over and reached for the drawer in the bedside table where she had stashed a candy bar. Chocolate, caramel, nuts, nougat. It had all the important food groups and would count for dinner, since there was no way she was going down to the dining room again and risk running into Chase Sanders.

Chapter 15

It took Chase another beer before he worked out just why Phoebe had walked out on him. When he did, he hooted in laughter and slapped the bar top so hard Paulie looked over at him. Chase waved him away and continued to eat his steak. Phoebe Ryan had thought he was coming on to her, not trying to make a business proposition. And she'd been offended.

An interesting reaction, Chase thought, as he speared a piece of asparagus. The steak, potatoes, and asparagus were excellent, mostly because he'd seen fit to bring in a top chef from the city. Sean Callahan had helped put the restaurant on the map, and Chase savored every bite of his five-star meal.

Still, he wasn't used to women saying no to him. For the most part, when he beckoned, even if it was with a crook of his finger, they came running. True, most of them hadn't engaged his interest for long, and none of them had half the mystique of Phoebe Ryan, who seemed to have inherited her grandmother's trick of appearing both aloof and alluring at the same time.

He speared a thick-cut steak fry as he watched the home-team batter knock out a home run. Phoebe Ryan had another thing coming if she thought she could get rid of him so easily. Chase wanted her talent, and now, dammit, if he didn't want Phoebe Ryan along with it.

Chapter 16

"You're making some good progress."

Lynn Masters appeared in the front hallway of Ivy House, startling Phoebe, who jumped and then turned. She smiled when she saw who it was. Lynn was wearing scrubs again, and Phoebe wondered if she ever took them off.

Phoebe wiped a hand across her forehead, drawing away some of the sweat that had accumulated. It was surprisingly warm for spring and she was feeling her exertion in the way her clothes were sticking to her, damp with sweat.

"Thanks." Phoebe looked around. She had made good progress. All of the big stuff was in the driveway, waiting for a rubbish removal company to come and haul it all away. She had scrubbed, swept, and mopped most of the first floor.

"This room isn't so bad." Lynn pointed at the large space that Phoebe had decided would be the living room.

"I think if I redo the floors and paint, we're golden. The kitchen is another story, but I'm having a new fridge delivered in a couple of days. In the meantime, I have some iced tea on ice. Want some?"

Lynn nodded and Phoebe led her towards the

kitchen. Here, she had already cleaned, and as much as possible, the space gleamed. Phoebe had hit the village supermarket, which was geared towards boaters, and had purchased a Styrofoam cooler, ice, drinks, a sandwich, and some snacks. Paper plates, cups, napkins, and plastic utensils were set out on the wooden table that she had decided to keep. Already, she was imagining the kitchen painted a warm cream, with new curtains, new appliances, and the cracked linoleum removed to reveal something wonderful, like the wide-board wood flooring beneath.

"I found this on my mom's bookshelf." Lynn thumped something on the table and Phoebe looked over from where she was pouring.

"I haven't seen that in ages," Phoebe said, glancing at the cover of the book Lynn had brought. It was Savannah's autobiography.

"I would have thought you had an autographed copy." Lynn said, taking the paper cup Phoebe handed her.

"No way. The critics panned it and it wasn't exactly a best seller. I am not sure they ever printed that many to begin with. I think it was just another flop that Savannah decided to ignore.

"Oh, well, my mom loved it. Read it over and over again. As if you couldn't tell."

"Really?" Phoebe took her paper cup and pulled out the other chair, sitting across from Lynn. "What for?"

"The good parts." Lynn dropped her voice.

"Full disclosure. I went through a Savannah Ryan phase too—I mean my mom made me watch all the movies, so I actually read the book too and wow. That's all I've got to say."

"You mean she talked about that?" Phoebe dropped her voice too. Suddenly the thought of her grandmother doing that was grossing her out.

"Well, not in detail. But I could read between the lines. That's probably why she didn't want you to read it. It seemed like she bedded half of Hollywood before she took on the East Coast blue bloods."

Phoebe reached across the table and pulled the book towards her. As Lynn had promised, it was dog-eared and worn, the paper cover faded. She looked at the face of her grandmother staring up at her from the cover. It had been a long time since Savannah Ryan had looked like that.

"You really do look a bit like her, you know," Lynn said.

Phoebe looked up and almost pushed the book away. "Oh, I don't know. I think I have more of my mom in me." She tried to keep her voice casual. Red-blond hair, blue eyes, the same sort of cheekbones. Sure, there were similarities, but Savannah Ryan had been breathtaking, with emerald-green eyes and a voluptuous figure, a true crowd-stopping beauty. She had been every inch a movie star.

"Besides, looks aren't everything. They didn't exactly guarantee her happiness," Phoebe pointed out. Her grandmother had died alone, leaving behind a string of lovers, but no one besides Phoebe to share her love with. When all you had were looks, it was hard to deal well with the passage of time.

"Well, I wouldn't mind being compared to her every now and then." Lynn laughed, a full, hearty laugh that echoed through the relative emptiness of the house.

"Like when she played Helen in that movie about Troy?" Phoebe asked.

"Or when she was the gangster bad girl. Now that was hot."

Phoebe smiled and though she wasn't sure why she said it, she did. "I have the jacket."

"You mean the leather one with the buckles." Lynn's eyes went round and she reached out and gripped Phoebe's hand.

"Please?"

Phoebe laughed. "It's in storage, but I promise, as soon as I can, I'll get it. You can try it on and play cops and robbers."

"You're amazing. That would be so cool. And to show you how grateful I am, how about you come over later and we can hang out? My parents are heading out for the weekend and we'd have the house to ourselves. You can stay in the spare bedroom, check out of the hotel? I mean, I don't think you're quite ready to move in here, even with my futon."

"A slumber party?" Phoebe asked, laughing.

"Come on, you're never too old for them. Trust me, it will be fun. My mom will even leave something for us to eat."

"Deal." Mrs. Masters really was a great cook.

Phoebe flipped to the center section of the book where there were photographs on thick paper. She leafed through them until she found the ones she was looking for. Savannah and Leland Harper. Phoebe scrutinized the pictures carefully. Now that she knew what to look for, she could see Chase in Leland. Leland had been a good deal older than Chase was now when he had married Savannah, but still you could see physical similarities, in the height, the dark hair, and the strong cheekbones, between the two men.

"So, I had drinks with Chase last night," Phoebe said, trying to keep her voice casual.

Lynn looked up, her eyes narrowing. "Just drinks?"

"Why do you sound so surprised?"

Lynn shrugged. "I don't know. When I last saw the two of you, I found it hard to believe that you could sit down and have anything as civilized as a drink with him. Though there's not many around here who wouldn't have a drink with him. He's kind of a local celebrity."

"Celebrity?" Phoebe asked.

"Yeah, I mean for Queensbay. He's some sort of champion sailor in Europe. Grew up here, sailing with Noah Randall."

"Noah Randall, the tech entrepreneur?" Phoebe swallowed. Noah had made a boatload of money selling his company and had showed up on the Hollywood scene for a while. Phoebe figured everyone was trying to get him to invest in movies, but apparently, he'd had the good sense not to.

"Yeah. Noah's from Queensbay too. He lives here with his wife, Caitlyn. Noah and Chase go way back. Anyway, Chase sailed for a while, and then he came back to help his dad run the family business. Basically, it was ship's chandlery down by the marina. Anyway, Chase jazzed it up and before you knew it, they were sending out catalogs and had a website. You know, North Coast Outfitters. They sell fancy boat stuff to rich people."

"I see," Phoebe said, though she had figured most of that out last night.

"Yeah, he's super-yummy. Oh, and supposedly, he loaned Noah the money to start his company."

"What?" Phoebe said.

"Oh, yeah." Lynn nodded.

That explained a few more things. Probably owns the restaurant too, now that Phoebe thought about the way the bartender had called him boss.

"Do you know what else he is?" Phoebe asked.

"Batman?" Lynn joked. "Or Bruce Wayne?"

Phoebe laughed. "No, a total horndog. He tried to come on to me."

Lynn's mouth dropped open. "Shut the front door. No way."

"Way." Phoebe flopped down on one of the folding chairs. She really needed to get some furniture in here. There were a few things in storage in

California that she had managed to salvage from the estate, but perhaps an actual shopping trip was in order.

"Whoa. So you're crushing on Leland Harper's grandson. It's like the romance of the century all over again." Lynn's eyes were alight and her hands were clutched to her chest.

"Don't go all romantic. I am not crushing on him. It was just a drink. One," Phoebe said, though she recalled it had been two. And they had spent most of the time head to head, baring their souls. Or, rather, she had provided him with a great deal of information.

"So a drink with Queensbay's resident hottie. I am sooo jealous. I mean, not really, since he's kind of a player."

"A player?" Phoebe asked.

"Oh, yeah. He's a really generous guy, shows up at all the benefits around town, which my dad goes to since he's chief at the hospital and my mom makes me go to since she figures I'll meet an eligible guy there, but he always, and I mean always, has a different girl on his arm. And they are all lookers. I think he actually brings the models from his catalog."

"The foul-weather gear ones?" Phoebe asked, hopefully.

"Nope, definitely the swimsuit ones."

"Oh. Well, anyway, it wasn't a date. It was…" She paused. What had it been? A date? A question about business? A "Hey, how about we get to know each other since our grandparents shagged each other" meeting?

"It is so totally romance of the century, part two."

Phoebe shook her head. "Please, I think it was more like the scandal of the century, and I'm not quite sure it's something that should be repeated."

"But all that passion. I mean Chase is so hot, way hotter than Leland. I mean Leland was kind of an old fogey when he and Savannah hooked up. Never quite sure what she saw in him."

Phoebe rolled her eyes. "It was probably the money. Savannah was excellent at self-preservation. Remember, she had a young child to support." Phoebe couldn't remember her dad talking much about his childhood, at least not anything serious. Fun, light stories about living with a movie-star mom, but he'd never known who his real father was and barely remembered Leland, his "stepfather."

"Well, Chase has got it all: looks and money. So are you going to sleep with him?" Lynn pulled up another chair, the metal feet scraping across the wood floor. Phoebe winced, but realized it didn't matter. The floors needed to be redone.

"Sleep with him? Why would I want to sleep with him? He, along with the rest of the village, was trying to buy my house because they think I am some sort of West Coast harpy who wants to tear this place down and build some sort of modernist white box."

Lynn waved her hand. "Don't worry, I put my

mom on it. She'll let everyone know that you're planning to restore the house to its former glory. Watch out: the ladies from the Historical Commission will be over here with old pictures and banana bread in about two days."

"Thanks, I think." Phoebe didn't really care for banana bread.

"So you don't want to sleep with him?" Lynn's voice was coy.

Phoebe sighed. "What I am saying is that he clearly wants something from me. I don't think it would be a good thing if I got involved, again, with someone who doesn't want me—only something from me. Besides, I barely know him. I'm not actually a 'buy me a drink and I'll go to bed with you' kind of girl."

"You know, there's no harm in trying it out. And just think of what the papers would say." Lynn's eyes went dreamy. "The fans would love it. It might be good for your business, you know."

Phoebe reached out and grabbed Lynn's hand. "No way. Don't even go there. If a reporter ever found out that Chase and I had even talked. Ugh. It may seem cool to be in the paper, but really, it's not. I left Los Angeles to get away from all that."

"OK," Lynn said, and Phoebe saw that her friend's eyes mirrored her own seriousness. "Mum's the word. But if you do sleep with him, I need all of the details, please."

"Lynn!"

"What," Lynn said laughing, "I'm a sleep-deprived resident who works at a children's clinic. All I see are moms and married dads. I need some vicarious thrills. Please."

Phoebe just laughed.

Chapter 17

"And just what do you think you're doing?"

Phoebe almost lost her balance, waved her arms, and then finally managed to hop off the rusty folding chair and land with a thump on the floorboards. They gave a little beneath her weight, and she swore as she felt the whole house shake.

Chase Sanders darkened the doorway, hands on his hips, filling the space, such that he was a silhouette against the light blue of the sky.

Phoebe stood, her balance regained and looked at him. It was hard to make out his features, but she was sure that there was the unmistakable curl of lips. Laughing. Chase Sanders was trying not to laugh at her again.

She kept looking at him and he lost the battle, erupting into a full-bellied laugh that Phoebe might have been tempted to join in with if she hadn't been the object of it.

"I was changing a light bulb." She tried to keep the prim tone out of her voice, but knew she hadn't quite succeeded.

"The light's out? Are you sure you shouldn't have had the electricity turned on first?" He took a step in and Phoebe could see that he had dispensed with the business attire and just wore jeans and a dark gray v-neck sweater that fitted him tightly, allowing a display of his chest. *Definitely impressive,* Phoebe thought.

"I did." And Phoebe had. She didn't mention that she had cable and internet. Really, it was none of his business.

Chase flipped a switch by the door, and behind him, the light on the porch went on and off.

"See. It works. But this," she pointed to the chandelier above her head, "doesn't. There were some light bulbs in the kitchen."

He moved in closer and she could finally see him now that he wasn't framed in the glare from outside. Chase pushed his sunglasses back on top of his head and reached out.

Phoebe reared back, but his hand gently touched her hair, pulled back in a ponytail.

"Cobweb," he said, and she could feel the warmth of his fingers brush along her scalp, sending a tingle down the back of her neck.

There was an easy smile as he cleared the cobweb away and shook his hand to rid himself of it.

"Thanks," Phoebe managed to mumble, not sure why him being here should suddenly make her feel like a kid on the first day of school; an odd mixture of fear, anticipation, and heightened senses.

"Let me." He held his hand out again and Phoebe followed his gaze to the light bulb she held in her hand. Wordlessly, she gave it to him, and he walked over to the fixture, reached up, and, barely standing on his toes, screwed it in.

"Old houses," he said. "Ceilings are never that high."

"It makes it cozy," Phoebe said automatically, feeling the need to defend her cottage.

"Or claustrophobic." He smiled at her. "Give it a try now."

It took her a moment to understand what he said, lost as she was in the deep, gravelly sound of his voice. Little kid, indeed. She was more like a teenager on her first date. Or like the wallflower who gets asked to the dance by the star football player.

Phoebe shook her head as she reached for a light switch on the wall. The wallflower and the football star were the stuff of movies—Carrie, for one—and she wasn't supposed to be thinking about men. She was supposed to be thinking about her new life.

The light blinked on and the hallway was flooded with light.

"A little too bright, but you can always switch it out with a lower-watt bulb when you're ready," Chase said, picking up the rusted chair and folding it. It squeaked, but collapsed under his capable hands.

"Where does this go?"

"Back in the kitchen, I suppose." Phoebe waved in that direction. She had no intention of keeping the chair, but right now, there weren't too many seating options available.

Chase walked down the hallway and Phoebe followed. He smelled like soap and fresh air, a hint of cologne, but nothing overpowering.

"So, what are you here for?" Phoebe didn't feel like waiting any longer, and truth was, she'd be happy to get rid of Chase sooner rather than later.

"I think you misunderstood me last night," he said, his dark blue eyes dancing as he looked down at her. She was wearing sneakers, and again she was aware of the height disadvantage that they put her at.

"Oh, I don't think so. I thought your meaning was quite clear."

He laughed. "I don't know, what's that they say… Sometimes, a sheet is just a sheet."

"Somehow, I doubt that where you're concerned," she shot back, thinking about what Lynn had told her. Phoebe had no need to get involved with players. She had learned that lesson already.

"Well, perhaps we can address that question later?" He let that hang there and, to her surprise, Phoebe felt herself considering it, thinking about just what it might be like to find out just what kind of sheets Chase Sanders had on that boat of his. She felt warmer all over, warmer than the day warranted.

"Sit, please. I want to talk to you." Chase's eyes were serious now, his mood changing suddenly.

"I'm quite capable of listening while standing up." Phoebe refused to be lured in by Chase's physical presence. Though the chair and the table were small, tiny compared to him, he still managed to look at ease, totally, utterly at ease.

"Fine. Doesn't matter to me. I just thought you might be interested in a business proposition."

Phoebe felt her body tense.

"What kind of proposition?"

"Not sheets exactly," he said, shooting her another smile. "But you had me interested enough to go and do a little research. I really liked your pillows, and my mom loved them. And so did half the staff at the store. And Joan Altieri told me the ladies of Queensbay are going crazy over the rest of your stock. I thought when you said you were a designer, you meant you went shopping with your friends and told them what to buy."

Phoebe reared up a bit. She had built Ivy Lane up slowly over the years, spending every spare minute on it. It was not some hobby.

"Just because I'm small doesn't mean I'm not serious."

Chase held up a quieting hand. "Everyone starts somewhere. Believe me, North Coast Outfitters was one crappy little shop in Queensbay when I took it over. I know you're small, but that doesn't mean you're not talented. Do you want to keep giving away your talent to talentless celebrities of the month, or do you want to share it with the world, on your own terms?"

Phoebe shot him a look. "How dare you come here and try and tell me my business. First my house and now my work?"

"That's not what I meant. I have a real deal for you, if you'll just calm down and let me talk."

Phoebe took a deep breath. Some of her friends in Los Angeles, Dean included, had been dismissive of her efforts, saying they were a distraction. What he had meant is that they were a distraction from what he thought was her real job working with his clients. She had a feeling he hadn't been happy about the success she had started to enjoy on her own. Now, part of coming here was proving to him that Ivy Lane was more than just a distraction.

"Fine. Talk." She held out her hand, in what she hoped was an accommodating gesture towards him.

"Well, I really liked the designs. At least on the site. Don't tell me you're sewing the pillows yourself, are you?" he asked.

She shook her head. "No, of course not. I create the design, get the fabric made and then I have a small workshop that sews the pillows for me. Then, they go to a warehouse, which handles all the shipping for me. I have a part-time assistant, a college student, who oversees it all for me."

"Smart. Leaves you plenty of time to create. And I guess market."

Phoebe shrugged. She hadn't done much in the way of marketing her designs. She'd had some luck there since she'd given some of her pillows as a housewarming present to a friend. The pillows then caught the eye of an interior designer, and soon,

Phoebe's pillows had started to pop up all over Los Angeles. But she knew she needed to do more. Going to shops like the Garden Cottage was a first step, but she would need hundreds more like it, across the country, if she wanted to make this a real business. Or one big customer with lots of shops, she thought, beginning to get an idea of where Chase was going.

"It's great stuff, but I was wondering... The website barely has your name on it. Why aren't you playing up the Hollywood angle?" There was real curiosity in his voice.

Phoebe looked down to the floor. "I wanted it to be successful on its own, not because I have a famous name."

Chase nodded. "OK, I get it. But you shouldn't hold yourself back like that."

"It's not up for discussion," Phoebe said sharply, drawing in a deep breath. Business deal or not, Chase could walk right out of here if he thought she was going to buckle on this.

"OK, so noted." He smiled to show that he wasn't put off by her tone. "Here's the deal."

Phoebe crossed her arms, interested in spite of her personal misgivings towards Chase. She had managed to do a little research on Chase Sanders. North Coast Outfitters was the real thing, a multi-million-dollar business with high-end customers, expanding every day. Getting North Coast Outfitters behind her would help her launch her fledging business much faster than she could ever do on her own.

"What kind of deal?"

"Well, I thought perhaps you could do some new designs, pillows, a little California cool, a little old-Hollywood-glamour type of thing, and we market them to our customer base. You make the design, do the samples and I'll take it from there. We'll offer them as a limited-edition set, promote the hell out of them and then see what happens. If my customers like the pillows, then we can try other things."

He was excited, she could tell, as the ideas were flowing out of him. She knew that his attention wasn't on her exactly, but it was still exhilarating to be swept up in his enthusiasm. For a moment, she could see it all mapped out—a limited-edition set of work for North Coast Outfitters, make her name known, then get herself into the pages of magazines. Her business would grow from there, and a Phoebe Ryan design would mean something simple, elegant, yet fun. Good taste for the next generation. Pillows, tablecloths, plates...and, yes, someday, even sheets.

"What's in it for you?" she asked, returning to reality. Nobody did anyone a favor like this without expecting some return. "You can't bribe me. I'm not selling the house, you know," Phoebe said, her defenses rising.

Chase smiled at her and took a step closer. "I know. You made your position very clear. Ivy House isn't for sale. I respect that. Especially since you're not planning on tearing it down. At least that's the word on the street." He gave her a small knowing smile, as if they shared a secret.

"But you know, I was able to take a marine hardware store in a sleepy little town in Connecticut and turn it into a successful online business."

Phoebe swallowed, suddenly lost again in Chase's sapphire-colored eyes, centered on the intent look on his face. Gone was the exuberance and in its place was a look of focus, of concentration. Phoebe remembered briefly that here was a man who had sailed through the edge of a hurricane to win a race. She supposed he wasn't a man to give in lightly or to second-guess himself.

"It's because I have a talent for knowing what people want and like. Me, I couldn't sew a pillow or come up with a design for one if you had a gun to my head. But I can spot when someone else has created something that people want. If you sign a deal with North Coast Outfitters, I will handle all those pesky details that you artistic types hate. You won't have to deal with suppliers or vendors or whether your name gets in the paper or if the shipment from the factory is late. I take care of all of that for you, so you can do what you do best."

"What's that?" Phoebe breathed.

"Create things." He was close to her now, so close that her vision was filled with him, with his dark, slightly unruly hair, his tan skin, the stubble on his face. She could sense his lips hovering near hers, and for a brief moment, just an instant, she had to close her eyes, break the connection between the two of them.

When she opened them, she found that he was watching her, a step back now, hands shoved into his pockets, one eyebrow raised.

"What do you think, do we have a deal?"

Phoebe hesitated only a moment before she nodded.

Chase smiled, looking highly pleased with himself. He stuck out a hand and she took it, their skin brushing, a bolt of electricity shooting through her. He held it just a bit longer than necessary, looking at her, a lazy, sexy grin spreading over his face.

"I'll have my lawyer send over some papers."

Chapter 18

"So, she took the deal," Noah said.

"She took the deal." Chase took a sip of his beer. Chase had wandered over to Noah's house after work, and now the two of them were holed up in the large garage behind it.

"Do you boys need anything else? I have to go out now." Caitlyn came in and Chase watched as his friend's whole face lit up.

"No, I think we're good. We have beer and a boat. What more could we want?" Noah said, giving his wife a kiss as he pulled her close, his hand touching her still-flat belly.

Chase watched, wanting to turn away, but didn't. Noah was so damn happy, married and soon to be a father that it was enough to make any other guy sick. Except that's not what Chase was feeling. Not envy, for while Caitlyn was beautiful and accomplished, Chase knew he wasn't jealous for her. Just of what she and Noah had together.

"Be careful, please. Let me know when you get there?" he whispered.

Caitlyn laughed. "It's just a few miles away. How much trouble can I get in? It's just dinner."

"Call," Noah said, his eyes narrowing, his

voice serious.

"I'll call. Of course. There's some stuff in the fridge for dinner if you boys get hungry. Just be careful using those power tools." She waved once more and let herself out and they heard the sound of her car leaving the driveway.

"Hey, Daddy, wipe the drool off," Chase said to his best friend.

Noah just shook his head. "Wait until it happens to you. Won't know what hit you."

"That will be the day," Chase said, but an image of Phoebe flashed through his mind as he said it. He could still feel the way the electricity had shot through him at her touch. He had hurried away from her, not because he wanted to, but because he so badly wanted not to.

"So you have a deal with the cool and collected Phoebe Ryan. What's next?"

Chase checked his watch. "Well, my attorney's drawing up some paperwork, and my marketing director is through the roof. Would think Phoebe was a movie star herself, she's such a Savannah fan. Coming up with all sorts of ways to market the collection. So we'll see. With any luck, we'll be able to have it ready for the next catalog."

"So you think this will help you get the house?" Noah asked, pulling back the tarp on the oddly shaped thing in front of them.

"The house?" It took a moment for Chase to figure out what his friend was talking about.

"Yeah, isn't this why you're wining and dining

her? So you can get her house? At least that's what you said the other day." Noah's eyes, shrewd, looked up at him.

"Sure, the house. I figure she'll be so excited, she'll have the place cleaned up and head back to Los Angeles in a couple of weeks. She'll be the next big design star, and she'll be so thankful to me that she'll sell me the house. No agent's fee or anything."

The words came out easily, but Chase knew he had stopped thinking about the house or even his business deal sometime during drinks with her. She had been refreshingly candid about her life during their dinner. And, of course, there was the way she looked at him. He couldn't quite get that out of his mind. She had wanted him to kiss her, he was almost sure of that. There had been that moment in the hall of Ivy House.

Chase shook his head, trying to clear his thoughts, but he couldn't. Her red-gold hair in a messy ponytail; her wide, sensual lips; her long, thin fingers—artist's fingers. He had felt his body hunger for her and knew that something would need to be done about that. Especially if she was the least bit willing. Oh, yes, if Phoebe Ryan gave him that kind of opportunity, he just might take it.

"Well, just be careful. I don't want to see it all backfire on you." And with that, Noah pulled back the tarp to reveal a boat. It was all wood, the paint chipped and peeling, the varnish bubbling, and there was a large hole in the bottom.

"Wow. It's a beauty," Chase said, running his

hands along the gunwale.

"I know. A Herreshoff America eighteen. Limited edition. Classic, yet easy to maneuver."

"And this is your next great idea?" Chase asked. Since Noah had sold his tech company, he'd been working head down on his next one, something to do with a new clean energy source. Noah was cagey on the whole subject, but Chase had told him that there was a blank check waiting for him when he was ready for investors.

"Hey, it's a wind-powered vehicle. Perfectly environmentally friendly."

Chase looked at his friend, staring him down until Noah came out with the truth.

"I wanted to do it for the baby. You know, his first boat."

"Do you even know it's a boy?" Chase asked.

"No and it doesn't matter, right? Girl or boy, it's never too early to get them out on the water."

Chase laughed. "I think they need to be able to walk first. But you're right, it's a beauty. It will be perfect when it's restored."

Chapter 19

Phoebe took a step into the shop. It was more than a shop, she supposed. North Coast Outfitters occupied prime real estate along the waterfront of Queensbay Harbor, adjacent to the Osprey Arms, and an easy place to stop for boaters and general tourists. She figured if she were going to make a deal with the devil, then she should get a better feel for him. Plus, she had some concerns over the terms of the contract, and it seemed more expedient to deal with Chase directly than go back and forth using lawyers, hers in Los Angeles and Chase's in New York. After all, the two of them were in the same town.

Large black-and-white posters hung on the walls of the shop, pictures of people sailing in boats, sunning themselves, generally enjoying the good life. She took a closer look at one of the pictures and saw that, sure enough, it was Chase, at the helm of a large sailboat, standing on the deck like a modern-day pirate, winds filled, water foaming at the bow. She swallowed. He even looked sexy in black and white, his dark hair blown by the wind, his eyes hidden behind sunglasses, his hands large and capable at the wheel. She swallowed, suddenly thinking that it might be better to just send her comments to the lawyer.

She heard it then, a trilling happy laugh, and a stunning woman with dark hair stepped into view. Chase walked next to her, one arm around her shoulder. He said something to her, and she looked up at him and laughed again. Phoebe tensed. He hadn't said he was single when she had given him the chance, but he hadn't claimed to be dating anyone either. Had she mistaken the vibes she'd been getting from him all along?

Phoebe almost turned, ready to hurry back to Ivy House, when she was spotted.

"Phoebe." Chase's voice was sexy, still tinged with the laughter he had been sharing with the woman on his arm.

Without bothering to disentangle himself, he walked over to Phoebe. The woman under his arm glanced up at him and then over at Phoebe.

"Hello, I'm Caitlyn Randall." She held out a hand and Phoebe couldn't quite miss the way the light caught the enormous diamond on her hand. Phoebe felt herself stiffen and plastered what she hoped was a cool and professional smile on her face as she shook the other woman's hand.

"Forgive me. Caitlyn, this is Phoebe Ryan, the new owner of Ivy House."

Caitlyn's eyes lit up and she glanced at Phoebe, speculation in her eyes. "Ivy House, you mean that beautiful old house just up from town? The one with the tower?"

"Yes, I suppose that would be the one."

"Phoebe recently inherited it from her grandmother, Savannah Ryan."

"Oh." Interest lit up in Caitlyn's eyes and Phoebe braced herself.

Instead of the usual questions, Caitlyn's look turned serious. "I am so sorry for your loss. I loved your grandmother's movies. All of them."

"Thank you," Phoebe managed to say, knowing she sounded stuffy, but she couldn't help it. So, this was Chase's type, this East Coast preppy looker. Caitlyn wore a simple wrap dress with knee-high boots and carried an understated leather bag. She looked like she would be equally at home on the deck of a boat in a retro two-piece or riding out on top of some great Charger, leading the hounds in snuffing out their quarry.

Phoebe thought she should have dressed better. What seemed to pass for California chic seemed hopelessly casual here. The morning had promised warmth today, so she had put on a pair of cut-off jeans and a flowing printed blouse and let her hair fall down loose, held back by her sunglasses.

"Well, good luck. Chase says you're planning on doing some renovations before you sell. I can't tell you how excited he is, he's been dreaming of Ivy House…"

"Caitlyn, surely you need to get back to work," Chase broke in smoothly. Caitlyn shot him a surprised look.

"Yes, the market waits for no woman," she

said and glanced over at Phoebe and then back to Chase.

"Be sure to say hi to Noah. Tell him I have those parts he wanted."

"I will. And you make sure you keep my little surprise to yourself. His birthday's coming up and I want him to truly be delighted."

"My lips are sealed."

Caitlyn turned to Phoebe again. "It was wonderful to meet you. Perhaps if you're going to be in town for a while, I can convince you and Chase to come over for drinks. Noah hates to drink alone."

"I'm sure that would be wonderful," Phoebe said, puzzled by the comment.

"Chase, I'll let you explain. Do you have a card, Phoebe? That way I can be sure to track you down. I find men are terrible with details like that."

Before Phoebe had quite realized what had happened, she had exchanged cards with Caitlyn Randall.

"Noah as in Noah Randall?" she asked. She remembered now what Lynn had told her and realized she had just come in contact with one-half of a power couple.

"The very same. We go way back," Chase explained, as if it were the most natural thing in the world, and Phoebe saw that it was for him. She smiled. Perhaps it was like having a tableful of Hollywood legends over for Thanksgiving.

When she had told Chase she had some questions about the contract, he had quickly ushered her out of the store and across the street to a set of offices above a modern row of shops. People were busy working, and they paid them little mind, except to say hi to Chase as she followed him down the open floor plan and into his own office.

"Coffee, tea?"

"Coffee would be great," she said. He pressed a button on his phone and ordered it.

"So you go way back with Caitlyn and Noah Randall?" she asked.

"Noah and Caitlyn live up along the east bank of the harbor. Caitlyn loves to entertain, so you better watch out. You will be getting a call from her. Oh, and she's a financial advisor, so she's likely to make sure that you're getting the proper rate of return on your investments, and you can totally trust her. She's like some sort of uber-mother hen."

"I still don't get the drinking-alone thing," Phoebe said.

"She's expecting. About three months along."

"Looks great." Phoebe felt her heart rate return to normal. So, the glow that hovered about Caitlyn had not been due to Chase's grin.

Chase gave a shrug and a smile. "Hey, when I knew him, he was just a computer geek who liked playing video games. Who knew where it would lead him."

Phoebe shot another look at Chase.

"What? Think I'm not refined enough for the likes of Noah Randall?"

"No, not at all. But you do seem a bit like

the odd couple," Phoebe said. There was a knock on the door and an older woman with reddish hair and freckles brought in a tray with a pot of coffee, cups, milk, and sugar. She set it down, reminded Chase he had a meeting, and left with a brisk, efficient nod in Phoebe's direction.

"We were an odd couple," Chase said, pouring her some coffee and then a cup for himself. "At first, but we both loved to sail. But I was better. So, Noah used me to win the Junior Cup at the Yacht Club."

Phoebe frowned. "What did you get out of the deal?"

Chase shrugged. "You'd be surprised."

"What does that mean?"

"It means Noah and I have been business partners for a long time. I invested in some software, and he invested in some hardware." Chase made an encompassing gesture and Phoebe nodded.

"Smart."

"And some luck. You never know where a friendship is going to lead you."

Chase's voice had dropped an octave and his grin was wolfish. "Caitlyn and Noah dated each other back when they were teenagers. I've known both of them a long time."

Something about the easy way he said it made Phoebe jealous all over again. Chase seemed to be suggesting he had known both of them—in different ways—for a very long time. They had been very comfortable together. But then she remembered the look in Caitlyn's eyes when she had said her husband's name.

"Well, it's nice to have old friends." She kept the wistfulness out of her voice, glancing around the office as she did so. It was spare, a modern place or, she realized as she studied it, more like a ship's cabin with lots of polished wood and discreet storage space. It was masculine without being overpowering. Unassuming, yet powerful and completely confident, much like Chase himself.

"So, you had some questions?" Chase's eyes sparkled, the sunlight from the expansive windows catching them. His eyes were a deep, deep blue and she felt herself drawn into them, and then remembered why she had decided to track him down in the first place.

"Yes. I thought it would be easier to talk face-to-face instead of going through lawyers."

"Quite right," he said, taking a sip of his coffee.

"Well, I'm fine with just about everything but this part." She handed him over a copy of the contract with the section highlighted.

He glanced it over and then looked over at her, amusement on his lips. "You're saying that we can use your name, but not Savannah's? Is there a problem with her?"

Phoebe shook her head, wiping her hands on her shorts. This was where she could have used some of Savannah's acting skill. A scene played out, Savannah done up as a gangster moll, staring down some scary mob boss as she negotiated for the life of her lover. Or maybe it had been for her brother. There had been so many movies, it was hard to keep them all straight.

"No problem with her. But I would just prefer to make a go of it on my name alone. I have no problem with the catalog or press releases talking about me, but I would prefer not to have my relationship with her mentioned."

"I thought you were close to her."

Phoebe swallowed. "I was. And that's why it would be nice to know people liked my work on its own merit. Not because of some old screen legend."

"So no trading on famous relatives." Chase took out a pen, crossed out a few lines of text, and put his initials next to it.

"Anything else?" he asked. There was a buzz on his phone. His eyes held her and the buzz was insistent. He pressed a button and his assistant's voice filtered through. "Your next appointment is here."

"That's all," Phoebe said. She knew she should go. They both had things to do, but something about his eyes pinned her in her seat and she felt a warmth spread over her, starting between her legs and crawling up over her body. She'd never had this reaction to a man just from his look. The question was what to do about it.

"Well, then I guess we have a deal."

Phoebe smiled. "I suppose so."

"Well, here's to a profitable friendship," he said. His eyes held hers and his intercom rang again.

She got up, pulling her bag with her.

"Thanks for stopping by. Next time, I'll give you the grand tour."

"That would be lovely," Phoebe said, feeling awkward. "I guess I'll be hearing from you."

"Consider the deal done. I guess you better get to work. Are you going to be heading back to California to get started? I have to get out to the stores there soon. I am sure I could look you up?"

Phoebe remembered what Caitlyn had started to say about the house, so she smiled, chin drawn up, and channeled her best Savannah look.

"You know, one of the best things about a job like mine is that I take inspiration wherever I can find it."

Chase had moved around the desk and they were standing close to one another. She could see the way his lips curled up in amusement, and she could feel in her stomach the way his low voice unnerved her.

"Are you feeling inspired?" he asked, his voice dangerously low.

"As it so happens, I have always found that being by the water fills me with a lot of energy."

He looked at her, a slow grin spreading over his face and she felt her body respond to him, heat licking through her as he took her hand to shake it and then brought it up to skim against his lips.

"Just creative energy?" he murmured.

"You can have my designs, but you can't have me," she responded.

"Are you sure about that? I told you: I always

get what I want."

She was stunned into silence for a moment, until the door opened, and the redheaded lady bustled in.

"Looks like that's my cue to go," she managed to stammer out, knowing she needed to get out and away from him.

Chapter 20

"Is that a hard hat?" Phoebe stopped in surprise, looking at what Chase had in his hands.

"Yes, it is. Safety first." Phoebe looked up quickly to see if he meant anything by that. There it was, just that sexy-as-hell Chase Sanders grin.

"But it's pink," Phoebe said.

"Well, it is for a girl." Chase said. He took a step forward and she saw that he was dressed casually in faded jeans and a v-neck t-shirt that clung to his chest and abdomen, which showed off how flat his stomach was and the nice taper up to his broad shoulders. *Stop thinking about his shoulders,* she reminded herself.

"A girl?" Phoebe turned her attention back to the hard hat that Chase was still proffering. "Excuse me... For a lady," he corrected himself.

"A lady." Phoebe put down her bag on the scarred wood floor and took the helmet from Chase.

"You said the other day you were going to fix the old lady up, so I thought I'd give you a little housewarming present. And see if you needed a hand."

"You can fix houses?" Phoebe heard the doubt creeping into her voice. She glanced around the room. Chase had found her in her studio, the light flooding in from the bank of windows. She had picked up some paint samples at the local hardware store, and there were large squares of them on the wall so she could decide between Café au Lait and Creamy Blond.

"No, but I know people around here who can. I would be happy to recommend some names to you. All good guys."

Phoebe nodded. She had wondered if she'd have to resort to looking through Yellow Pages to find the names of plumbers and electricians, and the thought had filled her with dread. Taking a recommendation from someone was a much better move. Still, it was a lot of interest on Chase's part for a house he professed to have no interest in.

"Do you treat all of your business acquaintances this way?" she asked, trying to keep her voice light. Right now, the room had one wall of built-in shelves, with cabinets on the bottom. She examined the hard hat more closely.

"I told you, we're partners now. Hopefully, very profitable ones," he countered.

Phoebe hefted the hard hat. It was heavier than she expected. "They really make pink ones?"

Chase laughed. "Not many. It's a special order, but I know a guy in the business."

"I'm sure you do." Phoebe took a sip of her coffee, still looking at the helmet. She wasn't sure what to do with it. Just how much demolition did Chase think the house needed?"

"You don't think I'm going to need it, do you?" she asked, trying to see if he had an opinion.

"You never know," Chase answered, still grinning.

"But..." Phoebe felt her mouth go dry. She thought about some new paint and curtains, but not any actual demolition.

Chase took a step closer to her and held out his hand. She wasn't sure what he wanted, but then he reached out for her coffee cup. Mesmerized, she let him take it from her and watched as he took a sip, her eyes locked on his, his on hers. Slowly, he handed the cup back to her.

"Thanks. I needed that. Look, I happen to have spent a few summers working construction. Thought maybe I could help you do a walk-through, get a sense of what needs to be done now, what can wait."

Phoebe felt herself swallowing hard, trying to forget the way his hand, warmed from the coffee cup, had burned against her skin and made her stomach do a flip.

"But we're not going to be breaking anything, are we?" Phoebe asked, surprised to find her voice was low, throaty.

"Not unless you want to."

Phoebe nodded. There was no reason for him to be holding her hand, but it had felt good. She decided not to dwell on it.

They wound up in the room she had decided would be the master bedroom. The floors were hardwood and she knew that they could be beautiful again.

"I know a guy who does floors. I asked him to swing by later, to take a look around, give you an estimate. They should be done all at once, upstairs, downstairs. That way, you can move in. You can always do your painting later."

Phoebe nodded. "It would be good if I could at least get a bed in here by the end of the week." Phoebe felt it, the slow burn of a flush. Somehow saying the word "bed" in front of Chase made her feel self-conscious. He had dropped her hand by this time, but was still standing close to her, and she couldn't get over the feeling of being on edge, like she had drunk five espressos in a row and the caffeine was buzzing through her in overdrive.

"Really? I didn't know you were in such a hurry to get set up. Is someone waiting for it?"

It took her a moment to figure out what Chase meant.

"I..." she stuttered, cursing her fair skin, feeling the blush crawl up her cheeks and to the roots of her hair.

"So you're just eager to get moved in?" he said, his eyes laughing at her.

"I'd rather not spend that much more time in the hotel. The Osprey Arms is fine, but I hadn't figured on making it a permanent home."

"I like that one." He had come up behind her, and pointed to the middle shade of blue on the paint chip Phoebe was holding. "I'm sure I could arrange a deal for you, since you're practically living there."

"Don't tell me... You know the manager." Phoebe said, the memory of the way he had seemed so comfortable at the Osprey Arms coming back to her.

Chase shrugged. "Maybe I do."

"Well, thank you, but I already did." The shade Chase liked was deeper than she would have gone for, but it was bold too. "I'm a grown woman; I can take care myself. I happen to have plenty of experience negotiating for myself."

"I am sure you can come down hard on them when you want." She could feel him, his bulk and heat behind, and the way his breath whispered in her ear and tickled her hair, which was up in a ponytail. She fought to control the shiver that ran down her spine and the little delicious flame of heat that flicked below her stomach, between her legs. Desperately wanting to put some distance between herself and Chase, she almost took a step away, but she couldn't; she was trapped there, loving the feeling of him close to her.

"I manage to get what I want most of the time," she managed to say in a husky voice.

"I can imagine." She turned slightly to face him so that her eyes were almost level with his chin. One of his arms was still around her and she could smell him, a mix of soap and spicy aftershave, melding together in a heady combination that made her knees feel just slightly wobbly.

His hand grasped her wrist and pulled her

closer to him. She met his eyes, could see that they were dark, liquid, as if consumed by something. His nostrils flared and he leaned in, smelling her hair.

"You smell amazing," he said, his voice a hoarse, ragged whisper. She felt any last inhibitions melt away, and she wasn't quite sure who moved first so that they were facing each other and she was encircled in the strong span of his arms.

It seemed as if time stood still, and Phoebe was aware of everything, from the fresh breath of air that wafted in from the window that was propped open to the sound of a bird singing and the whisper of the new green leaves in the trees. And then she heard the sound of her own heart beating and could hear Chase's ragged breath as his gaze roamed over her, taking her in, his blue eyes dark.

"What was that?" They sprang apart, and Phoebe's eyes traveled up to the ceiling. Dust trickled down and the hanging light fixture swung slightly. Her heart was thumping, and she had clutched her hands to her chest, no longer in the strong confines of Chase's arms.

It came again, another crash and then a scurrying sound. Chase's head was cocked up and he watched the ceiling. A slow smile came over his face.

"Squirrels, a raccoon maybe, in the attic."

"Yuck." Phoebe wasn't crazy about animals. Sure, dogs were fine and cats OK, but anything else... especially in her house, was just too off-putting to think about. Somehow, she hadn't thought about that aspect of living in the country when she'd been dreaming of Ivy House.

"Where are the stairs?" Chase asked. He was still looking up, completely oblivious to her, and it was with supreme disappointment that she realized he was not going to kiss her after all.

"Stairs?"

"To the attic." There was a touch of impatience in his voice. "They could be getting away."

"You're going to go up there?"

"Sure. How else are we going to get rid of them?" he said.

Call an exterminator, Phoebe thought, but didn't voice it. "What about rabies?" she said instead.

"I'm not going to catch them. I just need to find out where they're coming in from. And then we can set traps and get them out."

"Kill them?" All of a sudden, Phoebe didn't relish the thought of killing innocent animals. After all, in their minds, they had been there first.

"No, of course not. We'll set special no-kill traps, catch them and then release them. But we need to find out how they're getting in so they don't get right back in. So, the stairs?" he said again, his impatience marked with a smile.

Phoebe thought for a moment. "In the hallway."

She led the way out of the bedroom towards the door that led to a closet. It was big for one, an odd-shaped room above the stairs, and it had a round window in it. "Up there."

There was a trap door in the ceiling, with a rope hanging from it.

"You might want to stand back," Chase said.

"Are you sure we shouldn't call someone?" Phoebe asked. Chase had pulled a small flashlight from his pocket and was already pulling on the rope. It was stuck and he handed the flashlight to Phoebe as he put both hands on the rope, tugging hard.

With a squeak and a groan, the door came free and a cloud of dust fell down. Chase was quick, and he sidestepped the dust storm easily, pushing Phoebe out of the way so she was spared the worst of it. Still, grime swirled in the air, and she could feel it settling in her hair.

There was a ladder folded up against the underside of the door and Chase reached up and swung it down. It gave another protesting squeak and then there was silence. In agreement, the two of them paused and listened. The rustling had stopped, Phoebe noted with relief.

Chase put his foot on the bottom rung, tested his weight, turned, took the flashlight from Phoebe, and shot her a wink.

"If I'm not back in five, call in the cavalry."

Phoebe was about to protest, but then she remembered it was just an attic. She watched his amazingly cute backside disappear into the gloom above. There was a pause, silence and she half-expected to hear a scream; she could feel the tension erupting in her.

"Hey, Phoebe, you're going to want to see this."

Chapter 21

Phoebe put her foot up on the ladder and then stopped. "What is it?"

Chase chuckled. "Don't worry, this isn't going to bite you."

Somewhat reassured, Phoebe started up the ladder, entering the low enclosed space.

"Wow." Phoebe emerged into the dim light of the attic. It ran the whole length of the house, unfinished, rough wood, with nails sticking through the sloped roof.

"Watch your head," Chase said over his shoulder. He was ahead of her, his flashlight moving this way and that, illuminating an attic full of...stuff. Boxes, trunks, battered suitcases, coat racks filled with clothes, even an old dressmaker's dummy.

"The mother lode," Phoebe whispered. There were dormers along the length of the roofline, and the small leaded panes of glass provided some more light. Through it all, swarms of dust filtered and danced, caught in the sunlight.

"Is this her stuff?" Chase turned, the flashlight almost catching Phoebe full in the face before he lowered it.

"Savannah's?" Phoebe walked over to a stack of

boxes. In magic marker, the words, "*Mystic Moon,*" were written. It was the name of one of her movies. Phoebe ran a hand along a dress hanging on one of the coat racks. It had once been white, but now it was creamy, yellowed with age.

"She wore this in *Scott's Peak,*" Phoebe said. "And these boxes all have the names of different movies on them. Her movies. So, yeah, I would say this is all of her stuff."

"A whole career," Chase said. Phoebe looked up at him. He had an almost reverent look on his face as he scanned the collection.

"You're a fan," Phoebe said, the realization hitting her suddenly.

"What?" The flashlight jumped and Chase caught a hold of it, before he turned to look at her.

"You, you're a fan of the late great Savannah Ryan," Phoebe said, a teasing note creeping into her voice.

Chase smiled, with a slow cat-that-ate-the-canary grin, and said, "Of course I'm a fan of her work. Savannah Ryan made sex sexy back when I was a kid. I think there was only one movie where she took her clothes off, but even as a kid, you could see the sex appeal oozing through the screen. I saw every one of them. Even the bad ones. And she made some real lousy ones." Chase shook his head.

"Those were to pay the bills. She had expensive tastes and money poured like sand through her hands," Phoebe explained.

"So Savannah Ryan really didn't have a heart

of gold?" Chase said.

"She was complicated," Phoebe said, and it was a relief to admit it, even to Chase, who had probably believed it all along. She realized Chase had moved close to her so that there were only a few inches between his chest and her, and once again, she could feel the heat, the palpable pocket of warmth between them, like a current of live electricity snaking through them.

"You were saying?" Chase asked, and Phoebe remembered that she had been saying something.

"About a heart of gold..." Chase prompted. They were close again, just as they had been before in the master bedroom, the space between them just a fraction of an inch. She turned her head up so that their lips were almost ready to touch. Her heart skipped a beat and her breath hitched, knowing how badly she did want this—want Chase Sanders to kiss her—even though it was wrong on so many levels.

But for the life of her, she could not think of a good reason why she should pull away when his lips brushed hers. She moved into him, and his arms came around her, crushing her close to him, his lips finding hers, his hands strong and warm against her back.

Phoebe lifted her arms, her hands finding the back of his neck, brushing up to find his thick, dark hair, while his lips crushed against hers, exploring, inviting. A sound escaped, a moan, which she might have been embarrassed about if she hadn't been enjoying herself so thoroughly, all her senses engaged, feelings and need coursing through her.

Her lips parted, an invitation, and he took it, his tongue exploring, his teeth nibbling her lips, while his hands pulled her tighter and closer into him so she was possessed, so she couldn't have moved even if she wanted to. His tongue took hers and his arms brought her closer, and she slid into him, one leg in between his so she could feel his desire, hot and hard for her.

Phoebe lost all rational thought as his hands cupped her backside and then one came around to skim the edge of her waistband. Then, it was gone and his hand found her left breast, his fingers pulling gently at her nipple, which sprang to attention at his touch. His mouth moved down her neck, while one arm braced her back and she arched into him as his lips and teeth slid slowly down her neck, to the v of her t-shirt and then nipped lightly at her nipple, which puckered and pebbled under him.

She felt her knees go weak and a flash of heat and wetness between her legs. Chase stopped for a moment, his eyes darting wildly around, and then his hands picked her up and she was on something hard, a steamer trunk, while he kept kissing her, and she could feel that he was just as aroused as she was.

He looked at her for a moment, his gaze intense, lust darkening his eyes. She couldn't say anything, but just nodded at him to keep going. Not waiting for more, he kissed her again, and she rose up to meet him, as his hands traveled down the length of her shirt.

Chase pushed up the thin fabric of her shirt and found the sensitive skin. Hot hands brushed against her and she moaned again, arching into him, wanting him, wanting more.

Phoebe couldn't remember how long this went on because there was another crash and then a shout, loud and hearty.

"Chase, where are you?"

She sprang away from him, but his arms still held her, and he looked down at her, his eyes hazy with want and she felt her lips stinging from his attack.

"And that would be my floor guy." His voice was hoarse, ragged.

"Floor guy?" Phoebe repeated, glad he still had his arms around her, since her knees were shaky.

"This isn't over," Chase said, his voice a low, sexy whisper, and Phoebe almost felt herself sway so that Chase straightened her, brushed a finger along her jawline, before shouting to the intruder below.

"Up here. I'll be down in a sec." Chase took a moment to gain control of himself, while Phoebe sat up, straightened her shirt, and tried to fix her hair.

He turned and started down the ladder.

"Are you coming?"

Phoebe shook her head, hoping that it would shake the lust out of it. It did, but barely.

"I'll be down in a minute. I just want to look

around some more."

He threw her a smile and said, "Take the flashlight. We'll just be talking shop."

She watched as his head disappeared down the ladder and then let herself sag against a stack of boxes marked *Trafalgar Square* while she let her heartbeat return to normal. She closed her eyes. She had almost just had wanton sex with Chase Sanders on a steamer trunk belonging to her grandmother. What had she been thinking? And she had wanted it, desperately wanted what Chase had started. Or had she started it? Oh God, Phoebe thought, what was she thinking?

Chapter 22

Phoebe tasted a handful of popcorn kernels, deciding it needed just a bit more salt.

"Are you ready yet?" Lynn's voice echoed from the other room where a gigantic flat-screen TV was set up, the DVD player primed with a string of old Savannah Ryan movies.

"Just a minute." Phoebe added the salt and carried the popcorn into the family room. With Lynn's parents away, they had the house to themselves and were set up for another girls' night in.

It had been four days since Chase had come to Ivy House and found her. He had left soon after Jake, the floor guy, showed up. Jake was good to his word and promised her "the friend of a friend's" discount. What's more, he could start immediately. Until then, Lynn had offered a place to crash. Within the week, Phoebe would be able to live in Ivy House while fixing it up, and it was starting to dawn on Phoebe that this was it. The rest of her life was starting to unfold before her. It was unsettling and so the comfort of spending some time with a girlfriend, in a real house, was strangely appealing.

"Wine and popcorn. Who could have thought of a better combination?" Lynn said, grabbing a handful and taking a sip of the wine. She had traded her scrubs for a pair of cotton pajama pants and a faded sweatshirt. With her dark hair up in a ponytail and her glasses on, she looked more like a college student than a resident just a year or so out from being a doctor.

"I know, genius." Phoebe agreed. The Masters' family room was comfortable: a two-story space with a fireplace, overstuffed leather couches, and plenty of blankets to curl up with. Family pictures, including plenty of Lynn and her brother Kyle, decorated the shelves along with books and a few knickknacks, keeping the room simple and uncluttered.

"So which one are we going to watch fist?" Lynn held up two DVD cases.

"*Mystic Moon*, definitely," Phoebe said. "I think that one is my all-time favorite."

"Oh, good. Mine too." Lynn got up, popped it into the DVD player and flopped back down.

"I just love the costumes in this one. And Roger Dailey was such a hottie."

"She slept with him, you know? Before Leland, of course." Phoebe couldn't resist.

Lynn turned to her, her brown eyes big. "Really. That's so cool. I mean that you know all this stuff. It's like sitting here with Leonard Maltin, or that guy who runs the Actor's Studio and getting the blow-by-blow account.

Phoebe smiled. Even though Lynn was two years younger than she was, Phoebe was already feeling like she had made a true friend, something that had proved a bit elusive in her harried life in Los Angeles. Sure, she had colleagues and girls she went out with, but it seemed like there was always an undercurrent of competition with them. Whose design was going to get picked, which guy at the bar would take an interest in them, who had gotten the best purse or designer shoes.

At first, it had been exciting to be part of such a whirlwind and it had seemed to feed her creativity, but Phoebe had come to feel that it was more draining than energizing, and she'd felt that her inspiration had begun to suffer because of it.

"Well, you wouldn't believe what I found then."

Lynn's nose twitched while she thought about it. "The hat she wore in *Ghost Ship*."

Phoebe smiled as she explained what she and Chase had found in the attic of Ivy House.

"Wow, oh wow," Lynn breathed. "Do you realize how cool that is? Cool and valuable."

"Valuable?" Phoebe tensed a little.

"Yeah, to movie buffs. Not to be morbid, but since Savannah died, the online auction sites have been going crazy with her stuff—you know, autographs, movie posters. But there isn't much of it out there."

"Probably because she kept it all in that attic," Phoebe said.

"Well, I bet it's filled with cool stuff. Let me know if you want any help going through it."

Phoebe nodded. She hadn't thought much about the attic because she'd been busy working on her designs for North Coast Outfitters. And not to mention the fact that every time her phone rang or an email popped up, she had hoped it was something from him. Not a word from him, not unless you counted the crews of workmen he kept sending her way. Someone to haul the junk, the floors, even a lawn guy. Still, there hadn't been any presence of Chase himself for days.

"My favorite part," Lynn breathed a few moments later as Savannah Ryan and Roger Dailey kissed for the first time onscreen. Actually, the scene that had made it into the movie had been their tenth take. Savannah had confessed that she'd kept messing it up because she enjoyed the way he kissed. It had been before Leland Harper, if Phoebe remembered correctly, and Savannah had made a practice of sleeping with all of her costars.

"Chase kissed me." Phoebe didn't know why she said it. Perhaps it was the glass of wine she had already finished or watching the kiss on the screen that forced her to say aloud what she had been remembering for days. The bruising passion of Chase and his lips on her.

"What!" Lynn took the remote, paused the movie, so that Savannah and Rodger were frozen mid-kiss, and looked at her.

"Umm, why didn't you lead with that? So amazing. Is he a good kisser? I mean, he must be. He's just sex on a stick, isn't he?"

"Yeah," Phoebe sighed. She looked into her wine glass. There was no denying it. The kiss had been hot. Even now, at the memory of it, her whole body tingled, reliving the surge of electricity and lust that had shot through her while she was in his arms. She'd barely been able to think, glad that he had left her, but disappointed when he had finally gone.

"So it was amazing. Are you going to do it again?" Lynn was looking at her eagerly, her nose scrunched up, her face happy.

"I don't know. It's complicated." How do you explain the fact that kissing Chase was a bit like reliving someone else's history?

"What's so complicated? You think he's hot, he thinks you're hot. Shouldn't you just get together, you know, do the horizontal mambo?"

"Lynn." Phoebe threw a pillow at her, feeling the flush crawl up her skin.

Lynn caught it neatly. "Ahh, I get it. You're not the type."

"What type?"

"You know, the casual, hot-sex type. And he probably is. I mean he's gorgeous, rich, has a boat. And not to mention all the women he's been linked with. Arm candy, every one of them."

"I know." Phoebe had come to that very same conclusion herself, after flipping through several websites devoted to the East Coast's social bigwigs. Chase Sanders had been a regular, a sailor with a girl in every port...or a different one for every occasion.

He was a player plain and simple, and Phoebe, after being used for her personal connections all of her life, had no intention of becoming someone's arm candy again. No matter how delicious he might be.

"Still," Lynn continued, "there's always room for a fling. You know, the once-in-a-lifetime fling before you find Mr. Right."

"What makes you think there's a Mr. Right?" Phoebe asked.

Lynn smiled, looking completely self-assured. "Because there is. Everyone has a Mr. Right. Maybe you've just been dating the wrong guys, but you, especially, Phoebe, will find Mr. Right."

"You're such a hopeless romantic," Phoebe said, thinking that love was too complicated. Perhaps arrangements, with chemistry were a better way to go. Still, even casual flings took too much energy, energy that could be better put into her work and career.

"Love makes the world go around. Or at least hot sex keeps it rolling. You should totally go for it. You're not dating anyone. What do you have to lose?"

Everything, Phoebe wanted to say. Lynn had her pegged. There was nothing casual about her and from the moment she had seen Chase, she'd been attracted to him, with just a look from him sending her body into somersaults. And since he had flown out of Ivy House so fast that he'd barely said goodbye, she didn't even know if the kiss had meant anything to him at all.

"I don't even know if he meant anything by it," Phoebe said.

Lynn rolled her eyes. "Girl, you always know." With that, she resumed the DVD player, and Savannah and Roger Dailey's passionate embrace was interrupted by the sound of a gunshot.

Chapter 23

It was the Queensbay annual flea market and the bargain hunters, dealers, and junk sellers were out in full force. The sun was shining, with just a few of those super-white, cotton-candy clouds darting across a perfectly blue sky. A band was playing, there was the smell of coffee and grills going, families with kids dashed around, and groups of girlfriends prowled the tables.

Chase had bided his time after leaving Ivy House the other day. The force of what he felt for Phoebe, what he wanted to do to her, had him holding back, seeing if it was just some sort of madness, some sort of weird reaction to kissing the granddaughter of the woman who had been his first crush.

Perhaps there was some sort of residual lust build-up in the house, because all Chase had wanted to do was pull Phoebe to him and kiss her, run his hands over her long, lithe body, feel what he could do, how far out of control he could push her. Because that would be it. He had wanted to throw her down on that old steamer trunk, break through her air of studied casualness, and find what had to be a red-blooded woman below it.

But he sensed that while it might have solved

a momentary itch, Phoebe was a more complicated woman. She didn't trust him yet, and until he could prove that he wanted her, just her, she wouldn't be ready for what he had in mind.

So, he had done his research. It wasn't hard to figure out that she would be here. It was one of the town's biggest events, held on the stretch of grass and parking lots near the town dock and marina.

Chase saw Phoebe first, catching a glimpse of the red-gold hair, standing tall in the crowds. A smile creased over his face before he could stop it, and then he wondered what madness had him so happy to see her, a woman who'd not too long ago called him an arrogant son-of-a-bitch. Perhaps it was the way the sun caught the highlights in her hair or the way her cheekbones cut across her sculpted her face or the happiness that danced in her eyes.

He knew it well. "What are you after?" He slipped up behind her and put a hand on her elbow. She jumped in surprise, turned to him, and felt a tingle of anticipation at the changing expressions on her face. Surprise, delight and then the well-schooled look of indifference.

"What do you mean?" She tried to move back, but he was enjoying the feel of her, the way her body was pulled taut, full of tension, but not necessarily directed at him. No, her attention was elsewhere. He hazarded a look over his shoulder to see which table she was focused on.

"Don't look," she hissed, her blue eyes going dark, as she grabbed to spin him around in the opposite direction. He felt his skin go afire at her touch and an answering reaction between his legs. *If the woman had any idea how much she turned him on,* Chase thought, *she wouldn't be grabbing him like that in public.*

"Ahh, I knew it. So what are you after?" Chase looked over his shoulder again and watched sheer panic light up her eyes.

"Stop, you'll give it away." Her voice had dropped to an urgent whisper.

"I will, if you tell me what you're after," Chase said, pulling her closer to him, laying her arm on top of his.

"Owl salt-and-pepper shakers."

"Owls?" Chase was confused, but was enjoying the sensation of having her close to him. She was so intent on her prize that she seemed not to have noticed how close they were, the way she was letting him lean into her so that he could see the clear blue of her eyes, count the freckles on the bridge of her nose, and take in those full, wide lips, lips that he desperately wanted to kiss again.

Her eyes widened and she stiffened. "Oh, no, you don't." Her breath had become slightly ragged and she was leaning away from him.

"Don't what?" Chase feigned innocence.

"I know what you're trying to do."

"And just what am I trying to do?" Chase countered.

"You're trying to mesmerize me with your big hulking presence." Her eyes flitted around.

"Damn," she said.

"What is it?" Chase asked with amusement.

"That old biddy is looking at my salt-and-pepper shakers."

"Your salt-and-pepper shakers? The owls?" Chase said.

"Yes, the owls. They're ceramic and in prime condition."

"And let me guess: they're only a dollar each and you're worried someone else is going to steal the deal of a century."

"They're five dollars apiece," she answered loftily.

"Oh, my," Chase said with mock horror.

Phoebe made a face. "You just don't get it."

"I'm willing to be enlightened."

"Owls are going to be big next season. Those are perfect. The perfect inspiration pieces," she said.

Chase did hazard a glance over his shoulder now, and saw the pair of owls, only a few inches tall, gaudily painted in tangerine, brown, and that peculiar avocado green from the seventies. There was an older woman, gray-haired, dressed in tan polyester pants, a white cotton blouse, and a visor, poking around the other items on the table, but he could tell it was just for show. Like Phoebe, she wanted the owls.

"I think I can take care of this." He spun on his heel and sauntered over to the table, ignoring Phoebe's cry of protest.

Chase smiled at the redheaded woman who

was behind the table. He asked about an old beer sign, effectively blocking out the gray-haired woman who started to hover anxiously.

He examined the sign, made a big show of it, and then made his offer. The redheaded woman pretended not to be interested, so Chase took off his sunglasses, flashed a smile, and sealed the deal. He half-expected the lady in the visor to cry foul, but she just sniffed and wandered off.

Chase promised to come back for the sign and took his other package, walked over to Phoebe and handed her a bag with two objects wrapped up like miniature mummies in tissue paper.

"What's this?" she said, suspiciously.

"You can thank me later," Chase said, laying his arm across her shoulder.

Phoebe brought the bag up, poked around, and said, "You didn't."

"I did."

"How did you do it? I mean, what did you do? Pay full price for them?" Phoebe's voice carried a tone of disapproval.

"I simply made her an offer she couldn't refuse. The owls were part of the package deal."

"What package deal?"

"I got a great new beer sign for my man cave —and you have a pair of tacky owl salt-and-pepper shakers."

"They're not tacky!" Phoebe started to protest. And then she laughed. "OK, so, they're a little tacky. But you wait and see. Owls will be huge next season. How much do I owe you?"

He was seduced by the sound of her laughter. It was genuine, unaffected, and directed at him. He felt his heart soar and wondered how he could convince her to kiss him again.

"Like I said, these were part of the package deal. They're on me. Anything else you got your eye on? I'm a master negotiator."

"Yes, I've had some experience with that." He expected her to go cold on him again and wished he hadn't reminded her of how they met.

Instead, she smiled up at him, a flirtatious slant to her eyes. "There's an interesting vase three rows over, with a couple of ladies circling."

"Is it overpriced?" Chase asked.

"Absolutely," Phoebe said, her eyes crinkling up at the corners. She'd let him keep his arm over her shoulder for a while and Chase wanted nothing more than to snuggle her in closer to him, feel the heat of her body connect with his, brush his lips along the side of her face. He needed to stop thinking like that, he told himself. Otherwise, he would embarrass both of them in a very public place.

Still, he had her here, carefree and relaxed, and he wasn't going to lose that advantage. It was time to shake up Phoebe Ryan's expectations of him.

"Lead the way."

<<>>

Phoebe was painfully aware of the way the sun caught the lightened hairs on Chase's forearm as he shifted the gears of the Porsche. His presence overtook the car and she cast a quick glance at his profile. It was just about perfect, with a straight nose and strong chin, and when he threw her a quick look, one eyebrow quirking up as he accelerated up the hill, she felt her breath catch.

They had spent the entire day at the Queensbay antique fair and flea market, and true to his promise, he had negotiated deals for everything Phoebe wanted. It had become a game between the two of them, with Phoebe picking something outrageous and obviously coveted by more than one shopper. Each time, Chase had managed to get what she wanted, usually for half the price. Sure, he often wound up with something else, like a barstool to go along with his vintage beer sign, but Phoebe had gotten everything she'd had her eye on.

She had insisted on treating him to hot dogs and root beer, and now, with the trunk stuffed full of stuff—at least with what could fit—they were heading back to Lynn's house.

Phoebe knew that she shouldn't have let him drive her home, but Lynn, with whom she'd gone to the fair, had been paged into work early, and Chase had promised to make sure Phoebe would get home safely. He'd let his hand linger on Phoebe's back just a moment too long and her mind had gone blank, while her stomach tightened; she didn't have it in her to argue.

Now, when he looked at her, his sunglasses dipping just low enough so she could feel his gaze sweep over her, she felt everything tighten and a rush of excitement. His hand shifted gears and brushed along the side of her leg. Lust shot through her and she shifted in her seat, but not before she caught his triumphant smile.

Phoebe looked out the window at the green trees and houses flashing by. Suddenly, the air in the car had become too hot, too still, so she cranked the window open a little, breathing in a deep breath of fresh air, trying to clear her head.

Too soon, or not soon enough, he had pulled into the crushed shell drive of Lynn's house. The sun was starting to set, and she could see it cast its sparkling trail along the harbor in the distance. Before she could do it herself, Chase was out of the car and opening her door.

He held out a hand and pulled her up. She sprang up with such force that she wound up very close to him. Deftly reaching behind her, he shut the door. Still, his arms were around her and his face was very close to hers.

"Thank you," she managed to whisper. She could see the stubble on his face and the way his eyes darkened when he looked at her. "I had a nice time," she managed to stammer.

"A nice time?" he said with mock hurt. "Two of those whatchamacallem—topiary urns—for fifty bucks and you call that a nice time?"

She smiled and he caught her chin with his hand. She closed her eyes, overwhelmed, and when she opened them, she saw that he was looking at her intensely, his eyes searching, pinning her down.

Phoebe couldn't—wouldn't—let this happen. Chase was dangerous for her. She wanted him too much. And lust was never as simple as it was made out to be. Today, though, had been fun. It had only shown that he considered business, even if it was bargain hunting at a flea market, a blood sport. And that was all she was to him. Something to acquire.

He moved in and Phoebe felt the warm, smooth metal of the car beneath the small of her back. His chest was so close to her, she could feel the heat of it, sense the solid wall of muscle that was beneath his shirt.

Chase moved in closer, his lips hovering above hers. Before she could say anything, his lips trailed along her jaw and she felt her knees weaken. How could he make her feel this helpless, this wanted with just the lightest touch?

His leg nudged in between hers and she felt the strong, smooth strength of them, felt his arousal, and his lips found hers and she opened herself up to his kiss. Her hands came up to his neck and pulled him into her.

She didn't know if they stayed that way for a minute or five or fifty. She only knew that their mouths and tongues explored each other, each nibble and kiss and reaction matched the other's, until Phoebe felt as if she were melting, that if she did not have his warm, strong hands all over her, she would combust. Then, she felt something else.

Something that purred and then vibrated,

then rang and pierced their consciousness. Swearing, Chase pushed back from her, dug in his jacket until he found his phone. Not taking his eyes off her, he answered it with a terse "Yes."

Phoebe waited for her heartbeat to slow, for her heart to find its way back into her chest, for her knees to stiffen up. She looked down at the ground to find time to recover, let her hands smooth her ponytail back into place, all the while feeling her breathing grow more regular.

Chase put the phone back in his pocket.

"I have to go. Something's come up." He was looking at her intently, his eyes roaming over her like he wanted to possess her.

Quickly, he walked to the trunk, popped it, and took out the bags with her purchases. He placed them carefully on the side of the drive, and then he strode over to her, pulled her to him, and kissed her again, a hard, passionate, bruising kiss.

"Interrupted again, Phoebe. But I will be back. And don't try to tell me you don't want this any less than I do."

And with that he flashed his playboy grin, slung himself into the car and was off, the tires sending up a small trail of dust that settled slowly back to the ground.

Phoebe managed to make it to the first step of the porch before she collapsed on it, her mind spinning. What was she thinking, letting him kiss her like that? Again. Once she could understand, but she couldn't make a habit of kissing Chase Sanders. Of course, it was just lust, had to be.

Phoebe took a deep breath and heard the cry of a hawk, saw it circling overhead, looking for its dinner. Savannah had told her, warned her that men would use her, try to use Phoebe to get to Savannah. But Savannah was gone. And here was Chase Sanders, using all of his playboy charm on her, getting her to relax and like him, winning her over with five-dollar salt-and-pepper shakers, charming her pants off or trying to at least.

She leaned her head against the column of the porch railing, sighing. Because just a few minutes ago, she would have given a damn about history and been perfectly ready to have her pants—and just about everything else—charmed right off her.

Chapter 24

Chase had to take care of a manufacturing problem. It meant most of the night on the phone with a factory thousands of miles away. He'd had to head back into the office and when he was done, it was too late for him to head back to Ivy House, so he went right up to his own apartment at the hotel, a suite of rooms he'd fashioned into a bachelor pad when he'd bought the marina and the Osprey Arms. He had a long bank of windows overlooking the docks, and room service whenever he wanted. Even though it was late, he was too keyed up to sleep, so he poured himself a glass of single malt and sipped it while he sat in the dark and took in the view of the water.

He hadn't been able to stop thinking about her. Even when he was yelling and cajoling, his mind had slipped into wild fantasies. Not just of kissing of her, but of much more. Just how would her long, lean body look without one of her little v-neck sweaters? Or how her red-gold hair would spill across a pillow, or the way her supple legs would wrap around him as he rode her into wild release.

Or the way her eyes had flashed when she had laughed at him today, challenging him to track down ever more ridiculous items. The trouble he had gone to for a pair of pink-and-white-striped napkin rings. And it had all been a pleasure. Phoebe had been relaxed, her guard down, not eyeing him with distrust or keeping her distance.

He had been able to, for a moment, see the world the way she saw it, as a canvas of color and form, a palette of inspiration. She had been able to clearly explain to him how some of the things would influence her and how others just spoke to her, and she had enjoyed the hunt, the seeking of offbeat beauty, talking with all of the different dealers, learning where things had come from.

Chase shook his head. He wanted her; of that, there was no doubt. He had felt something the moment he'd walked into the house and there had been that odd feeling of recognition. True, she had looked a lot like Savannah Ryan that day, but she was as far from a movie star as could be. Phoebe was a jeans-and-sweater type of girl, who craved pretty, but not necessarily glamorous things. She could find a use for anything; even turn an ugly duckling into a swan.

He let himself breathe deeply, imagining the smell of her shampoo, the floral and citrus scent mixing with her distinctive aroma. What he wouldn't give to have her here with him right now.

Easy tiger, he told himself. He'd started out on the wrong foot with her and she was as prickly as a cactus. But still, if she thought to deny her attraction to him, she was crazy. She was a terrible liar and couldn't bluff worth a damn. She wanted him just as much as he wanted her. Chase glanced at his watch. The sun would be up soon and he hadn't slept.

He had a few things to do before he was ready for his next meeting with Phoebe Ryan.

Chapter 25

Phoebe awoke from a pleasant dream. It took her a moment to orient herself. And then she blushed. She had been having one of those dreams. Her face and body felt warm, suffused with blood, and there was an ache between her legs. It came back to her in bits and pieces, the dream, flashes of a dark head and blue eyes, the almost real feeling of his lips on hers, his hands stroking her, arousing her.

She pulled the covers up and buried her face into them. *Oh God,* she thought, *I am turning into a horny teenager.* The idea that an imaginary Chase Sanders, with his arrogant grin and big sexy hands, could have done that to her was just too much.

Before she could think more about it, her phone buzzed. Reaching for it, she tamped down disappointment when she recognized the number.

"Dean," Phoebe said, hoping the embarrassment didn't come across in her voice.

"Well, it seems like you have been a busy little bee," he said. It was cheerful, but Phoebe detected an undercurrent of disapproval.

"Oh," she said, grasping for words. She had left the window up and cool morning air filtered in, bringing her heart rate back to normal. The wild dream of last night receded.

"You saw the press release?" Phoebe had allowed Chase and his team to issue one. A brief notice that North Coast Outfitters and Ivy Lane Designs were collaborating on a new collection. Luckily, no one would pick up on the connection between her and Chase. But still it was out there, a flag in the sand, so to speak, that Phoebe was declaring for herself.

"Yes, I wish you had told me. I would have been happy to negotiate on your behalf," Dean said smoothly. Phoebe heard the clink of china and realized that Dean was already up, fully up, even though it was still very early on the West Coast.

"Well, thanks for the thought, but I did OK," Phoebe said. The terms had seemed fair enough; but then, she hadn't really asked for more, pushed, seen how much Chase was willing to give her. Dean was like a shark; he would never have acted that way on behalf of his client.

"Glad to hear. It's a good thing," he said, "I suppose. I am still working on wearing CallieSue down and knowing that you've moved on might be just the thing to make her want you back."

"Dean," Phoebe began. In truth, she hadn't thought once about losing the job to work on CallieSue's new line of country accessories and home goods. She had been too focused on and excited about her own business and designs to think about anyone else's.

"I know, I know, you said to leave it be. I

wasn't sure that heading out there was such a good idea, but who knew you would sign a business deal." He laughed again, but Phoebe had the sense he was dodging the point. Dean was probably sitting in his ultra-modern apartment, high up, with a commanding view of the city.

"Well, I think it's good for me. The house is wonderful," Phoebe hedged. It still needed a lot of work, but she was getting there. "And I've been feeling really creative, full of energy." Inspired, though Phoebe didn't say that.

"Well, I just want you to be careful, my dear. I checked a bit on the company you've signed on with. I hope you aren't dealing directly with the president, a Chase Sanders. He seems to have quite the reputation for himself."

Phoebe felt herself bristle at the implied warning. "He's not anything like the papers make him out to be..." she began, and then realized that she didn't know him that well at all.

"Ahh, so it was a personal deal," Dean said. "Listen, Phoebs, you know I am just looking out for you. I don't want you to get taken advantage of again." He said it gently, kindly and Phoebe felt her irritation slip away. Dean really did look after her; he always had.

"I know, I know," Phoebe acknowledged. "And it's just business, nothing like it was with Garrett. I mean, I have nothing to offer him besides my pillows."

There was a pause on the other end of

the phone and Phoebe waited, hoping that Dean wouldn't say anything that would make it awkward between the two of them.

"Well, I am sure you know what you're doing. And, well, now that you have a new job, I'm sure you'll be back here soon working again."

Phoebe laughed with him, not having the heart to tell him that she wasn't sure whether she was going back. She could work wherever she wanted to, at least for a while, and the thought of not hopping on a plane and heading back to Los Angeles was becoming more and more appealing.

<<>>

Her morning, after the phone call with Dean, went well. At least she meant it to, having every intention to focus on work. She'd made a great start on the collection for North Coast Outfitters, but she was fiddling with the first designs, doing her best to get them perfect. Memorable. Unforgettable.

"Don't be alarmed." Jake, the floor guy, popped up in front of her, a bacon-and-egg sandwich in one hand and the other hand clutched around a steaming cup of coffee. Phoebe was so startled she almost dropped the empty mug of coffee that she had been on her way to refill.

"Is there a problem?" Phoebe asked. Chase strolled in right behind Jake, hands stuffed in the pocket of his jeans, looking totally at ease in a leather jacket. He had on his expensive sunglasses, which he removed as his dark eyes gazed around the place.

"We're almost done," Jake said to Phoebe's unanswered question. "I know it still looks bad, but this is a messy job. I need another two days for the upstairs. And then you can really start to move in."

One more night. Lynn's mother had offered her the guest bedroom on a permanent basis while the floors were being done, but so far, she'd been able to stay in the house. Jake, since he was Chase's floor guy, was giving her a deal, which meant he worked on her house in between his other jobs.

"It looks beautiful." Chase gestured towards the living room. Phoebe had picked the darker stain. The wood had been restored beautifully and the floors gleamed, looking sharp and clean. Unfortunately, it only made the paint look more dingy. Phoebe wanted to take her time picking colors, and this way she could live in the house and restore it at the same time.

"Really, it does," Phoebe agreed. She supposed another night at the Masters' home was a small price to pay for perfect hardwood floors.

"Great." Jake took another bite of his sandwich and spoke around a mouthful. "Why don't the two of you get out of here so we can finish up?"

Phoebe couldn't help herself, gazing up the stairs, to the landing, and the attic piled high with the remnants of Savannah's life.

"Don't even think about," Jake said, watching her gaze. "You can't walk up there."

Phoebe laughed and held up her hands in mock surrender. "OK, I get it. I'll get out."

She thanked Jake and walked out the door into a beautiful spring day. She sensed Chase's presence behind her, but did not turn.

"So, fancy going for a sail?"

"A what?" Phoebe turned and looked at Chase. He was making a habit of just showing up and she could see he was serious, completely serious.

"A sail. You said you liked boats. Mine happens to be at the marina, and it's a beautiful spring day, with a nice breeze. There's a deli that will make us some nice sandwiches, a couple of sodas, maybe a glass of wine?"

"Are you sure this isn't just a chance for me to check out your sheets?"

Chase smiled, and she felt heat shoot through her. "As I was trying to tell you that night, I think there's a gap in the market. Boat sheets are boring, bland. And you, I mean, your designs seem anything but."

"So it's another business meeting?" Phoebe challenged.

"We boaters like to call it a pleasure cruise." He was joking, a cheesy-looking leer on his face. He topped it off with a wink and Phoebe had to laugh. But she felt her breath hitch and flame of desire lick through her as she gave serious consideration to the fact that she would be alone on a boat with him.

"Is it going to rain?" The sky was clear, but she could see a sort of haze settling over the harbor.

"Not until much later. Right now, it's a great day out." He'd pushed back his sunglasses so she could see his eyes gazing down at her, and she knew he wanted her to say yes. Phoebe hesitated for a moment, her brain screaming at her to say no, that she should go find someplace to hunker down, open up her laptop, do some work, but her body was sizzling with electricity, the thrill of being near Chase, of wanting to be near him.

"Fine. But I get to steer," Phoebe said.

Chapter 26

She had run upstairs to pack a bag and then dropped it off at the Masters' house, briefly telling Mrs. Masters where she was going.

"A sail. Isn't it supposed to rain?" Mrs. Masters said, glancing at the sky and then back towards Chase who had walked in with Phoebe.

"Oh, I think it will hold off. We should be fine," Chase said and then shifted uncomfortably from foot to foot. Mrs. Masters was giving him that look, the look moms used to give him when he came to pick up their daughters.

Phoebe came downstairs wearing khaki shorts and a collared shirt tied at the waist. A fleece was thrown over her shoulders and she had a pair of sunglasses and her camera.

"We'll be back later," Chase said, trying not to be obvious in noticing the way Phoebe's shorts showed off just about every inch of her long, tan, golden California legs.

He saw Mrs. Masters give him a look, so with one eyebrow raised and a smile, he turned on all of his charm.

"I promise I'll have her back in one piece, before sundown," Chase said, pulling his eyes away from Phoebe's thighs.

His charm worked. Mrs. Masters gave them some cookies and shooed them off. Chase drove them back down to the marina, where he ordered some food from the small deli near the docks. His boat was well stocked with water, soft drinks, and, as promised, wine and beer.

Chase wanted to put his arm around Phoebe and tell her that he wouldn't bite. Not unless she asked him to. But she seemed intent on keeping a distance between them, as if their kisses had never happened. Still, he felt a faint stirring of hope when he caught her looking at him speculatively from underneath her lashes while pretending to browse through the postcard rack in the marina office.

Perhaps she wasn't as cool as he thought. Ice queen was the thought that had come to mind when he'd first met her, but after their kiss, he'd had to re-arrange his thinking. She had been more like a fire demon, the way she had moved into him, arousing all of his senses, the way he had wanted the kiss to last forever, how he wanted to run his hands over her body, touch her, feel her. Each time, all rational thought had fled from his mind. Well, he'd had a few of them, like how he could get her alone and under him in a house without a lick of furniture and a pile of old boxes.

"Find anything?" Chase asked, his business taken care of.

She held up a picture of a large building that looked out over the water, a huge Victorian building, covered in lacy white trim, looking a bit like a wedding cake.

"The Queensbay Show House," Chase said, a small smile ghosting across his lips.

"Savannah used to perform there in the summer. I think that was when her agent was trying to revive her career."

Chase raised his eyebrows as he took the postcard for a moment.

"I know. It didn't really work. She never did have the best singing voice."

"Did you ever see her perform in one of her shows?"

Phoebe nodded, her blue eyes sparkling. "Not here—in Los Angeles. Still, it was a bit like magic. My nanny took me, but I got to go backstage where everyone was getting ready, see all these half-dressed actors sitting there, putting on their makeup. It's old and huge and bright and dark, all at the same time, and it was possibly the most exciting place in the whole world for a little girl."

Chase felt his heart tug. She had been lighthearted and free during the flea market, but she hadn't talked about her past. He realized he liked it when Phoebe let her guard down, when she actually talked about herself. He could almost see the little girl she had been, watching the chaos and excitement that was backstage.

"I bet you had your best dress on."

Phoebe laughed. "And I got to eat M&Ms and drink a Coke during intermission. It was a little slice of heaven."

"Well, then, let's go."

"What do you mean? It's been closed for years," Phoebe said.

"I meant we could sail past it. It will have to do, but there's a great little cove past there that we can tuck into and have our lunch."

Phoebe put the postcard back. "Sounds good."

<<>>

Phoebe might have been more comfortable as a swimmer than a sailor, but she knew how to handle herself on a boat. He watched as she hopped lightly aboard.

"Do you want me to stow this for you?" she said, pointing at the canvas bag packed full with their lunch.

"That would be great," he told her and got busy readying the boat for cast-off. They would motor out of the marina area and out into the wide expanse of Queensbay Harbor. The wind was coming off the land, so they would have a nice clear run up to the Queensbay Show House and then make the trip into Pine Cove. The cove was a decent-sized inlet off the Sound, deep enough for them to be able to go in, nice and protected from the wind and waves, anchor, maybe even take the little dinghy to shore and wade along the sandy shoreline.

When everything was safely stowed below, she hopped onto the dock, untied the mooring lines, and elegantly jumped back aboard. He powered up his engine and his forty-foot sailing cruiser moved away from the slip. Chase guided it out into the channel and towards open water, loving the feeling of the wind ruffling his hair, the smell of the tangy salt water assailing his nostrils.

"Don't worry, I'll let you take the wheel when I set the sails," he told Phoebe, but she merely nodded.

It was warming up and the pale pink of her shirt showed off the light tan of her skin. She looked content, sitting back on the cockpit seat, her head turned up to catch the sun.

It took more than a few minutes motoring slowly to make it out to open water. He gave the wheel to Phoebe, told her which direction to point the boat in, and got his sail up. In a moment, it snapped, caught the wind and the boat picked up speed.

Chase came back down in the cockpit and stood next to her. He felt her tense as he put an arm out to help her correct her course. When she had it, he cut the engine and there was that moment of pure, glorious quiet, the only sound a whisper of wind, and the smooth swish of water beneath the bow.

<<>>

Phoebe watched him move around the boat, capable and confident. He looked as good in a pair of rolled-up khakis and polo shirt as he did in his jeans and t-shirt, and she found herself focusing on the pull of his muscles beneath the fabric of his shirt.

He touched her and her body tensed, but it

was only a hand on hers, to help her point the boat in the right direction, and as soon as he did, she felt the boat leap to life below her, surge forward on the power of the wind.

Now he was sitting down, stretched out, hands behind his head.

"Aren't you going to watch where we're going?"

"No, that's what you're here for," he said with a smile.

"But I could hit something."

He shrugged. "It's the middle of the week, early in the season. I bet we have the water all to ourselves."

Phoebe looked around. The harbor was quiet, its high banks covered in a blanket of leafy trees, the sun sparkling and dancing on its surface.

"I guess we'll be safe."

"Just don't get too close to shore." Chase settled in and for all the world looked like he was going to nap.

Phoebe watched him for a moment and then nudged him. "Not fair. I didn't know you were going to make me do all the work."

"Work? You call this work?"

Phoebe sighed, looking at the harbor, at the houses nestled among the trees, at a bird, a hawk probably, flying overhead.

"No, this isn't work at all," she agreed.

"Told you nothing beats a sail for fixing what ails you." Chase sat up now and looked around. He scooted over and came and stood behind her, one arm coming around and touching hers. "A bit to the starboard," he said.

She had lost track of their course. She was supposed to be heading for the wedding cake. That's how she had always thought of the Queensbay Show House, a giant white wedding cake perched on the edge of the bank.

"I see it."

Chase was still behind her, close—too close—when he asked, "If you loved going to the theater, how come you never wanted to be an actress?"

"You mean like Savannah?"

"Exactly. You have the name, the face, and I am sure she would have opened the doors for you."

Phoebe swallowed, surprised that the memory could still pain her after all these years. Chase moved so he could see her.

"What is it? Tell me."

Lips pursed together, Phoebe shook her head.

"That bad?" he guessed.

"Worse," Phoebe admitted and then found herself smiling. "I was in first grade. We were doing a play, "Goldilocks and the Three Bears." I got to be Goldilocks, of course."

"Of course."

"Well, it wasn't just the hair. The teacher had figured out that Savannah was my grandmother and I think she held out the hope that if I got the lead, Savannah would deign to come."

"Did she?" Chase asked.

"Of course she did." Phoebe closed her eyes as the memory replayed itself.

"And..."

"I got stage fright, forgot my lines, and knocked down one of the walls of the Bears' house. Who knew Goldilocks was a comedy?"

"That sounds pretty bad. But you were just a kid."

"And I knew I wasn't cut out for it. And Savannah knew too. You know what she said?"

Chase shook his head.

Phoebe's voice changed, becoming richer, more ironic. "Don't worry, dear, the theater will survive quite nicely without you."

"Ouch," Chase said, but he was smiling, his teeth white against the tanned skin of his face.

"Well, it was the best thing that could have happened to me. I never had delusions of making it as an actress. Savannah helped me find my other talents. She was very encouraging that way. She's the one who kept sending me art supplies and books, even bought me my first computer so I could use a graphics program." Phoebe's voice had dropped back into her own.

"So, she wasn't the prima donna the press made her out to be?" Chase's voice was low, a dangerous growl, but she could sense the humor in it.

"Well, like I said, she was more like an Auntie Mame than an Auntie Bess, but I guess she did her best."

Surprised, Phoebe found her eyes tearing up.

She'd been so focused on taking care of Savannah, of sorting through things, that she had put her memories of Savannah far away.

"I always thought she was more like a fairy godmother than a grandmother. I could never call her Grandma. She made me call her Aunt Savannah. I mean, she was absent and forgetful, but then she could be generous to a fault.

"And now?" Chase asked.

"I miss her, but she was so sick at the end. Cancer. But I feel like in some respects, I never really knew what made her tick. She was an actress to the end, playing a role, keeping her secrets."

Chase laughed. "Well, everyone has those. Do you know that my grandmother didn't love Leland?"

"Well, of course she didn't."

"No, I mean before he ran away with Savannah. She thought she loved him, but they didn't love the same things. Leland liked the big life. My grandmother was more of a small-town girl."

"So?" Phoebe didn't know where this was going. So far, they had avoided the fact that their grandparents had been lovers.

"Well, let's just say Leland wasn't leaving a happy marriage behind. Or perhaps that Savannah didn't have to do much to get him to come."

"You know, Savannah always said he was the love of her life. It wasn't easy, but I think they were really, deeply in love. Passionate and stormy, but it was more than just an affair."

"And is that what you think love should be?" Chase asked, his eyes dark as he looked at her.

Phoebe shook her head. "No. I think that's the kind of love that doesn't survive. It consumes people, makes them resent each other. Savannah was a passionate person, but she could be passionate about many things. I think she could claim Leland was the love of her life because she didn't have to spend the rest of her life with him."

She glanced away, out over the water, swallowing before she continued. "My parents loved each other and I don't remember stormy at all. They seemed happy. Like my mom would smile when my dad came home early and my dad's face lit up when he saw her. They could count on each other. I think that's what love is."

"So no dark and stormy for you?" Chase's voice was dangerously low, and Phoebe looked at him for a long moment before she replied.

"I think dark and stormy could have its place, for a while."

Chase gave her his lopsided smile. "Good to know."

He'd taken off his sunglasses and his eyes were boring into her, laying her bare, and Phoebe felt a shiver run through her. She never should have told him so much and wished he wouldn't look at her that way. It made not thinking about that kiss all the more difficult.

"There she is." They sailed past the Queensbay Show House, which almost looked like it were about to pitch into the water. There was a large hand-lettered banner across the front, which read "Save the Show House."

"Guess it's fallen on some hard times."

"Yeah." Chase's hand was on her shoulder and he squeezed it. It was a simple, friendly gesture, but her body didn't respond that way. She wanted to move away, but here she was trapped in a boat, with not a lot of room to hide.

The Show House slipped behind him and Chase took over the wheel. He handled the boat through the channel out into the Sound, gliding past a long pile of rocks that guarded the entrance. Chase headed east, and they sailed along the wide-open water for a while, until he turned again towards the shore. He switched on the motor and she took the wheel as he dropped the sail. He came back and maneuvered them into a narrow passageway that opened up into a wide-open cove, ringed by marsh and trees. It was beautiful, Phoebe thought, and peaceful. A few houses ringed the shoreline, but it was quiet. She savored the calm, trying to drink it in, wash way the nerves she was feeling every time Chase's arm brushed against hers.

"They put this all together pretty quickly for you," Phoebe said. They were eating lunch, an array of bread, cheeses, and sandwiches set out before them. Chase had appeared with a bottle of cold white wine, and Phoebe accepted a glass, as much to settle her nerves as anything else.

"Nothing beats a sail and a picnic lunch. Hard

to do it, though."

"Why?"

Chase shrugged. "Work, life. You get older, busier, seems like it gets harder and harder to take a couple of days off to go sailing."

"What about your girlfriends?"

"Girlfriends?" One of Chase's eyebrows quirked up.

"You know, the ones you're always photographed with?" Phoebe asked pointedly.

"Ahh. Well, those. Somehow, I never seem to meet any who actually like to go sailing. They all say they do, but they think I mean on a motor boat. Once they realize that you have to do some work and that the cabin on any boat can be a bit cramped and that it's not all that glamorous, they always seem to get out of sailing."

"Guess you've been seeing the wrong ladies."

"If that was your way of asking if I am seeing someone right now, the answer is no. And, you, of all people, should know that the media has a way of exaggerating things."

"So you're not quite the playboy you've been made out to be."

Chase shrugged. "Let's just say those pictures are pretty much the whole story. I go out, I get photographed, and then my companion and I part ways, the press to the benefit of the both of us, but no further strings attached."

Embarrassed and relieved at the same time, Phoebe looked out at the water. She saw something swimming, a little head poking above the water, leaving a v-shaped wake. Once it got closer, she saw that it was a turtle. The little guy swam right past them, not even sparing them a glance.

"Ah, hell." She looked up and saw that Chase was looking at the sky. The clouds they had noticed before had rolled in, piling up with dark gray underbellies.

"Is it going to rain?" The words were barely out of her mouth when one large, fat raindrop fell into the cockpit.

"Here, get this stuff below," Chase said. "I'll take care of the sail."

Phoebe felt the wind getting kicky too, tossing the trees that ringed the cove, the light undersides of the leaves dancing in the wind.

She gathered up their lunch and brought it down to the table in the cabin below. She dashed back up, grabbed the bottle of wine and their water, and pulled down the hatch as soon as the rain began in earnest, a great sheet of soaking water.

Phoebe stood in the small galley, setting up their lunch again on the small table, while the boat rocked beneath her. Rain lashed against the portholes and she saw Chase's feet flash by. Then, there was a movement and he was in the cabin with her, big and wet. He was soaked to the skin.

"Ahh, you saved the wine. Nothing to do but to ride this out. I thought we had a bit longer, but the faster it comes, the faster it will pass by, I suppose. There might be some thunder and lightning, but I think we'll be safe here."

"I'm not worried," Phoebe said, though the boat gave a bit of a lurch, and she thought she heard a boom of thunder in the distance.

"Good. I'm going to find a dry shirt." He pushed past her towards the rear cabin, where the main bunk was. He didn't close the door and she could see him rummaging for a shirt, and then she got a glance of him as he crossed both arms over his back and hiked the shirt up. Muscles rippled in synchronicity, and she had a full glimpse of his flat stomach and the muscles that ringed it.

Phoebe felt her breath hitch and a tingle of lust shoot through her. No, she hadn't forgotten just how hot Chase was; she just thought that she wouldn't have to confront the shirtless proof of it.

Rain slammed against the porthole and then he was there, crowding into the small galley space. He reached behind her and poured a little more wine into their glasses. He was so close that she could feel the heat rising off him, smell his rain-slicked skin.

"We'll be OK," he said.

"I'm fine," she answered automatically, but she wasn't. Her heart was racing and her skin felt too warm. She half-turned, but found he had her trapped. She would have to push past him—touch him—if she wanted to get to the relatively open space of the cabin. Still, it was all so small, there was really no place to escape him.

"You're shaking," he said, his voice dangerously low, and she felt the reaction between her legs, aware she was thoroughly aroused by him. She made a study of him, taking in the dark, too long hair, his thick eyebrows, one of which had a faint scar under it; the tanned skin with the shadow of a beard on it and the way his shoulders stretched the fabric of his worn t-shirt.

"What are you nervous about?" he asked, and his hand moved closer to her. His hands were still on his hips, but now he moved them to either side of her, truly trapping her. She looked into his eyes and saw an answering need to her own in them. She had to look down and away, and her body shifted so she was against him, feeling his strong, lean legs brush against her thighs, and then the evidence that he was just as aroused as she was.

"This is a bad idea," she said, automatically. His hand came up and stroked the side of her cheek, and she shivered at his touch.

"It doesn't have to be." One finger caught her under the chin and lifted it up so he could look at her.

"You're beautiful," he said, his breath hoarse and he pressed in closer to her. She rose up to meet him and their mouths met. She found his lips and they took and tasted her, while one of his arms circled her and pulled her close. Phoebe moved her own arms up and around his shoulders, finding his neck and pulling in to him, the need to be close to him filling her desperately.

"Chase," she murmured.

"Tell me to stop now," he pulled back a moment and looked at her, his eyes deep, dark, filled with want, "while I can, and I will. I'll go up on deck and get us back to shore. Or..."

Want and need were coursing through her, and she could feel her desire for him rising in her. She shook her head and said, "Don't stop. We have a storm to ride out."

He spoke no more, but his mouth assaulted her, his tongue taking, testing, teasing, while one hand traveled down her neck, skimming her skin, until it found her breast. He cupped it, teasing her nipple, which responded to his touch, puckering beneath it, growing to fullness. Phoebe felt herself give a small moan and heard Chase's satisfied chuckle. Slowly, leisurely, his hand traveled over to her other breast, and he brought that one to arousal.

She kissed him harder, feeling him grow hard against her as his hand traveled down her shirt, to her waistband. His hand was as warm as fire on the bare flesh of her stomach. One of his knees pushed into her legs, spreading her open. His strong arms lifted her up so that she was balanced on the edge of the counter. He pushed in between her and slid a hand down inside her shorts, finding heat and her wetness. Phoebe moaned for him and wrapped her legs tightly around him.

She heard a small crash, realizing it was just the sound of a knife falling into the galley sink.

With a practiced, swift movement, Chase put both hands under her, pulling her close to him. She wrapped her legs around him and he pulled her back from the counter. In a few short strides, he had her in the cabin, throwing her gently down on the bunk.

Above her, she could see rain bubbling and dripping down the clear hatch cover, see that the world outside was gray. Inside, though, in the dim light, all she could see and smell was Chase, the mix of his soap and aftershave, as he pushed her back on the berth. He stood above her, and he took off his t-shirt, revealing the solid-muscled chest she had only glimpsed before. She sat up and ran one hand over his chest, the slight dusting of dark hair, tracing it down to the waistband of his pants.

Chase stopped her, took her hand and kissed it, then nibbled on her fingers. "Take off your shirt," he said, and Phoebe, after the merest hesitation, peeled it off.

Before she could cover herself, he stopped her. "Let me look." She felt emboldened under his scrutiny, and she reached behind her and unclasped her bra, throwing it off to the side.

Chase smiled at her and his hands skimmed across her breasts, bringing them to life, her nipples tightening further under his touch. His other hand found her shorts, and he undid them, pulling them off her, taking his time. Well, her body ached for him.

He was above her, knees on either side of her, dark and handsome. He caressed her breasts, kneading them so that her back arched. Her hands came up to reach for him, and he took them, pulled them over her head, pinioned her there, while his mouth found one nipple, then the other. One hand trailed down her body, finding the thin scrap of fabric between her legs. He moved there, and Phoebe knew he could feel her heat, her need. Slowly, teasing, he brought his hand inside her, and she bucked with pleasure.

He touched her then, finding her spot, while his mouth ravaged her body. His fingers kept pushing her to the peak, a wave building and building until she was there, her body writhing and twisting underneath him, his weight pinning her, until she reached it, reached the crest and let it wash over her.

She opened her eyes, saw him watching her, his hands lightly stroking her. She saw that he was ready for her, his pants straining. Phoebe sat up, her hair spilling across her shoulders and pulled him towards her, opening his zipper, pulling down his underwear, until he burst free.

She stroked him and his eyelids fluttered as he bent down to kiss her, his knees spreading her apart. His hands moved over her, bringing her back to arousal, as he slid himself into her, testing, gently, as she pulled him towards her, and he thrust into her, the two of them rocking together, the boat bobbing in the waves underneath them as he brought her again to the edge, their rhythm driving them both to the edge. This time Phoebe kept her eyes open, as Chase's eyes gazed into hers, as they both went closer and closer. Her hands wrapped around his back and when he came, she went with him, both of them tumbling down the sweet sea of pleasure.

Chapter 27

Chase opened his eyes. He was on his back, staring up at the roof of *Windsway*'s cabin. Phoebe was half next to him, half on top of him, tangled around him. He could smell the flowery scent of her shampoo, the slightly spicy whiff of her perfume. She moved and one of her breasts grazed against his chest, and he felt himself grow hard again.

He ran a hand through her hair, while his other hand trailed down her back. She shivered against him, the movement sending waves of desire over him.

"Wow, babe," he said, and she turned to him, so he could see her eyes, which looked more green than blue in the light. Above them, he could see that the skylight was less wet and that the dark gray seemed to be giving way to a lighter sky.

Her hand lay on his stomach and he could feel it sliding, stroking.

"So that was good?" He thought he detected a note of satisfaction in her voice.

"Good doesn't quite do it justice," he said and was rewarded with a pleased smile. His heart jumped a little at that, and he realized that the thought that he had made her happy, made her feel pleasure, made him happy. It was a new sensation for him. No one had ever complained about his lovemaking. In fact, with most women, he was more concerned about how much he enjoyed himself. But he had a need to please Phoebe, to drink in every bit of her long, lean body, feel her move and cry out with pleasure underneath him, know that it was all because of him.

"The boat's not moving as much," Phoebe observed.

Chase squinted through the porthole. "Looks like the storm is passing by. We may even see some sun." The water was calmer now, and the *Windsway* barely moved beneath them.

"I guess that means we could go home now," she said. Her hands were still roaming over his stomach and then they dipped a little lower, and he felt himself ready again, ready to have her, this time to take her slowly, lazily, to watch her carefully, to see her enjoy every minute of it.

"We still have a few hours of daylight left," he said, pulling her on top of him. He kissed her and she returned it, her hair falling down in a gold curtain around him. He rose up and pulled her closer to him, his hands teasing her breasts, lightly pulling her nipples until she threw back her head in pleasure, arching and bowing her back as he slid lower down, finding her sex again, urging her on, higher and higher, until she was almost at her peak. Then he slid into her, holding him tight to her, and thrust into her, watching her eyes fill with pleasure and heat.

She arched her back and grabbed his head. His lips raked down her neck and to her nipple, and he teased it and pulled it tight in his teeth as she called out his name in pleasure. Resting his hands on her hips, he held her tight as she rode him to the crest of a powerful orgasm. He waited and watched until he sensed she was near, could feel her closing like a hot velvet fist around him, see in her eyes as she came. Then, as she crested, he allowed himself to come, following her over the edge until she sagged into him, spent, and he fell back, dazed.

Chapter 28

Dark was falling as they motored into the Queensbay Marina. The weather had broken, treating Chase and Phoebe to a magnificent sunset, the sun streaking the sky above the water a rainbow of purples and reds. They had fallen into a comfortable silence after they had finally decided it was time to return, Chase giving her directions as she guided the boat, while he took care of the sails and coiled lines.

Phoebe loved the feel of the wind ruffling her hair, the way her body felt relaxed, sated. The sex had been some of the best she'd ever had—nope, make that the best she'd ever had—and when Chase came down to stand next to her, one of his strong hands settling on her to help her steer the boat, she sunk into him, loving the feel of him, the presence of him comforting her.

They docked the boat together, with help from a friendly deckhand, and as Chase checked the lines, they heard a voice calling them.

"There you are," Lynn said as she came up to them. "Nice boat."

Something in her smile had Phoebe guessing that Lynn had a pretty fair idea of what they had been up to. Luckily, dusk was settling and it hid the flush that was spreading across her cheeks.

"My mom sent me down," Lynn said, apologetically. "She wanted me to invite you both to dinner. I texted, but with the storm and everything, you know, she got a little concerned. Typical mom."

Phoebe wouldn't know, but she wasn't upset. It was strangely nice to be worried about, even if she had been in capable hands. She sent a look to Chase and he answered with one of his own.

"So, dinner?" Lynn turned to Chase. "The Randalls are coming."

Chase looked at her, then laughed. "Noah's coming?"

"Yes. Noah and his wife are big donors to the hospital and the clinic, so my parents wanted to thank them. When Noah heard Phoebe was staying with us, he wanted to make sure you were back in time for dinner."

"I'm sure he did," Chase said drily.

"I don't know," Phoebe said, hesitating, feeling nervous. She wasn't sure she was ready.

"My mom promised to be good," Lynn whispered.

Chase jumped down lightly on the dock. "A home-cooked meal. Sounds great." He held out a hand for Phoebe and she looked at him. He was standing there in his khakis and a fresh polo shirt, looking perfectly relaxed, like he hadn't just spent the afternoon doing that with her.

With Lynn grinning at her and Chase offering

her his hand, Phoebe had no choice but to take it.

Chapter 29

Dinner was surprisingly normal. They'd pulled into the Masters' house and Chase took a beer from Lynn's father. The two men sat on the back deck overlooking the water, talking boats and sports.

Phoebe had run up to her room to change and freshen up, trying desperately to get the "I've just had the most amazing sex of my life" look off her. Her lips were swollen and her cheeks reddened from where his stubble had roughened them, and when she looked in the mirror, all she could think about was them, naked and twisting.

She splashed water on her face, changed into a sundress, sandals, and a sweater and ran down to help in the kitchen. Lynn shot her a look and there was a knowing smile on Mrs. Masters' lips, but neither one of them said anything as they brought drinks and appetizers outside.

The Randalls had arrived by then. Noah was almost as tall as Chase, but with light brown hair. Caitlyn gave Phoebe a hug, explaining to Noah that they had run into each other in town. She was wearing a sundress and Phoebe could see that she was glowing, whether from her condition or the way

Noah's gaze lingered over her, she couldn't tell.

Chase introduced them and Phoebe could feel Noah appraising her with his eyes, while one arm held his wife close. Apparently, she passed because he smiled and shook her hand easily. The sun was setting, turning the water into liquid gold, and a light wind rustled the tall trees in the Masters' yard. It was a great view and Lynn had snuck in and changed the playlist on the radio to something fun and upbeat.

Chase made room for Phoebe to sit next to him and she did. His arm lay casually across the back of the settee as they made conversation.

"So," Caitlyn said, sipping a club soda, "how are you enjoying our little town of Queensbay?"

Chase's knee brushed against her, and Phoebe had to fight to keep her attention on Caitlyn. "It's very relaxing," she answered.

"Glad to hear it. Chase said you've started work on the house. How is that going?" Phoebe nodded. "Yes, that's the plan, at least." Phoebe wasn't quite sure what else to say, since she didn't know what she planned to do with it.

"Hey, Phoebe," Lynn said, sitting on the arm of one of the wicker couches, "the clinic is running a kid fair soon to raise money. Think you could run the art booth for them, you know, since you're creative and all that?"

"It's for a great cause," Caitlyn said, her hand unconsciously rubbing her belly. "Noah's agreed to be in the dunk tank."

"That I've got to see," Chase said, punching his old friend's arm.

"Only if we take turns," Noah said.

"Hey, Chase, maybe North Coast Outfitters could donate some things, to use as raffle prizes? It is for a good cause." Lynn said hopefully.

"Lynn, you're hopeless," her mother said, as she passed around a plate of hors d'oeuvres, but Phoebe could tell she wasn't upset by her daughter's forthright comment.

Chase laughed. "Well, if Phoebe's in for being creative, I suppose I'm in for some dough. Just don't make me finger-paint." There was the general sound of laughter, and Dr. Masters reappeared with fresh beers for the guys and more white wine for Lynn and Phoebe.

Phoebe caught the look that had passed between Caitlyn and Lynn, plus Caitlyn's knowing wink, and knew that one of the goals of the dinner had been to get her and Chase to agree to help out with the fair. She guessed that Lynn knew it wouldn't hurt to have the granddaughter of Savannah Ryan running a booth. The girl was relentless when it came to protecting and guarding her clinic, she had to give her that. At least it was for a cause Phoebe could get behind.

The rest of the evening passed quickly, with steaks and salad eaten al fresco, laughter, and good conversation. Noah and Chase even told a few stories from their days at school, which had even Dr. Masters roaring with laughter. Phoebe felt alive, a warm glow suffusing her, from the good food and the company.

She saw the way Lynn's parents looked at each other with affection and the way Noah was overly solicitous of Caitlyn and her comfort. There was no fiery passion here, just warmth and love. For a moment, Phoebe's heart constricted and she knew this was what she wanted, more evenings like this, sitting out by the water, surrounded by friends and family.

She hazarded a glance at Chase, saw him laughing at something his friend said and wondered if he could ever want the same thing. He wasn't a settling-down type and was cynical about love. Would he want to be sitting with her here, a year from now, hanging out on Ivy House's own terrace, listening to music, laughing with friends, or would she already be old news to him, another one in his long string of flings? Though he had made it sound like he wasn't as bad as everyone thought.

He caught her looking at him, and he flashed the smile, the one that made her toes curl and her stomach clench. She held his gaze and she could feel herself frown, the sadness growing on her face. Before she could dwell on that anymore, Lynn pulled her into a movie trivia game against her mother and Caitlyn.

"That was awesome," Lynn said at the end of the game. Phoebe had won hands down, easily beating Lynn's mother, who was shaking her head in disbelief.

"I've never beaten her," Lynn said. "Not once."

Caitlyn laughed, but Phoebe could see that she looked tired. Noah wandered over at that moment.

"I think it's time I took my wife home." Noah thanked the Masters and then turned to Chase. "You heading back to the village?"

"Yes, in a moment," he said. He too thanked the Masters, told Lynn to give him a call about the kid's fair, and then turned to Phoebe. They stood awkwardly. She was aware that everyone seemed to have drifted off to give them some privacy, but Phoebe kept her distance.

"I had a nice time," she said, her voice even. He looked at her, a strange smile playing on his lips. He glanced over her shoulder and then took a step towards her. When she began to move back, he pulled her into his arms and covered her mouth with his for a hot kiss. He broke away and whispered in her ear, "I feel like a teenager saying good night to my prom date."

His head gestured and Phoebe turned. Mrs. Masters was hovering, her motherly instincts kicking into overdrive.

"Not at my prom," Phoebe whispered. "I was eighteen and a legal adult and no one cared what I did or who I did it with."

"Does that mean you'll come back to my boat with me?" Chase asked.

Phoebe took a step back, remembering what she had felt earlier. She and Chase had an undeniable attraction, which they had officially satisfied. And that was it. It had to be. They couldn't possibly want the same things. She had to be careful here; otherwise, she would get hurt.

"Not tonight," Phoebe said.

"You're sure you don't want to see where this takes us?" Chase said, his look smoldering into her.

Phoebe jerked her head in the direction of the Masters' house.

Chase glanced over her shoulder and Phoebe could all but feel Mrs. Masters' concerned gaze boring into her. "Perhaps tonight is not the best night for it." He agreed, and she felt a rush of disappointment.

"I could always sneak out after they've gone to bed," she said as she leaned up into him, "...come meet you."

"Tempting as that may be, I don't think you'll get far. Until next time?"

His lips brushed quickly and fiercely against hers and he was gone, disappearing into the dark of the night, towards the street, his car, and the short drive to the marina.

Chapter 30

Chase could kick himself. He tossed and turned in his bed, thinking how easy it would have been to go back and wait for Phoebe to slip out of the house. She was a grown woman and he was a grown man. Neither of them were teenagers, but he knew that Dr. Masters wouldn't go for it. He barely let his own daughter out of his sight, and he wasn't going to let Phoebe go wandering off either.

She had seemed happy tonight. A bit skittish at first, sitting there with his friends and with Lynn, but later she had begun to relax. He wondered if she could be happy away from her life in Hollywood. Queensbay wasn't exactly a backwater, but glittering parties and palm trees weren't a part of their repertoire. Would dinners at the Yacht Club and afternoon sails be enough for her?

Chase wondered why he was worried about that. This afternoon had been intense, more than intense; it had been the best sex of his life. He wasn't a choir boy, by any means, but he'd certainly been pickier than he'd let people believe when it came to actually getting into bed with a woman. Sure, the image of a playboy suited him and his company: a sailor with a girl at every port. The image had been created a long time ago to help him get endorsements for his sailing career and it had seemed to work when he took over North Coast Outfitters.

But it meant he generally met a certain kind of woman. Tall, athletic, gorgeous, but usually with an agenda, one that included using him to help themselves. Phoebe was the first whose arm he'd had to practically twist to take his help. And she was making it difficult by not allowing him to use her connection to Savannah. Still, he could understand her desire to make it on her own.

Chase tossed the covers off and got out of bed. He wasn't going to sleep anyway. Pulling on a pair of jeans, he walked into the living room and threw himself on the couch, where he could look out and see the water. The lights of the marina were dimmed now, and boats bobbed peacefully in their slips. It was calm, quiet, and well ordered, and when he had come here as a kid to work in his dad's store, he had dreamed of this. Of looking over it all and wanting it, wanting it to be his. And now he had it. But it just wasn't enough anymore.

He scrubbed his hands through his hair. It was almost morning: time for him to get up, maybe take a run, work out some of these kinks.

Truth was, it wasn't enough anymore because he wanted something more. Sure, he thought it had been the house, but once he had seen her, all of a sudden, it had been her. He wanted Phoebe Ryan, in his bed, but now he wasn't ready to let her go.

As the sun rose, its rosy fingers painting

streaks in the gray dawn sky, he smiled. He had a plan. Every good sailor needed a course, a strategy to get from A to B, to win the race. And if there was one thing he was good at, it was taking his time and working a plan.

Chapter 31

"Sorry about dinner last night," Lynn said, shaking her head. "Would you believe me if I told you it was Caitlyn's idea?"

Phoebe pushed the coffee table out of the way and kicked the rug so that it unspooled across the sheen of her newly refinished floor.

"Really? I hadn't guessed."

Lynn scowled at her sarcasm. "Yes, she wanted to get to know you a little better. And get you and Chase to help out with the fair. She's great, but a little relentless when it comes to making things happen. Not that I'm not grateful, since the clinic needs every penny it can get, but, well, I wouldn't want to say no to her."

"Glad I didn't," Phoebe said, and she was. She was happy to help.

"Nice rug," Lynn said, "but I don't know why you want to put all the furniture down when you still have to paint."

"Not all the furniture." Phoebe pushed back a strand of hair that had escaped from her ponytail. "Just enough so I can live here and move out of your spare bedroom. Besides, it's good to live in a house for a while before deciding on the paint. You need to see how the light plays in the room."

Lynn laughed. "Well, when I finally move out of my parents' house and into my own place, promise me you'll give me some decorating advice. I spend all of my time in baby-blue scrubs and around vomit-green walls. I'll need all the help I can get."

"Color is easy," Phoebe said absently, her mind drifting.

"I don't suppose you found any lost treasures up in the attic?"

"I've barely had time to go through it." Phoebe had been busy working on the designs for North Coast Outfitters and handling the existing orders for business.

"There's no time like the present." Lynn jumped up.

"What are you talking about?"

"Please, I'm totally dying for a chance to poke around Savannah's old stuff."

Phoebe hesitated for a moment. It was her stuff to poke through if she wanted. She'd been avoiding it, unsure if she was ready for what she was going to find. Phoebe took one look at the expression on her friend's face. It was so eager.

"Get ready for some dust," she warned her as they made their way up the stairs and to the attic.

"Wow, Savannah really was a packrat," Lynn said, as she moved a stack of old clippings aside. "Look, a bra." Lynn held up a black lacy number.

"Ugh. That must have been from a movie. I don't think she would have kept it otherwise."

"Yeah, but which one? There's nothing in here that says which one."

Phoebe walked over, looked at the bra, then looked at the stack of clippings. "See, these are all reviews of *The Black Orchid*. It was a throwback to film noir. The bra was probably a part of it."

Lynn closed her eyes, "Oh, yes, now I remember. Wasn't she the fallen lady with the heart of gold?"

"Something like that. So, I guess the black bra was an integral part of the costume."

"You know, sewing up knife wounds may not seem that glamorous, but at the end of the day, I'm glad I don't have to sit around in my underwear in front of a million people," Lynn said.

Phoebe shook her head. "Never seemed to faze Savannah. And she could pick up any object in her apartment and tell you what movie it was from, who her costar was, whether it was a hit or a flop."

They were quiet for another minute, before Lynn asked her.

"Are you going to tell me about it or make me use my imagination?"

Phoebe groaned. "Was it that obvious?"

Lynn nodded. "Absolutely. If I hadn't fallen asleep so early last night, I would have gotten it out of you then. So…"

Phoebe couldn't help the smile that stretched across her face. "It was pretty unbelievable." Just the memory had a smile flooding across her face and heat spreading across her body.

"Wow. And you let him walk off last night? You didn't go back for seconds."

"I think it would have been thirds. Or fourths," Phoebe said, failing to keep the smugness out of her voice.

"Argh, you're killing me. Not really. Keep talking, just because I work crazy hours and barely have time for a shower, let alone a date. I need my vicarious thrills."

"Like I said, it was pretty unbelievable. But somehow I don't think your mom was too keen on me slipping away with him for a night of steamy sex on his boat."

Lynn rolled her eyes. "Yeah, moms can be like that, even when they're not your own." As if realizing what she said, Lynn's face contorted. "Man, I am so sorry. I shouldn't be complaining about my mom…"

"…when I don't have one," Phoebe finished for her lightly, trying to put Lynn back at ease. "Don't worry about saying the wrong thing. You shouldn't be sorry for having a mother, even though she sometimes annoys you, just because I don't. That's life."

"Wow, you sound so serene about it," Lynn said.

Phoebe laughed. "Therapy. I had a lot of it after they died. And then one day, I realized I had to keep on living and so did other people. And it's sort of nice to know someone's looking after me. I think it probably kept me from making a mistake."

Lynn snorted. "What sort of mistake is Chase

Sanders?"

Phoebe didn't know what to say. Sex with Chase had rocked her world. It had never been like that with anyone else, the physical sensations. But there was more. More to him and to the sex. She was afraid she was getting entangled.

"It's funny," Phoebe said. "All my life, guys have been into me because I was related to Savannah Ryan. Struggling actors, wannabe playwrights, even my old boss—they all thought there was something more to me because I was related to someone famous."

Lynn sat on an old steamer trunk. "OK, so I get it. You had your own weird version of groupies. But what does that have to do with Chase?"

Phoebe looked at her and there it was like a sucker-punch in the gut as she said it aloud. "I think Chase might be the same way."

"What do you mean? He doesn't seem that way."

"Associating with the Ryan name would be great for his business. I told him I didn't want Savannah's name mentioned, at least until everyone can judge my work for what it is, but I know he thinks I'm being foolish. I don't think he can resist the allure of the romance of the century—the modern-day version—at least from a marketing perspective."

Lynn looked at her, so Phoebe pulled out her phone.

"My friend sent this to me," she said, as she

called up the headline. "Déjà vu—Ryan Revives Famous Love Nest." It's short on details, but it talks about how I inherited the house and am intent on bringing it back to its former glory. It goes into Leland and Savannah."

Lynn took the phone from Phoebe and scanned through the article. "So?" she asked.

Phoebe took her phone back and glanced at the article. "It might only be a matter of time before someone makes the connection between this house and the fact that Leland Harper's grandson lives in this town. And then it will be romance of the century, part two."

"And you think that's a bad thing?" Lynn asked.

Phoebe shook her head. "It would be if Chase was behind it. I told him that I didn't want to be known as Savannah Ryan's granddaughter anymore. I have to stand on my own two feet, on my own talent."

"Surely you don't think?" Lynn asked.

Phoebe shrugged. She hadn't had a chance to ask. And besides, Chase had promised he wouldn't, but perhaps he couldn't be trusted.

"For what it's worth, it totally seems like he's into you," Lynn said carefully, taking a sip from her water bottle.

Phoebe leaned back against a box. "I don't know. Maybe." She looked at the picture again. She wondered how the press had gotten onto her efforts to restore Ivy House? And would this be the last of it? The story did mention Ivy Lane's website. She'd already seen a jump in orders today. Perhaps, it would be good for business to play up this angle.

Lynn shook her head. "I don't know, but I think the way he keeps showing up here, finding you at the flea market, buying all of that stuff...I think he wants to be with you. Phoebe Ryan—you—not anyone else."

Phoebe wanted to believe her friend, she really did.

Chapter 32

Chase found her, after dark, in the attic. Phoebe looked up, startled, hearing the tramp of steps and then was reassured when she heard his voice calling up the stairs. She had forgotten to lock the door again, and there was Chase's head popping up into the opening of the attic.

She had turned on the light and plugged in one of the lamps that was lying around, so she hadn't noticed it growing dark outside. Phoebe was annoyed that so much time had passed—she had meant to see what the light looked like in the living room around dusk. She felt herself filled with nervous anticipation when Chase fully emerged into the attic.

"You've been busy," he said, by way of a greeting.

She looked at him, standing there with his hands shoved in his pockets, rocking back and forth on his feet, looking like his usual cocky, assured self.

"I brought dinner. Chinese, I guessed," he said, still smiling, "Since you didn't bother to answer your phone or reply to my texts."

She shrugged. "Chinese is fine," she answered coolly.

"What are you doing?" he asked, one eyebrow arching up.

She had to swallow to bring her body under control. Had she really thought that just once with him would be enough? That she could respond to him calmly, rationally.

"Just sorting through some old things. Savannah left a treasure trove of stuff here."

He came over closer to her and she could smell him, his warm dusky scent.

"Is that a photo album?"

He took it from her. "You do look a lot like her, you know."

Phoebe nodded. "My poor mom. She was dark, but my dad was light. I got all of the Ryan genes. Whenever I was with Savannah, people thought I was her daughter. She liked that better than being called a grandmother. Always concerned with what people thought."

"Is that why you're against using her name?" he asked.

"Savannah lived and died by what the public thought of her. She was obsessed with it. She let them paint her as a home wrecker, a bitch—a slut, even—if she thought it would keep them interested. She was always the actress, never herself, because she was always playing a part."

Phoebe looked up at Chase, who was holding her tight in his arms. "I don't want to do that. I don't want to be someone's publicity piece or be used to sell something. I want to be myself. The papers will take anything and turn it around. You'll say it doesn't matter, but if it starts to make you money, you feed into it, you let it happen because you think it's for some greater good. And what's more, people believe it. The most outrageous things, they'll believe, and then you start to buy into it."

"If they want a show, give it to them."

"Exactly," Phoebe said, looking down. Her hands were dirty and she probably had dust smudges on her face. "But I don't want to be the show."

"Hey," he said, catching her chin in his hand, "what's bringing all this on?"

"I told you I'm not an actress, Chase. I'm Phoebe, not Savannah. I'm not some sexy blond bombshell with a smart mouth and a plucky sense of courage."

He smiled. "I like you just the way you are. Sure, I liked Savannah's movies, but unlike all those Hollywood types, I can separate fact from fiction, and, Phoebe, I know the real deal when I see it, when I feel it."

"No," she said in frustration, "I'm just a private person. I don't like being used." She pulled out her phone and showed him the article from earlier, about her and Ivy House.

He glanced at it and shrugged. "It didn't come from me."

"That's it." Phoebe felt a flash of anger. "How can I be sure I'm not being used? You told me yourself that you do things all the time for publicity's sake."

"Used? You think I'm using you to further my business?" His voice rose a bit, and he put both hands on her shoulders and pulled her close to him.

"You're the one who drew up the contract," Phoebe pointed out, her voice sounding breathy even to herself.

"And I changed it. Before we had sex. So, I wasn't using you then. Or would you like me to tell you that I am using you?"

Phoebe gasped as his lips brushed against her hair, nipped at her earlobe. "For your body, that is, 'cause, babe, you have one hell of a body. And your hair. I can't forget your hair. Or your lips," he had whispered. "I know I am definitely using you for your lips."

Phoebe felt her body respond to his words, the heat starting between her legs and spreading throughout her. It was just one article, one of the minor gossip sites, easy to forget.

"I guess being used isn't so bad," she said as his lips brushed along her jaw.

"Feel free to use me back. Whenever you want. Because what happened yesterday was pretty good, better than good. I would hate to see all that go to waste because you're afraid I'm after your famous name or your house."

"You're not after the house?" Phoebe managed to breathe. "Or my name?"

"Babe, I thought you knew what I'm after," he said, pulling her into him, nudging her legs apart as he pushed his leg in between them. She tightened over him, feeling heat lick through her.

His hands slid around her shoulders.

"Then we should give them something to talk about, don't you think? Give them a real show, ride this little thing to the end," she said, wanting it, wanting him.

Unbidden, Phoebe wrapped her arms around Chase, and he pulled her close, his hands fisting in her hair.

"I missed you," he said when he came up for air, and his sapphire eyes held her, turning her into liquid on the inside.

"I was right here," she told him, and then words and thoughts left her as his hands found the tender flesh of her breasts through the thin fabric of her t-shirt. She responded to him as he touched and tugged and pulled.

"Do you have a bed yet?"

"Second floor," she managed to breathe out, as his hands cupped her bottom and he swung her around.

Suddenly, she found her feet leaving the floor as he lifted her up and over his shoulder. In a flash, he was down the attic ladder, and she had a vision of her hallway swirling before her as he found the right door. They were in the bedroom now, where all she had was her bed, a dresser, and boxes.

Chase had found the master bedroom with ease, the only door on the second floor with light spilling out of it. He nudged the door open with his foot and headed for the bed, just a lumpy futon. He lowered Phoebe onto the comforter and stepped back. She reached for him, but he stepped out of the way, surprising her.

He let his eyes roam over her, from the way her red-gold hair spilled over the pillows, the way he could see her nipples ready for him underneath the thin fabric of her t-shirt, to the way her jean-clad legs seemed to stretch on for miles.

Her blue eyes were bright, alight with desire and her hands reached for him again. He took them, held them, holding and kissing her long, elegant fingers one by one.

"We have no need to rush this time," he told her.

"I thought you had dinner waiting?" she teased.

"I plan on feasting right now," he said as his hand circled her belly button and brought on a shiver of pleasure. Chase wanted to take his time with her, and savor every moan, shiver, and bit of pleasure he could give her.

"Last time, it was fun."

"Fun?" Phoebe sat up, ready to be offended.

"Fun. But I don't think I got to take my time, really figure out what makes you tick." His hand brushed in between her thighs, and even through the thick fabric of her jeans, he felt her body respond.

"That works," Phoebe managed to say, as his hand hooked the waistband of her pants, and he pulled her towards him. She tried to reach for him again, but he moved out of the way.

She sat up and he lifted her shirt off and tossed it on the floor. His hands cupped the lacy fabric of her bra and he brushed his hands over them. Phoebe's back arched and Chase unhooked her bra, tossing it to the side. Her breasts sprung free and he lowered his mouth to feast on them, feeling her come alive beneath them. Her hands held him close, and he started on the button of her jeans.

He took a moment, breaking free, and peeled them off one leg at a time, until she was naked except for her lacy cream underwear. He touched there, felt the evidence of her arousal, and peeled those off too. She was naked before him and he stroked her, watching as her head fell back and her hips rose to meet him.

Phoebe had never felt so wanton, so full of desire. So far, Chase had used nothing but his mouth and his hands on her, but her whole body was alight, tingling from his touch. Her hips angled up to him, as he stroked her sex, while his other hand brought her nipples to attention and his mouth ravaged hers, his stubbled skin brushing against the sensitive surface of her cheek.

Her fingers found the buttons of his shirt and she managed undo them, and she let her hands roam along his back, his chest, and his flat abdomen, and then she dipped below, found that he was aroused, hard for her, but still he kept up his assault, demanding that she do nothing but let herself be taken, and she did, riding the waves of pleasure until he slipped inside her and she wrapped her legs, pulling him deep inside of her, clenching around him, matching his rhythm as she moaned his name and he answered with hers. Then, she tumbled down into darkness, her body releasing as she felt his release wash over her.

Phoebe lay still, very still. Chase was on top of her, a dead weight that did not seem to want to move. His arm was on her stomach and she gently tried to wiggle free.

"Sorry," he said and rolled over to the side, pulling her close to him. His hand stroked her hair and his mouth nibbled on her shoulder.

"I suppose that was worth the wait," Phoebe said after a moment, after her heart stopped thudding quite so fast and the blood had receded from her ears.

His arms encircled her, pulling her in tight and close and, for a moment, Phoebe felt that she could stay like this forever, in the circle of his arms, happy and satisfied.

"It was for me," he said, his teeth nipping at her ear.

Chapter 33

They got cold. And hungry. Night had fallen and the breeze from the open window had become downright cold. She felt herself shiver, and Chase got up, pulled the throw from the bottom of the bed over her, and started dressing. Her heart sank at the thought of him leaving, but she tried to keep her face from showing it.

He only buttoned two buttons and pulled his jeans up, leaving the top undone.

"Where are you going?" she asked.

"I heard your stomach growl."

"Did not," she started to say, just as it did so again.

One eyebrow went up.

"I'll bring it up here," he said. Phoebe looked around. Her comforter was a custom silk one that she'd designed herself and had shipped to her. As romantic as eating in bed sounded, she couldn't bear the thought of anything happening to it.

"Oh, no you won't." She pulled the blanket around her and swung her legs out of bed, hunting for her clothes. "No eating in bed."

"Doesn't that depend on the menu?" he said, pulling her to him. She wasn't sure that they would make it downstairs, but then her stomach growled and he let her go.

"I'll go set everything up," he said and bounded from the room. Phoebe watched him go. The expression on his face was like that of a very happy puppy.

She took more than a moment, running a quick shower and finding a pair of casual linen pants, a fresh t-shirt, and sweater to wrap herself in. The hot water sluiced over her, and she tried to clear her head. It means nothing, she told herself. She shouldn't let herself get too wrapped up in him. It couldn't be permanent. Not for him, and that was what she wanted. Sooner or later, someone was going to get hurt. But for now, she told herself, just enjoy the moment.

When she went downstairs, she found that Chase had made himself useful. He'd moved the kitchen table into the dining room and found candles. He'd opened a bottle of wine and set it out amid the takeout cartons.

"I didn't know what you liked, so I got a little of everything," he said, appearing in the soft candlelight. Music was playing, probably Coldplay, and even without a rug or curtains or a fresh paint job, all of a sudden, it felt right, Phoebe thought; it felt like home. Her breath hitched and her heart lurched. Home. It was what she had been trying to find for a long time.

Chase held out the chair for her and she glided into it. "We have moo shu, lo mein, chicken, and broccoli..."

Phoebe went for the moo shu, while Chase seemed to be happy with a lot of everything. It took a while before he brought up the attic.

"I thought you'd be busy arranging furniture."

"So did I. Lynn wanted to poke around Savannah's things and so we did."

"Did you find anything interesting?" Chase asked.

Phoebe shrugged. "Nothing too out of the ordinary. Just those old photo albums."

"Savannah's?"

"And some from my parents, from before I was born. I didn't really know where they went. Haven't thought about them in a long time. The pictures, I mean. It was weird seeing them."

"Why?" Chase asked.

Phoebe thought for a moment before she answered. "They were so happy. And in love. With each other. I remember it and seeing the pictures brought it all back to me."

"I'm sorry," Chase said, but it was more a question.

"Don't be. It made me happy. Sad too, but happy. Happy that they had that. It was so different from what Savannah and Leland had."

Chase's chopsticks paused midway between his plate and his mouth. "What do you mean?"

"My parents had a steady type of love. I don't remember them ever really arguing. Their relationship was even, steady. But then I think about Savannah and Leland."

"What about them?" Chase's eyes were dark in the candlelight, intently looking at her. Phoebe didn't know why she pressed on, but she had to.

"Their love was intense. Leland gave up a lot to be with her. Savannah even gave up her career for a while. It burned so hot, their love, it consumed them. He was jealous of her acting, but she couldn't not do it. In the end, they loved each other still, but they were at each other's throats. At least that's what all the stories said. It was like they were so on fire for each other, it burned them out."

It hung in the air between them. Chase looked at her for a long time, before he took her hand and gently pulled her towards him, up from the table, into his arms. She looked at him for a long time, staring at his face, and finally he stood up and she did too. She led him up the stairs and into her bedroom.

Chapter 34

Chase stayed the night. He had offered to go back to his apartment, but Phoebe had simply thrown him a look and pulled him towards her. She didn't want him to go, liking the warmth and strength of him. He didn't seem to mind, wrapping himself around her.

It was the weekend and they stayed together the whole time. He helped her move things from the shed into the house and watched as she rearranged. They went shopping for groceries, making themselves pasta. He lamented the lack of a TV, but she made it worth his while.

Monday morning came around and Chase had to go back to work. She sent him away with a bang and the house felt strangely empty without him, but she was ready to start getting to work. She had a contract to fulfill after all. There were also some phone calls and emails from Dean asking her when she was coming back. There were emails from her workshop asking if they should purchase more materials to keep up with the new orders. Her landlord was asking if she wanted out of her lease since he had another interested party.

While she had spent the last couple of weeks

in a sexual fog precipitated by Chase, life was going on around her. Decisions needed to be made, decisions that had nothing to do with Chase Sanders and more about how she wanted to live her life. Did she want to run her business from Los Angeles? Her whole life had been there. She had never meant to make her stop in Queensbay permanent, had she? There was nothing to say that she and Chase couldn't keep their relationship going, for a while at least, cross-country. And besides, as Chase said, they were just riding this thing out, seeing where it took them.

So what to do? Phoebe sat in the room at the back of the house, her own little studio. In Los Angeles, she'd never had this much space and it was glorious to be able to walk, to pace, to think as she worked. She had seen pictures of it in the photo album. It had been fitted out like a country gentleman's study, with leather-bound books and dark wood. Now it was white, with gleaming floors and a row of windows that looked out over the backyard and the harbor. Phoebe had come to love this room and her ability to watch the light as it moved over the water.

Her new desk had come, and she and Chase had assembled it, laughing as they tried to figure out the instructions. It was huge, with plenty of room to spread out, and she sat at it now, letting her mind wander, just drawing. When she was done, she looked at what she had created: a pattern of concentric rings in bright pop-art colors. She smiled and pulled her laptop towards her. Ivy Lane was doing well, the mention of her restoring the house driving a lot of traffic to the site.

Things were starting to take off for her and it was time to get really serious. Perhaps, it was time to give Caitlyn Randall a call. She was, by all accounts, a financial advisor and a whiz with money.

The days passed. Both she and Chase were busy with work, including a quick business trip down to Florida for Chase. He was gone only a few days, but when he arrived, he had sauntered in, taking her to bed almost immediately. Then, he was gone until the weekend. The weather was beautiful and they took another sail, threw steaks on the grill, and shared a bottle of wine with Lynn and her parents.

Weeks went by and she and Chase slipped into a pattern. He would stay with her all weekend and then head down to work. They spent most of their time together at Ivy House, but she went to his apartment once, above the Osprey Arms.

"Why do you live here?" she asked. Room service had delivered some fried calamari, and they were eating it on the small balcony attached to his suite.

"I like to keep an eye on things," he said, dropping his eyes as he squeezed lemon on his plate.

"Eye on what? Surely, you get to see enough boats during the day from your office. You have a water view there."

He said nothing and slowly she put it together. "You own this. The marina, the hotel?"

"Yes. I own it. I have a manager, but it's a part of my holdings."

"So you're building up quite the little empire," she said. It made sense how the bartender had called him "boss" and the way her hotel bill had been suspiciously low.

"Sort of. I'm not bad at organizing things, figuring out how to give customers what they want, whether it's a new piece of foul-weather gear or a great place to bring their families for a summer cruise or to a hotel with a great view."

"Are you partners with Noah?"

Chase shook his head. "On some of the things. I was one of his first investors when he started his company. Then, over the years, I leveraged that to invest in some other things. Sometimes Noah joins in, sometimes my brother does, sometimes I do it alone. My brother, Jackson, he's working in New York now, but he comes out on weekends in the summer to sail and hang out. Hopefully you'll meet him?"

The question hung in the air. They hadn't talked much about the future and Phoebe didn't know if she wanted to.

"That would be nice," she said absently. She took a sip of wine as someone blew a foghorn, a signal for the launch to come pick them up.

"Do you always treat your investments like this?"

"Like what?" he asked.

"Wine and dine them?"

"Sometimes, I go out for business dinners," he said carefully, his fork hovering in midair. "I take a personal interest in all of my affairs."

"Affairs?" Phoebe didn't know why she was pushing. Everything was going well. She had been designing like mad, and Chase's own house design team was a dream to work with. He'd even sent Tory over to redo her website and now the orders were coming in, several a day. But her work for the collection was almost done. In another week or so, there would be no real reason to stay in Queensbay.

"I meant business affairs. In the most traditional sense," he said, humor lighting up his eyes.

She had begun to think that she could build her business from anywhere. She'd been ducking Dean's calls, knowing that if she told him what she was thinking, he would try anything to convince her to come back to Los Angeles. He'd been calling and texting almost daily since she had mentioned the deal with Chase.

She was starting to build a life on her own terms, but she wanted to be more than an investment to Chase, something he would hand off to be managed when she had fulfilled her end of the deal. So far, he'd given no indication that it was anything but smooth sailing, but then again, he hadn't asked lately if she were planning on staying or going.

"You're not jealous I discovered that new sweater designer in England, are you? I like her stuff, but I told you, she's an old salt dog, almost fifty, with a Scotsman for a husband. I feel like he's going to run me through with his bagpipes if I even so much as look at his wife."

Phoebe laughed. When Chase had told her that he was going to England for a few days, she had wondered what she would do if all his designers were given the same treatment as her. They had never talked about the status of their relationship as easily as they had slipped into it. She realized that she had just assumed Chase was a one-woman-at-a-time type of guy, but she had no proof.

"Hey, that's not jealousy I see, is it? Imagine, the fair-haired California babe being worried about some lady who knits sweaters in the dark and cold."

"Well, when you put it that way, but surely there must be others. You seem to have quite a stable of talent you're developing."

Chase shrugged, but his eyes were serious. "That's part of what makes North Coast Outfitters successful. Luxury and high-quality goods you can't get everywhere. It takes time and attention to do that."

"I know," Phoebe said. She felt restless. They were supposed to be meeting up with Noah and Caitlyn to listen to some live music at Augie's—Lynn, too, if she got done with her rounds—but there was something that was making her edgy.

"You don't think I'm stepping out on you, do you?" Chase asked, his voice low.

"No. I don't know." She was standing by the railing now, looking over at the bustle of the harbor below. The sun was starting to set and boats were streaming in to get settled for the night, couples were walking about arm in arm and kids raced up and down, playing or enjoying ice cream. It was a happy scene, full of life and Phoebe glanced up. Ivy House was just visible, its tall tower poking up among the trees that were now fully covered in their summer coats. Even from here, she could see that the house needed painting, one of those big-ticket items she had decided to put off. Still, it was there, a landmark, looking down over charming Queensbay, watching the town, protecting it.

Did she want to be part of this life? She could work from anywhere, she knew that, whether it was Queensbay or Los Angeles or some other place she'd never been to. But would she want to stay in Queensbay, in Ivy House, if Chase wasn't part of her life? She looked over at him. He was sitting there, his big frame at ease in the comfortable chair.

"Phoebe, I haven't been with anyone else since I met you...since before I met you and, more importantly, I haven't thought about anyone else. I know my PR department has tried to paint a different picture of me, but like I told you, that was just for show."

"Was?"

"Every sailor needs to find a home port," Chase said. He held out a hand and she took it, and he pulled her onto his lap, cradling her there.

He didn't say it, she noticed. He didn't say the words that she wanted to hear. Only promised her that he was being faithful for now. Phoebe swallowed hard and leaned her head into his shirt, feeling the steady beating rhythm of his heart. She had her answer. She was in love with Chase Sanders, a man who saw her as another one of his business investments. Savannah had warned her about giving her heart away too freely. But she hadn't ever, not to Dean, not to anyone. Chase had her, if he wanted her, but he'd never said he wanted the same things from her, from life, as she did.

"Are you OK?" he whispered into her hair. All of a sudden, she felt sick, her heart pounding, her stomach churning.

"No, you know, I think maybe I better sit this night out."

"What?" He pulled away from her, searching her face.

"No big deal, I'll just walk back to the house. You go, I know you were looking forward to seeing the band. So don't change your plans on account of me."

"But, let me drive you at least."

Phoebe shook her head, resolute. "No, I think the fresh air would be good."

"I'll walk you home. Do you want anything, soup or something? You barely ate anything."

"No, I'll be fine. You'll be late if you walk me home and, besides, if I don't feel better, I know a doctor or two."

She gave him no more time to think, but was already opening the sliding door into his living room, finding her purse, slipping into her shoes. He trailed after her, clearly puzzled, one hand running through his hair.

"Are you sure?"

She leaned over, gave him a quick peck on the cheek. "I just need some sleep, some rest. Listen, I don't want to get you or especially Caitlyn sick."

"I'll call you later." His voice trailed down the hallway after her as she moved quickly to the stairs, intent on getting out of there as quickly as possible.

The rest of the hotel passed in a blur and she emerged onto the sidewalk, breathing the fresh air, feeling the thudding of her heart in her ears. She was in love with a man who wasn't capable of it. How could she have let this happen?

Chapter 35

It took Chase a moment to spot her amidst the throng of kids surrounding her. She was at a booth and apparently making some sort of giant sculpture out of newspaper strips applied to a tower of blown-up party balloons. Paper-mache, Chase remembered from an art class long ago.

Her hair was pulled back in a sleek ponytail, and she was layering strips of soggy newspaper as the kids called out suggestions to her. She had a whole crowd of them enthralled or rolling on the floor with laughter. Phoebe looked beautiful, relaxed, unconcerned and in her element. Any of the shyness or the iciness he had seen was gone, focused as she was on creating and working with the kids.

She lifted one of them up, a little boy with shaggy blond hair and blue eyes, so he could slap a piece of newspaper strip on what was rapidly becoming some sort of not-so-scary monster. Overjoyed, the little boy clapped his hands, and as Phoebe set him down, she ruffled his hair.

Chase's heart clenched. It was at that moment that the sun emerged from the clouds and a shaft of sunlight shot down; Phoebe was momentarily suffused with light, and Chase felt the ground shift beneath him as his whole being attuned to her. He couldn't stop staring at her, feeling that this was finally the moment, the moment when he felt his world shift, the planets align, and stars shine brightly.

Phoebe was his everything. He always thought that love was something he wouldn't experience. It seemed like something for other people. He wasn't that type of guy. He was a wanderer, an adventurer. Women, in his mind, were wonderful creatures. They smelled good, they were fun to be with and most of them made him happy, at least for a short while.

But none of them, until Phoebe, had ever been able to make him feel alive. Sure, he'd had an adrenaline rush from steering a fifty-foot boat along in rough seas or from the thrill of concluding a business deal, but this was something different. Something inexplicable and heart changing.

"She's a natural." Chase was jolted out of his reverie by Lynn.

"What?" It took a moment for Chase to come back to reality.

"With the kids. Have you ever seen a dozen five-year-olds sit still for this long? And the monster was all her idea. Anyway, thanks for hooking us up with a tent guy. The fair benefits the clinic, so every penny saved is more for them. Thanks so much."

"My pleasure," Chase managed to mumble, his attention back on Phoebe. A natural. A creative, talented, beautiful, sexy woman.

Phoebe finally saw him, gave him a curt nod, and then her attention was caught by a little girl tugging on her hand.

Phoebe bent down to listen as the little girl whispered a suggestion that they make pointy teeth for the monster, but her mind was elsewhere. She wondered how long Chase had been there watching her. But now, he was there, giving her a look, something different from the usual steamy ones he threw her way. This one had been intense. It had been the look of a drowning man, who had just realized that the last ship had passed him by. But before she had time to dwell on it, the kids took up the chant of "pointy teeth, pointy teeth," and she was drawn back into the real world.

<<>>

Phoebe packed up the last of the art materials into a large plastic bin. Her feet hurt and she was tired, but energized.

"That was a lot of fun," she told Lynn as they broke down the card table. Chase had disappeared after a while, and she hadn't seen him again.

"Thank you so much. It was our best year ever, so I hope that means that the clinic will be able to get some new equipment."

"Well, I'm glad you talked me into it," Phoebe said, taking a moment to stretch.

"Let me help you with those." Chase appeared beside them, a smile on his face. Phoebe looked at him, searching for the look he had given her earlier. He took her scrutiny in, but gave away nothing as they continued to clean up. They packed things away and it wasn't until he was walking her to the car that he whispered in her ear, "Let's go home tonight, just the two of us."

She didn't need to ask where he meant by home, but the thrill that shot through her, as he took her hand in his, wasn't lust; it was something entirely different, and she knew that as much as she had pretended that this was a casual affair, it no longer was.

Chapter 36

The moon was full and it came in through the window, suffusing the room with light. Phoebe sparkled like silver and he brought her to him, kissing her gently, sweetly. Slowly, he undressed her, reverently addressing her body with his mouth, feasting slowly and fully on her. Something had changed for him and he wanted to savor her. So far, whenever he had been with her, it had been wild and passionate, the ice queen with the fire dragon underneath. But tonight, now, he wanted to savor every minute of her. When she tried to rush him, he just shook his head and held her hands, letting his fingers brush over her, gently teasing and testing, watching her as the pressure built, knowing she was practically begging for release. Still, he decided to torment her a little more, taking his time as his hands roamed over her, as she writhed and moaned with pleasure.

Finally, she sat up and pulled him to her. "Now," she whispered, and when he smiled, she said, "Please, I need you."

He was undone then and he pushed himself into her slowly, feeling her hot wetness close around him, hiding him tight. He pulled in and out slowly, and as her hips rose up to meet him, he moved faster and she matched his rhythm. Thrust for thrust, they moved together in a slow, steady beat, pushing them higher and higher towards the edge. They reached it together and he gave one more moan and dove into her fully, and he watched as her eyes filled with pleasure. He held back no longer and followed her over the edge.

Afterwards, they lay together, and she fell asleep beside him, curled around him and, for once, he hadn't been thinking of the best way to disentangle himself without waking the woman next to him and making his escape.

No, instead, all he wanted to do was pull her closer to him, breathe in the scent of her hair, feel the rise and fall of her chest underneath his hands. He had stayed that way, unable to sleep, trying to understand just why he felt this way about a woman whom he'd only known a short time. This was totally different from what he had felt about the other women he'd let into his life.

Now he lay awake in the early hours of the morning, listening to the sway of the branches outside the window, hearing the sound of a warning buoy gently toll in the distance. He'd understood what she said about love. His own parents were reasonably happy, but he'd never given much thought to what he wanted. He had been too focused on winning at sailing and building his business to get entangled emotionally.

None of his other girlfriends had stayed long,

and he'd grown tired of them long before he found some way to set them free gently or they'd wised-up and gotten out. Phoebe wasn't fragile or a delicate flower. She didn't need to be protected. She was self-contained. Talented.

Phoebe hadn't held back on him tonight. He'd finally had all of her; she'd given freely. He didn't want to let that go. That realization made him pull her tighter to him, causing him to kiss her hair, trace a finger down her bare back, relieved to see the way she murmured and turned, arched towards him.

Chase wasn't sure whether he'd ever have enough of her, the way her red-gold hair blew in the wind or her blue eyes sparkled when she found something she thought was beautiful or interesting or the way her nose scrunched up and her freckles blended together when she concentrated. He knew that he'd bought his way into her life. She wouldn't have stayed if he hadn't offered her a job.

He fought against that thought as he kissed the nape of her neck, running his hand along her spine, cupping her buttocks to him, until she turned, her eyes awake, her mouth reaching for him. Chase wrapped himself around her, nudged her legs gently open, and pushed all thoughts of tomorrow away for the moment.

Chapter 37

Chase rolled the living room rug up to the legs of the couch and draped a drop cloth over it all.

"What are you doing?" Phoebe said, appearing in the doorway. She had slept later than she had meant to and woken to an empty bed and the smell of coffee. She had brushed her teeth, but skipped the shower. Her phone had been lying on the table next to her and she flipped through it. That's when she had seen it.

"You said you're ready to paint in here."

"You're painting?"

He looked at her. She had wrapped her robe tightly around her as if that could be her armor against him and the world.

"Is there something wrong with that?"

She forced herself to keep calm. "I take it you haven't checked your phone today."

He shot her a smile. "I was otherwise occupied." He took a step towards her.

She held up her hand. "Don't."

Concern creased his face as he looked around. His phone was on the shelf and he walked over, flipped it on, and scanned it.

"Phoebe," he looked up.

She shook her head. "This has your fingerprints all over it, Chase. How else would they have known where to get those photos! God, I'm practically naked in one of them."

"You're in a bikini. A really hot bikini, I might add," Chase said.

Phoebe fought down the tears that had threatened to overtake her. The press had gotten a hold of their relationship and their business partnership. It was personal and detailed, rehashing everything about Savannah and Leland, Phoebe's parents, Ivy House, and the deal she and Chase had struck.

There were half a dozen pictures of them kissing, holding hands, and sunbathing on Chase's boat. There were even pictures of Savannah and Leland and the whole history.

"This is the kind of publicity money can't buy." Phoebe shook her head. "Sure beats dating the odd model for this kind of press. I hope you're happy."

Anger darkened Chase's face and his eyes turned almost black. "You think I did this?"

"Who else? Who else would know this stuff? Where to find us, or all of these details about Savannah and my parents? They even have my favorite ice cream. I told you no press and you let them into our lives. Into this. I thought we had…"

Phoebe broke off before she embarrassed herself. Chase had never promised her anything more than a good time. Light and sweet. And she should have never expected more from him. But somewhere along the line, she opened herself up to him, thinking that maybe there could be something more between them.

"Look, Phoebe."

"Save it. I asked one thing of you...that this would be private..."

"I'm sorry, I had..." Chase looked contrite, she would give him that.

Phoebe shook her head. "All my life, people have wanted to be with me, get close to me because of my family. They didn't care that I collect salt shakers or that I love mint chocolate chip ice cream or that I'm ticklish. They never cared about me, only what I could do for them."

"I'm sorry." He was angry now. "Look, I'll talk to my PR guy, straighten it out. Listen, babe." He walked over to her and rubbed her arm. "I'll take care of it. It will be fine."

Phoebe swallowed hard and closed her eyes. She couldn't look at him. "Don't, please don't. Just go. I can't do this."

"Phoebe!" Chase looked at her, but she turned and pointed towards the door.

"Fine." He came closer to her. "I'll give you some time to think it over."

Chapter 38

Chase felt no better after yelling at his PR director. Sam Waterstone had sworn the story hadn't been entirely his doing. It was too good an opportunity to pass up, and Chase had never objected before when a picture of him and a date showed up online or in the papers. So, Sam had given in and now the media had it, and they loved the parallel between Chase and Phoebe and Leland and Savannah. In fact, all of America loved the parallel, from what Chase could see.

Chase refused all requests for an interview, which he knew might only make the story grow faster. But he didn't know what else to do. He knew if he said anything, his words would be twisted, and the media would make his relationship with Phoebe into a big deal. He didn't want her getting the wrong idea. He didn't want her to think he was in it just for the benefit to his bottom line.

Chase swung around in his office chair, thinking about Phoebe. The way she had looked at him, a look full of betrayal. She had told him how much she hated being used because of her connection with Savannah. How she wanted to make a name for herself, on her own. And now it seemed as if he was doing just that for his business because sales had gone up fifty percent since the story broke, and Chase knew that this was the kind of exposure that would cost millions of dollars to buy. And here he had it because of a few pictures of him and Phoebe kissing.

He looked again at those. Someone had gotten them with a long-range lens, a picture of a heated embrace, in front of Ivy House. And then, of course, the reporter had dug up another picture of Leland and Savannah in almost the same pose, in almost the exact same place. Chase hadn't wanted to read the comments section, but he did and stopped when he saw red. Had people no sense of decency? He wanted to punch some of these guys for what they were saying about Phoebe. It was complimentary, but lewd. Didn't they know she was taken?

But was she? She had all but kicked him out this morning. And all he had wanted to do was help her paint. Or let other people do it while he took her for another sail. There was a side creek he had wanted to explore, and he thought he could convince her to enjoy a lazy afternoon of sun and other things.

Would she let him back in? Could he convince her that this hadn't been his doing? Or that it was to her benefit? Every story mentioned her designs and she would have to benefit from all the press too. Chase checked his phone. He had left her half a dozen messages, but she hadn't returned any of them. Any more messages and he would be considered a stalker. He got up. Sitting in his office wasn't doing any good. He needed to go fix things.

Chapter 39

"I saw Chase," Lynn said as she opened another box. Phoebe's things had started to arrive from California and Lynn was helping her unpack. "He stopped by the clinic; we had a thank you ceremony for all the sponsors."

It had been almost a week since the story broke and she had been hounded by calls from reporters. She had refused them all, even unplugging her phone and letting everything on her cell go to voicemail. Besides, she'd been too busy trying to fill all the new orders that were coming in. The story had been good for business, just as Chase had said it would be.

Phoebe stiffened and then said nonchalantly, "He was one of the sponsors, so it was nice of him to come."

Lynn looked at her in the fading light. "I don't think he was there to check up on his donation."

Phoebe shrugged, trying to show that she didn't care. Why, then, did she want to cry all of a sudden?

"I think you should talk to him."
"What?"
"He looked upset."

Phoebe snorted. "He's upset because his little ploy backfired. He knew…" Phoebe stopped herself.

"Look, I know you think he was using you because of Savannah and maybe that's how it started, but I don't think that's the way it is. You didn't see the look on his face."

Phoebe swallowed.

"Lynn, I just can't. I don't think I can trust him again."

Lynn was about to say something else, but there was a knock on the door. Phoebe looked up, her heart jumping.

"Are you expecting anyone?" Lynn asked. Phoebe shook her head tightly, but she knew, even as she walked to the door, that Chase wouldn't have knocked.

"Dean."

"Phoebe, there you are." Standing on her porch was Dean Grant.

"Dean." She gave him a hug, feeling a small surge of pleasure. All of a sudden, it felt nice to see an old friend.

Dean gave her his typical European greeting, a kiss on each cheek, before holding her at arm's length.

"The salt air seems to agree with you," Dean said. He was impeccably dressed, as always, in a light jacket, matching trousers, a robin's-egg blue shirt, with a paisley pocket square that complemented everything.

Phoebe was glad that the dusk hid her flush.

She knew that Dean was lying. If anything, the recent turmoil with Chase had left her with some sleepless nights.

"Dean, this is my friend Lynn Masters."

"Pleased to meet you," Dean said politely, but all his attention was on Phoebe.

"You haven't returned any of my phone calls. And…" he lowered his voice, with a glance at Lynn, "I need to speak with you."

Phoebe sighed. She didn't know if Dean was being dramatic, but she hadn't returned his phone calls either, which, he supposed, was why she needed to be tracked down.

"OK," Phoebe said. Dean hesitated.

"You know what, why don't I just clean up this stuff for you," Lynn said. "You two can just run along."

Dean flashed a smile of perfectly white teeth. "An excellent idea. How about dinner, Phoebe? There's this cute little place up the road, the Osprey Arms? Do you know it?"

Did she ever, but Phoebe just nodded. She wasn't exactly dressed for dinner, but it was Dean and not a date, so she supposed that in a few minutes, she could make herself presentable.

Dean had waited for her patiently at the house while she cleaned herself up, and then they walked down to the Osprey Arms together. For a moment she panicked, but then calmed down. She was pretty certain she wouldn't run into Chase because he mostly ate in his room. And so what if she did?

"So, Chase Sanders?" Dean looked at her over his scotch, his gaze unreadable.

Phoebe didn't really want to talk about her involvement with Chase, so she took a sip of her wine instead.

"Last I heard, you thought the man was the devil incarnate," Dean pointed out, but his voice didn't hold any bit of lightness.

"Things change," Phoebe hedged.

"They do. I leave you alone for a couple of weeks, and I find you're reliving the romance of the century. In every way?"

Phoebe decided to ignore that question. She didn't want him to get the wrong idea, but there was no use denying the fact that there was something downright date-like about the corner table and the low lights of the Osprey Arms' formal dining room.

Phoebe smiled at that. "It's like you said: the fresh air, springtime. It does something to a girl."

"Well, I hope that your designing is going well?"

"I've been working on some designs," Phoebe hedged.

"You know, I've been talking with CallieSue. She's very intrigued now..." Dean said.

"Is that what you wanted to talk to me about? I told you I wasn't interested in working with her." Phoebe felt her blood began to heat. CallieSue had probably gotten "intrigued" with her as soon as all the press hit. She wasn't some no-name designer now. She was a bit of a celebrity herself.

"Just a moment." Dean held up a calming hand.

"I don't think CallieSue has developed a better sense of style in the last couple of weeks." The waiter arrived with their first course: a salad for her and soup for Dean.

He took a look at the bowl, sniffed and shrugged, as if resigned to indifferent food since he was outside of a city.

"Not bad," he proclaimed, and she had to wait as he had added a pinch of pepper and had another spoonful. He took another spoonful, and she could tell that he was actually enjoying himself. In the meantime, she pushed the leaves of what she was sure was organic, locally grown, lettuce around her plate as she waited for Dean to get to the point.

"Be that as it may, I think she's more inclined to listen to your ideas now." Dean stopped and put his hand out and covered hers. She was surprised by his gesture.

"Phoebe, I care about you. You know that I have only ever had your best interests at heart."

"What are you talking about?" Phoebe felt her heart race a bit in her chest.

"Well, it's not just CallieSue who is interested."

Something in Phoebe stirred. She knew that this was why Dean was here. He had something bigger to tell her.

Dean smiled, as if reading her mind. "Listen,

I know you must miss your life in Los Angeles and here's the perfect chance. You won't have to ride the Savannah coattails—you'll be your own woman. I know how important that is to you; I realize that now."

Phoebe was flabbergasted. "Dean, that's the nicest thing you've ever said to me."

"Really, it's just the truth," Dean said with a smile, his spoon hovering over his soup.

"So who is it?" Phoebe said, even more overwhelmed. It was more than she could have hoped for, more than she should have expected.

Dean leaned in and whispered the name. Phoebe looked at him, aware that her mouth had dropped.

"But that's huge...she's already...she goes by one name."

Dean smiled, enjoying her reaction.

"Why me?" Phoebe managed to whisper.

"Why?" Dean threw back his head and laughed. "Because you're talented." His hand reached across the table and touched hers. She fought the urge to pull it back from him, and his smile was more than just a smile, seductive almost. "How many times have I told you that?"

"All the time." Phoebe managed to remove her hand and dropped it into her lap. Her heart was beating fast. "So, back to Los Angeles?" It was a tremendous opportunity, one she would have killed for even just a few weeks ago.

"Yes. She's based there, so she would definitely expect you to be there, plus she's going on tour in a month, and I think you can expect a fair amount of traveling as well, so you two can continue to work together." Dean scraped up the last bit of soup and looked at her.

"Oh, you're worried about, what, the house here. I am sure you could get a good price for it. It's a waterfront property, right? Or I suppose you could keep it as a vacation retreat, fly back a couple of times a year."

Phoebe thought longingly of her dark-stained floors, newly finished and gleaming, a rug thrown casually over them, just begging to welcome some furniture, and Ivy House, begging to welcome happiness and life back into it.

"Only a couple of times a year?" Phoebe asked.

"Well, of course. Look, it's a big job, and I need to know that you're all in with me on this before I go back to her. It would mean a lot of money, prestige. You could do anything you want. Maybe a TV show and certainly a full line of housewares sold at a major store. The sky's the limit. Already, the press is buzzing about the possibility."

"Dean, that's so generous of you." Phoebe was at a loss for words, for not only had she thought of Ivy House but also had a fleeting thought of Chase. If she went back to Los Angeles, would she see him again? Would he miss her as much as she would miss him?

Savannah's words came ringing back to her:

Never rearrange your life for a man...

Smiling, Phoebe reached out and took Dean's hand. "You'll let me think on it for a few days?"

Dean smiled and brought her hand to his mouth for a quick friendly kiss. "I knew you'd come around."

Chapter 40

Phoebe was daydreaming. Or thinking. She had started out the day productively enough, working on designs, but it was too lovely a day to be inside. So, she had wandered out to putter in the backyard and plant some of the annuals she had bought in her new flower pots.

She sat on the stone step of the terrace, with the view of the harbor spread out below her, the sky a cloudless blue. Everything was peaceful, but her mind was whirling with the offer Dean had made her. After Savannah had died, it seemed like the last thing she wanted to do: go back and work for someone else. But now, here was an opportunity to work with a huge name, an international presence. A collaboration, Dean had said, with her name linked. Even more so than her North Coast Outfitters deal, it would jumpstart her business.

She had told Dean she had a contract with Chase, and Dean had only smiled. "I am sure we can arrange something mutually satisfactory to both parties to get you free and clear. And back on a plane to Los Angeles. She wants to get started pronto."

Phoebe knew she needed to speak to Chase directly. See if he even cared that she would be backing out of their deal. At this point, he probably wouldn't, would he? His phone calls and texts had started to tail off.

Well, she had been the one to tell him to go, so she had no one to thank but herself. The gossip pages hadn't slowed down one bit, and she was pretty sure that a photographer was stalking her. Instead, the papers kept going over Leland and Savannah's affair and marriage, and drawing parallels to her and Chase.

Well, she had known what she was getting into, right? Chase had all but told her that he was a player. That this was a no-strings-attached, heated affair, a giving into feelings—of lust—which they couldn't ignore. But somewhere along the line, it had changed for her. Love. She wasn't a lust type of girl. Sure, just the thought of Chase's wolfish smile, deep-blue eyes, and dark tousled hair made her knees weak and panties wet, but it wasn't enough. It wasn't enough to keep her going. She wanted a life, a real life, with someone she loved and who loved her.

Maybe it didn't have to be the house and white picket fence—goodness knows, Los Angeles wouldn't be that. But perhaps it meant that she could find someone who wanted the same things she did: a committed relationship, a family. And what had Chase told her? *Let's just have a good time babe and see where it takes us.*

Well, it had taken her too far. She couldn't sleep in her bed without being woken up by thoughts of Chase and memories of how they had been together. A hot flash of desire and loss seared through her, and she closed her eyes to clear out the memories. Maybe she needed a fresh start. Coming back to the past, to the place where she thought love lived, maybe she was kidding herself. It was just a house, not a piece of magic. She couldn't get her parents back and maybe she couldn't be happy here without Chase. Already too many bad memories.

Chapter 41

Footsteps crunching on the gravel path shook her out of her melancholy thoughts.

"When were you going to tell me?" Chase came upon her suddenly. Phoebe reared back. She had been planting primroses in the empty planters that flanked the steps of the stone terrace.

"Tell you what?"

"Your new deal." Chase tried to keep the anger out of his voice, but he saw her flinch.

"How did you..."

"You don't think I read the business papers, the websites. Everyone's all abuzz that the brilliant Phoebe Ryan is designing a collection with Serena, the hottest international pop and movie star. I thought you were over that, Phoebe. I thought you had committed to your own designs."

He pulled out his phone and showed her. Phoebe gasped. She had had no idea. There was a picture of her and Dean having dinner at the Osprey Arms, drinking champagne and the headline, "Phoebe Ryan makes a new conquest." She couldn't bear to read the rest.

"It's not..."

Chase cut across her. "I understand. You're a

California girl, right. You can take the girl out of Hollywood, but you can't take the Hollywood out of the girl. You're putting your career first. Just like Savannah. I suppose this was a fun little game for you while you and your gentleman friend cooked up a way to make a big story out of it."

Now she rose up, truly angry. "You're the one who told me it was no strings attached. You're the one who said, 'Hey, babe, let's enjoy the moment'. And if I recall, it was your PR director who cooked up the 'Romance of the Century, Part Two' story. You're the one who said our relationship was good for business."

Chase froze, his own words thrown back at him. "I..."

"Look, I gave you your designs and you can use them however you want. You've already made sure the world knows exactly who I am, so feel free to say whatever you have to sell more of them. Our business deal has run its course."

"It wasn't about the deal..." Chase said. She could see him fighting to keep calm and she felt her wall coming up, the one she retreated behind when she needed to avoid hurt.

"What was I supposed to do, Chase? You made it clear that you were just in it for a good time. I need to think about my career. This is the opportunity of a lifetime, in case you haven't noticed."

Chase ran his hands through his hair. "I thought this..." and he gestured all around him, "meant something to you. What about your own designs, your work for North Coast Outfitters? Us?"

"It's just a house. A house that needs a lot of work. I need to keep moving forward."

"And going with him is that?" Chase asked, his voice quiet, his face hard.

"This opportunity isn't about that," Phoebe corrected him. It wasn't about Dean.

"Well, then." Chase looked at her, his eyes dark and hooded. "I guess I'll wish you good luck." She could hear his voice catch, but he pushed through.

Phoebe felt her eyes glitter with sudden tears, but she stood firm, quiet.

"Thank you. I guess I'll be seeing you."

Chase laughed bitterly and swallowed, giving her one long last look before he turned and walked away.

Phoebe watched him, not knowing if she had made the worst mistake of her life. How had it come to this? She knew that if he just turned around once, she would be undone; she would go to him, pull him to her, and beg him to forgive her, to take her right there, take whatever she had to offer. Even if it was a lust-only, no-strings-attached kind of a deal.

Phoebe just sat on the rough stone step, the cold seeping through her jeans and into her body. The sun was setting and still she sat, letting the world go dark around her. That's how she felt about her whole world. It hadn't been ideal, how Chase had found out about Dean's offer, but he hadn't even let her discuss it with him, let her see how it might all work out. Because there was nothing left to work out. She thought what they had meant something. But then he had thrown it all in her face. What did she think that Playboy of the Month, Chase Sanders, was going to settle down with her in a small house overlooking the water and watch while she sewed pillows? That he would ever want to settle down, make a home, make a family? And with her, of all people?

What had she been thinking? That she could undo Savannah's mistakes? That somehow the Savannah–Leland history could be rewritten? It never would have worked out, she told herself. But if that were the case, then why did she feel like this? She'd made no final decision. She'd only be toying with the idea of going back to Los Angeles.

Truth was that she hadn't felt the kind of peace she'd felt in Queensbay in a long time. Ivy House had been a magical place to her and it still was. How could she leave it? But what choice did she have?

Phoebe let her eyes travel over the sweeping expanse of the harbor, down its broad length, across the darkening shadows of its hills. The water had steeped into her, even in such a short time. It had allowed her to find her creativity again, to find her playfulness, to find more purpose. Or had it all been Chase? He'd never made any promises to her. In fact, he had been more than upfront about what he had wanted from her.

"Phoebe? Are you OK?" Lynn's voice called

out, and she could hear footsteps coming around the path.

Phoebe looked at her and wiped her face.

"What happened?" Lynn came to her, a stethoscope still around her neck, in her scrubs with cartoon characters.

"The bastard, what did he do?" She wrapped her arms around Phoebe and hugged her close.

"It's over," Phoebe managed to say before letting the tears come.

Chapter 42

"Don't you have someplace better to be?" Noah looked at him. Chase had wandered back to Noah's house and was now in the barn, sipping a beer as he watched his friend sand down the bubbled varnish on the little skiff.

"Work was a little slow," Chase said and shrugged when he caught Noah's disbelieving stare.

"I'm the president of a multimillion-dollar company, and I can take the afternoon off and visit an old friend when I want to."

"Did you just call me old?"

"That's not what I meant." Chase scrubbed his hands through his hair. He hadn't been able to sleep or think straight since his last conversation with Phoebe. It had gone even worse than the one before that. And she had thrown his words back in his face.

"Do you think I'm afraid of commitment?" he asked.

Noah looked startled and then he said carefully, "I think that in the past, you've been the type of guy who was offered a lot of options and hadn't felt that any of them were right at the time."

"You make it sound like a business deal," Chase said.

"You look like hell," Noah said affably. Chase knew he should have been irritated, but it was hard to ignore the truth.

"It's Phoebe."

Noah paused his sanding to take a swig of his own beer. "Thought it might be. What did you do this time?"

"Why do you think it was me?" Chase said. "Maybe it was her."

Noah just looked at him.

"What?"

"Seems to me that she's the kind of girl who wants someone who's all in," Noah said after a moment.

"What do you mean, 'all in'?"

"Well, seems to me that she's fixing up that house, trying to put down roots, and she wants to share it with someone—but really share it with someone. Not just a stranger passing through the night warming her sheets. Only thing casual about her is her decorating sense."

"So, she's looking for someone to be all in?" Chase still wasn't sure what Noah was talking about.

"She's looking for a commitment. Maybe it's marriage, maybe it's not. Never can tell these days, but she's in love with you."

"How do you know?"

"Let's just say I know how it feels to be in love with someone and not be sure how they feel about you. And to tell you the truth, you have the same look about you."

"But she's ready to close up everything here and move to Los Angeles, and she didn't even tell me. She doesn't want me. She's putting her career ahead of me."

"Did you ever give her any reason not to?" Noah said. "Didn't she get mad at you about the newspaper articles first? Did you ever give her any reason not to think that you weren't just using her for your business?"

"She knows I would never do that," Chase said sharply.

Noah shook his head. "Does she?"

"But why would she go back to him?" Chase was sure that it was this Dean Grant who was pushing her to go back to Los Angeles.

"Well, at least she's getting something in return from him, right? What were you offering her? Or, more importantly, did you ever tell her what you were offering her? Remember, my friend: men and women speak different languages. You think you're showing her how you feel, but she wants to hear it."

"That's it? That's your great advice?" Chase was angry. "We're great together. How could she not know?"

Noah shook his head. "See, different languages. You're showing her when you need to come out and tell her. All in, my friend, all in."

Chase thought about that. It was true. She'd never really said that she wanted to go back to California—just that it was a great opportunity. And he never asked her to stay. Or worse yet, he never asked her if she wanted to make it work. He had just assumed that she would be willing to take whatever he gave her.

"She wants me. All of me," Chase said with some amazement. Women had wanted him before, but they had usually wanted his money or his lifestyle or some combination of both. In return, they had been willing to warm his bed, but not one of them had really wanted all of him. They had wanted to catch him.

"I think you're finally getting it. I don't think she bought into any of this romance-of-the-century stuff you cooked up."

"I didn't cook it up," Chase began, but then stopped. He certainly hadn't prevented it, figuring it was good for both of them. But she hadn't wanted any of that either.

"I mean, do you think that stuff is true? This whole crazy love thing? Savannah and Leland...that wasn't love, was it? It was just self-destructive lust, right?"

Noah smiled, a dreamy one, as he sanded down the wood on the boat. "Love takes many different forms, my friend, and when it comes to you, you shouldn't fight it. Always seemed to me like your grandfather and Savannah Ryan were all in."

Chase stood there glowering as he thought about it.

Noah laughed and continued with his sanding as he asked, "So, what are you going to do?"

Chapter 43

"Phoebe Ryan?" Phoebe answered her phone, only half paying attention. She was thinking of packing, trying to sort through the things she might want to take with her and the things that could go into storage. She had already contacted the real estate agent about the possibility of renting Ivy House out again and someone at an auction house about making a full catalog of Savannah's stuff. The money could go to charity, Phoebe thought.

"This is Robin Smyth from *Hot Style*." Phoebe perked up. *Hot Style* was one of her favorite reads, filled with all sorts of up-and-coming designers and products.

"I wanted to discuss featuring your line of pillows and accessories in an upcoming issue and on our website and TV segments. Your work recently came to our attention, and I think it would be a great fit in our next issue."

Phoebe stopped what she was doing, trying to breathe. "You want to feature me?"

"Yes, we just love your stuff. Plus, I heard you're restoring an old house. And that it belonged to Savannah Ryan. Listen, I was such a huge fan and was so sad when I heard your grandmother passed away. I just think that since you do such great stuff and if we can tie it in with her work, well, then it would be like the artistic torch is being passed from one generation to the next—even if the medium is different. What do you say, are you interested?"

Phoebe smiled and she could almost hear Savannah's raspy voice saying, "You finally got your big break."

"I don't suppose this has anything to do with all the rumors going around now, does it?"

There was a pause. "Well, to tell you the truth, I got a call from at least four other designers who told me that they just had meetings with Serena about working on a collection together."

"Oh," Phoebe said.

"I guess her agent and manager are really shopping around. I am sure it would be a great opportunity for you, but I really like your stuff, even without someone else's name attached to it." Robin emphasized the word "your," and Phoebe felt her heart beat a little faster.

"Plus, I am a sucker for cute little Victorian house with water views."

Phoebe laughed. "Apparently, I am too. So, no matter what happens with the Serena deal, you want to feature me?"

She could hear Robin shuffling some papers. "Yes. And between you and me," she said, dropping her voice, "I hear she's a total nightmare to work with. And a total attention hog. Listen, it's your business, but something similar happened with her clothing line. She went to ten different design teams before she found one that she stuck with, and they have a total non-disclosure agreement. They can't tell anyone who they work for. And worse yet, they can't put out anything of their own."

Phoebe let that all sink in.

"Great. Now," Robin continued, "I'm not promising anything, but many of the new designers and companies we feature, they see quite a jump in their business. Are you prepared to handle that?"

Phoebe looked around the study and her big workspace. Her sketches were spread out on it. She had been sorting through them, deciding whether any of them were worth keeping. There was a decision to be made here.

"I'm ready to handle it," Phoebe said.

<<>>

Lynn had come over with a bottle of champagne when she heard the news. "I am so excited for you."

Phoebe was nervous, but she could feel the adrenaline and the champagne kicking in. Excitement. Purpose. There was a chance that nothing would come of it, but she had to be true to herself.

"I think, maybe, I'm being manipulated." She told Lynn what she had learned from Robin Smyth.

"I don't think Chase would do that," Lynn began.

Phoebe shook her head. She had done a little more research after getting off the phone and realized that Robin had been right. Supposedly, Serena was not known for sharing credit for design ideas. And once Phoebe had looked a little more closely at the press release about her collaboration with Serena, she saw that the language was intentionally vague about how committed Serena was to Phoebe.

"Not Chase."

It took Lynn only a moment to put it together. "Oh, you think Dean is trying to get you away from here and Chase. I knew he was the villain."

Phoebe rolled her eyes at Lynn's dramatics. "Not a villain. Just being pretty aggressive in pursuing me. I think he's doing what an agent does, spinning the media to make the situation work to his advantage."

"So, you're not going to get me backstage passes to a Serena concert?"

Phoebe shrugged. "Maybe, maybe not. I still know a few people. But I don't think I'm going to be working with her. It's my life, my terms this time."

"This means that you're not leaving?" Lynn's face broke into a smile.

"No, I'm not leaving," Phoebe assured her, knowing in that moment that she really did belong here, that she wanted to be here, to give this a real try.

"I'm glad. I would've missed you," Lynn said, and, impulsively, Phoebe hugged her.

"This means more margarita nights at Augie's."

"I can handle it if you can," Lynn said.

Phoebe took a sip of her champagne, savoring the bubbles. She would need to tell Dean her official decision. But not now. For now, she just wanted to savor the moment.

"Imagine, a major magazine wants to do an article on me..." Phoebe said, feeling her toes tingling.

"So cool. And you don't care that they're going to mention Savannah?" Lynn asked.

Phoebe shook her head. She had thought about this too. "It finally feels right. Like the editor said, an artistic torch being passed from one generation to the next. I think Savannah would have been proud. And happy."

"Have you told anyone else?"

"I haven't talked to Dean yet." Phoebe shook her head. She wanted to keep him out of this opportunity.

"That's not who I meant," Lynn countered.

Phoebe turned to face her. "It doesn't matter if I stay or go. Chase and I want different things. I want to settle down and, well, I don't think he's the type."

"Did you ever tell him that's what you wanted?" Lynn said, taking a sip of her champagne.

They had nearly polished off the bottle of champagne and were digging into a bag of potato chips when Phoebe got the text.

"Ugh, it's Dean. He wants to see me. I guess he wants his answer."

"Can't you text him back?" Lynn suggested, licking the salt off a chip before eating it.

"No. I think a part of him wants to make sure I'm back in Los Angeles. Unless I can explain it to his face that I plan on turning down this amazing opportunity and why, he'll think I'm delusional.

"Are you rational?" Lynn asked, gesturing to the half-empty bottle of champagne.

"I poured you more," Phoebe said with a snicker.

"Ahh, no wonder I feel all floaty and wonderful. I'll hold down the fort while you're gone. Have you got a TV yet?"

Laughing, Phoebe tossed her the remote. She texted Dean back and ran upstairs, changing into a sundress and a pair of high-heeled sandals. Using her sunglasses as a headband, she fluffed her hair, grabbed her bag, and was ready.

Chapter 44

Chase kept pounding on the door. Finally, he heard footsteps and when it opened, he almost barreled in, but stopped.

"Where is she?" he demanded.

"Hello to you too," Lynn said. She was wearing jeans and a t-shirt, not her scrubs, and her hair was in a messy ponytail. He could hear the sound of the TV in the background, and he saw a flash of the screen and almost did a double take until he realized that it was Savannah and Leland on the big screen and not Phoebe and himself.

"Lynn?"

"She had to meet someone. You really upset her, you know. How could you? You know that's the one thing she hates, being used because of who she is."

"I wasn't using her," he said, the panic rising. "Where is she? Who is she meeting?" he demanded again, dread hitting him hard.

"Why is that any of your business? She said your deal is over. She did what she was supposed to, and whether she stays or goes has nothing to do with you."

"She's staying?" Hope filled him.

"Yeah, but not because of you. In spite of you. It's all over the TV now—all the entertainment shows are replaying all these programs on Savannah and Leland. Phoebe's all over the place, the poor little Hollywood girl. She never wanted anyone's pity, you know."

"I know. Listen, Lynn, I didn't leak the story. At least not on purpose."

"Fine, I believe you, and I bet she does too."

"Then, what's the problem?" Chase could hear the frustration in his own voice.

Lynn rolled her eyes. "You've got to tell her, you big dummy. Tell her how you feel."

Chase tried to tamp down his impatience. Lynn was obviously buzzing and he needed her to focus.

"Where is she?"

"Who, what? Oh, she went to go talk to Dean. About the job offer. Down at the hotel."

Chase felt his stomach flip. No way he trusted that guy. Sure, Phoebe had said he was a true-blue friend, but Chase had a feeling there was more to the story, at least on Dean's side.

Chapter 45

"Couldn't we go someplace more private?" Dean took her arm and tried to guide her away from the dock.

She took a deep bracing breath of air and decided. It was almost fully dark now, and the lights along the dock were coming on, one by one. Music from the Osprey Arms' outdoor terrace drifted over, and the air was warm, a hint of summer to come.

"This is fine." All of a sudden, Phoebe didn't feel like being in a more private place with Dean. Public was good enough for her.

"I need to say I think you're making a big mistake." Dean stepped up to her and pulled her up to him, his light eyes searching hers.

"He's not good enough for you, Phoebe. I'm the one who was there for you. I want you to share everything with me. With your name and talent and my help, there's no saying where you could go."

He lowered his lips to hers and pulled her in tight. He tried to kiss her, but Phoebe jerked back, putting a hand out against Dean's chest, holding him off.

"I know you did it," she said. "You leaked the

story about the collaboration with Serena. Is it even true? Does she want to work with me?" Anger crept into her voice.

His hazel eyes were confused. "But you're making a mistake. He's not good enough for you, and all of that romance-of-the-century stuff was complete crap. He can't love you, not the way I do."

"As opposed to what you're doing?" Phoebe said coldly.

"Phoebe, please." Dean pulled her close again and she knew he was going for another kiss. His eyes were intent, serious, but the look in them quickly turned to surprise when he fell back. All of a sudden, the dock was crowded.

"Chase, don't." Phoebe was too late.

Chase had already spun Dean around. "Get your hands off my girl!"

"Your girl…" Dean turned back to look at Phoebe. "See, Phoebe, I had to save you from yourself. Is this why you're giving up the opportunity of a lifetime. For this buffoon?"

"What did you call me?" Chase's eyes narrowed.

"Phoebe, I am so sorry." Lynn followed closely behind Chase. "He wanted to know where you were."

Phoebe looked around. Chase and Dean were squaring off against each other, both of them in some sort of fighting stance. She swallowed hard. Dean worked out quite a bit at the gym and was a black belt in karate. But Chase had the more muscular build, like that of a street fighter.

"I can't believe you think you can step in and ruin her life. She's throwing it all away."

"What are you saying, I'm not good enough for her?" Chase's voice was dangerously low. "Do you think you're better for her than me? How dare you try to get between us?"

Phoebe felt the tension rise. She was about to step in between the two of them. She wasn't sure who said what or who went for the other first, but she saw Chase's arm shoot out and Dean staggered back, into Phoebe. She teetered, started to lose her balance, and reached out to grab one of the pilings to steady herself.

"Oh, no," she heard Lynn say, and then Phoebe felt herself falling, heading for the murky waters of Queensbay Harbor.

It was cold, Phoebe thought, as she hit the water and began sinking. The shock had her hesitating a moment before she was ready to kick herself back up to the top. All of a sudden, there was something around her waist, pulling her up, up towards the fading light of the surface.

"Are you crazy?" Chase yelled when they hit the surface. Phoebe gasped in breaths of air, unable to answer. The water was cold and she was shivering. A crowd had gathered and there were flashlights being shone their way.

"Come this way, there's a ladder," someone called. Phoebe coughed, realizing she had swallowed more salty water than she had thought.

Chase's arm was still around her as he towed her against the current and towards the walkway.

Strong hands lifted her up. Phoebe looked around. Dean was sitting, holding his nose, while Lynn hovered over him. Someone had a first aid kit and she had broken out an ice pack. She glanced up, gave the thumbs-up sign.

Phoebe felt Chase's presence behind her. "Does someone have a blanket?" he called out and, in a moment, she felt something draped over her. The police were there and so were the paramedics.

"I'm fine. I'm fine." Phoebe waved them away.

Everyone was looking at her, at them. "I can swim, you know." She pulled the blanket more tightly around her and started walking off the dock.

Lynn stood up, but she waved her away. Phoebe stopped in front of Dean, who looked up at her, an ice pack on his nose.

"Dean, I'm really not going back to California. I don't want the job and I don't want you. And that has nothing to do with him." She nodded towards Chase. "I'm staying to pursue my business. And you and me, we're done."

Dean stood up. A lock of his blond hair fell across his eye, and he tried his best to work his charm as he stuck out his hand. "It's my loss. But good luck, I guess. When you change your mind…"

She ignored his outstretched hand. "I'll know who not to call." And with that she kept walking.

Chapter 46

Chase found her by following the wet footsteps across the front porch, through the front door, which she hadn't locked, down the hall and to the terrace. She had lit a fire in the fire pit and changed, though she was still wrapped in a blanket, sitting on the new outdoor couch she'd had delivered.

It had taken him a good hour to straighten things out with the police. Luckily, Dean, like Chase, hadn't wanted to make a big deal out of it, so they shook hands, Chase with his stomach aching from Dean's nicely placed roundhouse kick, and Dean with a shiner that made him look more like a biker than a preppy Hollywood type.

She was drinking tea, wrapped in a soft blanket, staring out at the water. The sun was well down below the horizon, but the last streaks of purple-pink suffused the indigo sky.

"I'm sorry," he said, deciding to lead with an apology.

Her face didn't turn. He could see her exquisite profile, the long straight nose, the way the fire picked up the red-gold highlights in her hair.

"Why did you come today?"

"I came because I thought you were going to

Los Angeles with him, for him," Chase said, and felt his hands clench and then unclench.

"Dean?" She had turned now, surprise lifting her voice.

"Yes. I thought you were going to walk out of my life and I was crazy. Crazy that I would lose you."

He came around the couch and dropped down in front of her.

"What are you doing?" she asked.

Chase took her hands in his. They were still cold and her hair was still damp, probably from her shower. She smelled like her flower-and-citrus shampoo.

"Phoebe Ryan, I love you. I love you because you're you. Stubborn, caring, loving despite never being loved, because you're talented and creative. Because I can't think straight when you're around. Because when your blue eyes look at me, I would do anything for you."

"You did jump into the water after me. I was on the swim team or didn't you remember?"

"Shh." He put a finger to her lips. "No sarcasm. I am trying to tell you something here."

She shook her head, lifted her chin. "Then just say it, Chase Sanders."

He smiled. "Phoebe, I love you. Every single thing about you. From your fuzzy slippers, to your silly salt-and-pepper shaker collection, to the way you look in the morning when the sunlight hits your hair on the pillow, to the way your skin smells in the rain. I love you and I want to spend the rest of my life with you. I love you because you're you. And no one else. Will you marry me?"

Chase looked at her, barely breathing. Slowly, excruciatingly, she reached up with her hands and brought his face close to her. She laid a gentle kiss on his lips and breathed the word, "Yes."

They sat there on the couch, entangled in the blanket, watching the dying embers of the fire. It was fully dark now and frogs had grown loud around them.

"So, about this house," he started to say.

"Oh, no you don't."

"I was thinking that we might need to expand it, just a little bit. You know, so you have a proper studio and there's plenty of room for the kids to run around. That's if you want to stay here. If not, I am sure we could find something else."

Phoebe's mouth shushed him with a row of kisses along his cheek.

"We can't leave Ivy House. It's magical."

"Romance of this century," he agreed, as his mouth caught hers and kissed her.

Want a preview of the next book in the series? Check out Chasing A Chance, Lynn & Jackson's story...

Chasing a Chance – Book 4 of The Queensbay Series – Lynn & Jackson's Story

Chapter 1

Lynn Masters stood with sore feet and the beginnings of a knot in her back, looking over the patient board and saw with more than a bit of satisfaction that it was just about clear. If the clinic managed to avoid an outbreak of the flu, the common cold, or even a minor trauma, it could mean an early night for her. Sighing at the thought, she debated whether she wanted a cup of the gunk they called coffee or if she could make it through to closing time without another shot of caffeine.

After this shift, she was off duty for three days and her thoughts were excited as the prospect of a break stretched in front of her: empty days with nothing to do, the first real break she'd had in weeks. As far as pediatric residents went, she was senior enough to be at the top of the food chain, in terms of schedule but still, someone else had always called in sick or they'd been short-handed and she'd kept saying yes to working overtime. So now she was well and truly due for some time off and she planned on enjoying every last minute of it.

Skipping the coffee, she made her way down the hallway toward the front desk to start updating her charts. The Queensbay Sailors' Clinic, which had started life in the nineteenth century as a home for destitute sailors, had entered the twenty-first as a facility to provide cost-effective medical services, mostly to women and children. It tried hard, it really did, to be bright and cheerful, despite the dilapidated air about the place. Over the years, it had been housed in a small house, an old church, and other various spots around town, but now was in a building which someone had told her had once been a sail maker's loft. It was a big and spacious, but it hadn't been well-taken care of over the years.

The clinic took up the entire first floor. The second floor was mostly empty, except for a resident psychic who kept sporadic office hours. Her clients climbed up a set of rickety iron steps attached to the outside of the building to have their fortune told. Many of them headed straight down to the clinic, right after their psychic readings, where invariably Lynn would find something wrong with them.

Curious, Lynn had stopped by to see Madame Robireux once, to ask her how she knew there was something physical ailing her clients, but Madame, in true soothsayer's fashion had only waved her heavily ringed hands over a crystal ball and given an enigmatic shrug and started talking about auras. The psychic had offered to read Lynn's own aura, but she had declined, deciding that if was something wrong, she preferred to discover it the old-fashioned way.

In truth, the whole building had the air of an aging woman of the night, with great bones, the last vestiges of beauty not quite gone, but with a general sagginess, as if the whole thing was ready to slide in on itself.

The chairs in the waiting room were hard and uncomfortable and the tables in the exam room were old and the vinyl covers were cracking.

To counteract this, the staff and volunteers had made the inside of the clinic cheery enough, with murals painted on the walls, depicting scenes of oceans and jungles and even a more fanciful one, showing unicorns and fairies in a forest. The kids loved all of them, always stopping to search for their favorite fish or animal each time they came.

And Lynn loved it too. She had poured her heart and soul into her time here at the clinic, helping to raise money for it, donating her own time, and taking pride in watching her patients—kids—grow. She had even started a special program for some of her higher risk ones. Called Healthy Kids Now, she focused on getting her youngest patients exercising and eating better. Sure, everyone knew the basics —eat better, move more—but putting it into practice was harder, even if the parents were on board. Everyone was busy so Lynn had worked to make the program as simple and as easy to use as possible. The successful results were starting to roll in and she'd even received some attention from the medical community. She'd had half a dozen requests to write or speak about it to other clinics and doctors and was trying to field them all.

Lynn strolled the halls, well-being and contentment flowing through her. Sure she might have a bad case of sore feet, but there was nowhere else she would rather be. As she approached the front desk, she saw that the main receptionist, Lori, and her friend Sue, one of the nurses, were there, head bent down, deep in discussion.

"Can you believe it?" Lynn listened with only half an ear, finding the screen on the computer where she needed to sign in; she began inputting information. The two women had worked in the clinic together for years and were best friends. They were always gossiping about something or the other, whether it was what some celebrity had been wearing or who was beating whom on some reality show. Seldom was it of any true concern to Lynn. There had been a time when she might have been interested in all of that, but the last years of medical school and her residency had left little time to keep up on current events, of any kind. Besides she was more of a classic film kind of girl.

"We have a month," Lori hissed to Sue.

"And where are we going to go?" Sue sounded angry. "I've been here for eight years, and just like that they're going to..."

The two of them hushed when they noticed Lynn and in the silence she plainly read guilt.

"What? Is there something wrong with me?" Lynn did a quick scan. She was wearing scrubs and her white doctor's coat. She'd only had one vomiter today, and she had managed to sidestep the projectile launch. Lunch had been turkey on rye, no mustard or mayonnaise, so she knew she hadn't been messy there.

"Is it my hair?" she asked, touching the long ponytail she kept her wavy, dark locks in.

The two women just shook their heads. "You look fine, girlfriend. So fine you better go find a boyfriend."

Lynn shook her head. The two women were always razzing her about her love life, or lack thereof. Being a med student didn't leave a lot of time for dating. Of course, now that she was just about the real deal, a full doctor, the women had told she was a catch. They had even threatened to start setting her up on blind dates, just like her mother, if she didn't start going out on her own. It was just that she knew herself. Her relationships had always ended badly and she was in a good place right now, so why mess with it?

"Nice try, ladies. Fess up. What were you really talking about?" Lynn leaned in and dropped her voice. She knew that Sue and Lori loved to gossip not just about showbiz but what was happening in real life. They were a true treasure trove of information and couldn't keep anything to themselves if they had something really juicy to share.

"Well..." Sue matched Lynn's low tone and threw a glance over her shoulder, "you didn't hear it from us, but word on the street is that the clinic is closing at the end of the month."

"Closing." Lynn's mouth dropped open and to her it felt like the bottom of her stomach dropped out.

"Shhh!" Lori and Sue said at the same time, and Lynn muttered a sorry.

"Aren't they always saying that?" Lynn kept her voice down. The Queensbay Sailors' Clinic was a town institution, but it generally ran on a shoestring budget and for as long as Lynn had worked there, there were always threats in that it was one month away from closing its doors forever. Still, she had planned on it being around and had even accepted a permanent position once her residency was done. She had never thought she'd be out of a job so soon.

"But this time it's for real. Mr. Petersen's finally selling and the new landlord wants to turn this place into a day spa. We need to find new space within the month or it's lights out."

"A day spa!" Lynn was too incensed to keep her voice down and Sue gave her another angry look as she shushed her.

"You heard us, girl. This place is going bye-bye to make way for a day spa."

"What do you mean bye-bye? Can't we just move to another location?"

Lori shrugged. "Mr. Petersen hasn't raised the rent on us in years. It would be difficult to find another location like this. And even so, that would take time. The lease is up at the end of the month. That doesn't leave long for the Director to find us another place and get it up and running."

"But that's not right!" Lynn said, feeling her anger rising. The clinic served an important need here in town. It couldn't just go away. And then there was the question of her paycheck. And the new apartment she had just signed a lease on. And her Healthy Kids Now program she was planning on expanding. She felt her head began to throb and her heart beat a little faster. This was so not good. It couldn't be that everything she had worked for the past ten years was going to evaporate in a matter of weeks.

"You tell us! Oh, look. Now she's getting angry; but I don't know what's that going to do," Sue said, shaking her short, fluffy red hair.

Lori laughed bitterly. "Don't go thinking this is like some patient of yours you can go and fix, Lynn. You'd be better off spending your time looking for another job."

Lynn pulled herself out of her own sense of injustice and looked at the two of them. "What are you going to do?"

Lori shrugged and looked at them over her half-moon glasses. "I've got a standing job offer to run my cousin's dental practice. Offered me a thirty percent raise."

Sue nodded. "I've got a lead in on a job at the hospital. Night shift, at least at first, but still it pays better."

"But..." Lynn looked at them. The two ladies didn't appear too concerned, only resigned. "The clinic is an institution, right? It's been here since the town was first founded. Are you going to let over hundred years of history go down the tubes without a protest?"

The two other women looked at her, then at each other, and Sue said, "When you put it that way...I guess so."

Lynn fisted her hands and said, "I'm not going down without a fight."

Sue and Lori exchanged looks as Lynn gathered her stuff and propelled herself out the door.

Lori pulled down her reading glasses and her eyes followed Lynn's exit. It was her best look, the one she used when she was going to pronounce something she felt was important. "Lordy. Think that Mr. Petersen knows enough to get out of the way when she's a coming?"

Sue shook her head as she watched Lynn's retreating back, "No way, she's tiny..."

"But mighty," Lori finished for her.

Books In This Series

The Queensbay Series

Love small town contemporary romance? The discover Drea Stein's Queensbay series. Nestled on the shores of New England, Queensay is the town where love is in the air. Get to know the couples of Queensbay as they live, laugh, learn and love...

Dinner Fort Two - The Queensbay Series Book 1

Darby & Sean's Story

Rough Harbor - The Queensbay Series Book 2

Caitlyn & Noah's Story

The Ivy House - The Queensbay Series Book 3

Phoebe & Chase's Story

Chasing A Chance - The Queensbay Series Book 4

Lynn & Jackson's Story

With You - The Queensbay Series Book 5

Tory & Colby's Story

All That I Want - The Queensbay Series Book 6

Colleen & Jake's Story

Truly Yours - The Queensbay Series Book 7

Lydia & Lance's Story

About The Author

Drea Stein

Drea Stein is the author of the Queensbay Small Town romance series.

Copyright

Copyright © 2016 Andrea "Drea" Stein

All rights reserved. No part of this publication may be reproduced, distributed, or transmitted in any form or by any means, including photocopying, recording, or other electronic or mechanical methods, without the prior written permission of the publisher, except in the case of brief quotations embodied in critical reviews and certain other noncommercial uses permitted by copyright law. For permission requests, write to the publisher, addressed "Attention: Permissions Coordinator," at the address below.

GirlMogul

309 Main Street

Ste 101

Lebanon, NJ 08833

www.labelleviejournal.com

Publisher's Note: This is a work of fiction. Names, characters, places, and incidents are a product of the author's imagination. Locales and public names are sometimes used for atmospheric purposes. Any resemblance to actual people, living or dead, or to businesses, companies, events, institutions, or locales is completely coincidental.

V 21

Made in the USA
Monee, IL
10 April 2023